A collection of heartwarming romance stories that revel in the magic of celebrations—and celebrate the joy of love.

ELAINE FOX
"The Anniversary That Never Was"
"Elaine Fox demonstrates a virtuoso understanding of American class divisions and attitudes...a carefully created romance every bit as entertaining as *My Fair Lady.*"
—*Romantic Times* for *Untamed Angel*

KATHLEEN NANCE
"Ever a Bridesmaid"
Ms. Nance was a Golden Heart award finalist in 1997 for her debut novel, *Wishes Come True.*

CONSTANCE O'BANYON
"Go for the Gold"
"Constance O'Banyon is dynamic. Wonderful characters. One of the best writers of romantic adventure."
—*Romantic Times* for *Desert Song*

BOBBI SMITH
"Lottery of Love"
"With dashes of humor, passion, adventure and romance, Ms. Smith creates another winner that only she could write!"
—*Romantic Times* for *Renegade's Lady*

Elaine Fox
Kathleen Nance
Constance
O'Banyon

Bobbi Smith

Celebrations

LEISURE BOOKS　　　　　　　　　　　NEW YORK CITY

A LEISURE BOOK®

February 1998

Published by

Dorchester Publishing Co., Inc.
276 Fifth Avenue
New York, NY 10001

ISBN 0-8439-4350-5

The Anniversary That Never Was

Elaine Fox

*To my mother, my grandmother, and Bernice Washburn, the
strongest and wisest women I've ever known.*

Chapter One

Thank God he wasn't coming, Gwyn thought, staring out the window at the grassy sweep of lawn. Caterers scurried from the tent to the house and back again, hauling glasses, ice, tablecloths, and trays. One group of workmen pounded at the wooden base of a bandstand on the south end of the patio, and another strung lights around the stone perimeter.

He'd been invited, she knew, but her grandmother had assured her more than once that he wouldn't be there. Still, she pictured him showing up, envisioned him among the party guests, casual and self-assured. Davis Hilliard. *Dr.* Davis Hilliard, she reminded herself.

She thought she could see him without emotional trauma—it had been two years, after all. But she didn't want it to be today. Not when she'd just arrived, not before she talked to her grand-parents about coming back to stay. And certainly not for this party, the celebration of her grand-parents' fiftieth wedding anniversary. For inevi-tably there would come that moment when she'd catch his eye by accident—perhaps across the cut-ting of the cake—and they would both have to think the same thing: this might have been *our* anniversary.

"I'm so sorry, darling. You tell him we'll miss him terribly, every minute. And I'll have Swordfish save him some cake. Yes, dear, you know—the butler. We call him Swordfish, just for fun."

Gwyn turned at the sound of her grandmother's voice and pushed her hair back to fasten the pearl-drop earrings she'd been holding.

Bernice Curry, tall, slim, and moving with the grace of a twenty-year-old, entered the room with a portable phone propped between her cheek and her shoulder. Her gracefully veined hands held a long scarf that Gwyn knew she intended to tie around her neck in a dramatic, artistic fashion. She marveled again at the youth and energy of this seventy-year-old woman, feeling as she had doz-ens of times in the past that she herself was much older at heart than her charismatic grandmother.

"No, of course it's no trouble, dear. You just stay home and take care of that cough of his. We wouldn't dream of having him venture out of doors for our little celebration. Absolutely not. No, it's no trouble at all . . . Swordfish would be *happy* to do it. You know how he dotes on the little ones."

Gwyn smiled at this. Swordfish was her grand-mother's dour, sour-faced butler, a chronically unhappy man who'd been with her grandparents for years, to everyone's mystification. Bernice had taken the name from a Wodehouse novel, Gwyn thought, which might be the only reason the pompous man didn't revolt against it. For Bernice to be threatening to send him somewhere with cake for someone's child meant that Bernice was seriously displeased with whoever it was.

"Yes, yes. All right. Love to Sid, too. Bye now." She dropped the phone from her shoulder to her hand and clicked it off with her thumb. "Well," she said, "that ought to teach her to cancel at the last minute."

"Who was it?"

"Linda Brady. Not that she's indispensable to the party, of course, but it's because of her little Jimmy that we arranged to have that wretched clown. 'But what will the *children* do?' she kept wailing, until I finally relented and invited the annoying man to don his nose and play his kazoo for the children, or whatever it is he does. I tell you, that woman gives me a pain. And she dotes too much on that child."

Bernice swirled the apricot-colored scarf around her neck and tied it in front of the mirror.

"I told her the Booths' children were perfectly happy with the ponies at the last party," she continued. "But no. Jimmy must have a clown. Jimmy'd be *devastated* without a clown. I tell you, she gives that child more than the boy even wants. Promise me when you have children, Gwyndolyn, you won't spoil them rotten."

"I promise, Gran." Gwyn watched her tie the scarf and wondered if now was a good time to

11

broach the topic of moving back to the guest cottage. Now that Gramps was retiring, he wouldn't need the downstairs for his medical practice. And the upstairs was already set up as an apartment. She could use the old offices as a studio if he decided to clear out his equipment, and she'd already gotten a lead on a teaching job at the Southwalk Academy, the high school she herself had gone to.

But she didn't relish the idea of telling Gran—strong, independent, energetic Gran who was always so proud of her—that she'd been laid off. Or that she was just too tired of trying to make it as an artist in the city to look for another gallery job. The truth was, she'd been living hand-to-mouth for too long trying to support her artistic career, the inspiration for which was increasingly difficult to maintain under the stress of making a living. She was, simply, tired. All she wanted to do was come home for a while.

"Now," Gran said, turning from the mirror, scarf ends fluttering with the movement, "let's get you straightened out."

She took Gwyn's hands in hers and held her arms out, looking her over from head to toe with a critical eye. "No," she said, shaking her head. "There's nothing I can do to help you, darling. I'm afraid you're perfect."

Gwyn laughed. "Careful, Gran. I'll start to think you're finally losing your eyesight. I'm far from perfect."

"So tell me, why didn't you bring a date, hmm? Not seeing anyone?" Bernice tucked a lock of Gwyn's dark hair behind her ear and brought her fingers around to cup one of the pearl earrings. "These are pretty."

Against her will, Gwyn blushed.

"Are these the ones Davis gave you?"

"They're the only ones that go with this dress—"

"Yes, they have that nice, antiquey look. And the pearl is the exact same color. Oh, he had exquisite taste, didn't he? Do you never hear from him?"

"Of course not, you know that. I haven't heard from him since he left for the Baltics."

"That's right. Well, he is back, you know. Your grandfather heard from him just a few weeks ago." Bernice arched an eyebrow as she examined the earring.

"But you said he wasn't coming today, right?" Gwyn's stomach gave a little flip. "And he's living in Charlotte?"

Bernice dropped the earring and moved back to the mirror. "That's right. Though I understand he's not seeing that woman anymore, that stockbroker." She adjusted the folds of the scarf at her neck.

Gwyn watched her. Her thick white hair was swept back from her face in a short, striking cut that accentuated high cheekbones and clear, sharp eyes. She was still beautiful, still willful, still all too perceptive.

Though her grandmother didn't know— couldn't know—that this was a particularly painful day to be talking about him, Gwyn wondered if she had some ulterior motive for bringing Davis up. Two years ago their wedding plans had been confidential. They'd wanted to get married on her grandparents' anniversary—a plot that would have pleased her grandparents tremendously, she knew. Then came the blowup.

After that, of course, the plans had become superfluous. Gwyn had let no one know how devastated she'd been by the breakup, or how this particular date gave her a melancholy ache. But still, it seemed odd to be suddenly talking about Davis Hilliard when his name had barely come up between them for the last two years.

"I think a stockbroker would be perfect for him." Gwyn picked up a hairbrush and ran it through her shoulder-length curls. "I imagine them all to be so . . . driven, you know. Just like him. And of course there'd be all that money to invest."

She couldn't keep the cynicism from her voice, and Bernice shot her a hard look.

"When did you become so contemptuous of money?"

Gwyn put down the brush and looked away, waving one hand as if to flick away her own mood. "I'm not contemptuous, not of money—just the relentless pursuit of it. It was always so important to him to make his fortune, his *own* fortune."

"But that's admirable."

"Yes, in a way, I suppose. It's just—" She paused. Did she really want to start thinking about all this again? It was humiliating enough that her own attempt at success had been so disastrously misguided, financially. Davis's pursuit and attainment of his goals seemed to cast a shadow on her own chosen path. Particularly in light of the fact that she was now in the position of wanting—needing—to move back home.

"He didn't have room in his life for anything else," she explained at her grandmother's piercing look. "That's all. I thought life should be about more than making money. He didn't." Gwyn laughed despite herself. "So I went off and didn't make any. And he went off and made a fortune."

"I don't think he made a fortune, dear. That work he did in Latvia was hardly paying the bills."

"Yes, but it set him up pretty nicely when he came back, didn't it?"

Bernice shrugged. "*Now,* certainly. He learned a lot. But he paid a price for that."

Despite herself, Gwyn turned toward her. "What do you mean? What price?"

Her grandmother smiled at her over her shoulder. "He lost you."

Gwyn scoffed. "I believe he considered that a bargain."

Bernice studied her a moment before turning with a fresh air of purpose toward the door. "Well, never mind all that now. There will be plenty of young men here tonight, and I expect you to dance with each and every one of them. The Carlsons' son is in town for the weekend. I always thought he was such a handsome devil."

"Devil being the operative word there, Gran. He was always a little too smooth for my taste."

"If smooth bothers you, there's always Ben Inman."

Gwyn giggled as she followed her grandmother from the room. "I believe I still have a deformed toe from ballroom dancing with him in high school. What's he doing now?"

"He's a lawyer."

A moment passed before they both began to laugh.

"Perfect," Gwyn said. "He's making a *living* stepping on toes."

Davis Hilliard felt the sun warm his face and depressed the accelerator a little more. The car picked up speed and the wind whipped over the convertible's windshield, through his short hair, buffeting his sunglasses. He couldn't have felt better. He'd had enough cold to last him a lifetime, and May in North Carolina was nothing short of perfect.

He reached down and turned up the radio, drumming his thumbs against the steering wheel with the beat. God, it was good to be home. And on a picture-perfect day like this one, it would be heaven to be back at the Currys'. Of course, Gwyn wouldn't be there. Bernice had made sure he'd known that, though he wasn't sure if she'd informed him thinking he *would* come or thinking he *wouldn't*. He wasn't sure how much Gwyn had told them about the breakup.

Well, it would be easier without her there, he thought, feeling some of his good mood drift inexplicably away. He turned down the radio. He had a lot to talk to Arthur Curry about and having Gwyn there would only be a distraction.

Though he was curious about her. How was she these days? Was her painting still making her happy? Did she still have that recklessly curly hair? Did her eyes still seem to actually sparkle when she laughed? He pictured the dimple that showed on her right cheek when she smiled and remembered himself kissing it on one of a thousand occasions.

He blew air into his cheeks and let it out slowly. No, she was probably still in New York, living the artist's life she'd always wanted. Good for her, he told himself, nodding. Yes, good for her. She'd wanted that life and she went after it and she got it. When he was in Latvia, Art Curry had sent him a clipping about an opening of hers in New York, complete with pictures of some of her paintings. She was good, he thought. Then, again, *good for her.*

For a second he let himself imagine her face as she slept, her hair tumbling over her shoulders and that incredibly soft skin. She had the most amazing skin. He shook his head again. Then he reached down and turned up the radio.

It would be nice to see the Currys again. Art and Bernice were the most eccentric family on the point, and people were drawn to them because of it. They were always doing something interesting, always had some fascinating thought or activity going on. They were a constant, invigorating challenge to the senses.

In fact, it was mostly due to Art that he'd become a doctor. All those afternoons spent in Art's offices, helping him clean up and listening to his diagnoses, had inspired him. Of course, most of that time he'd been hoping to catch a glimpse of Gwyn. But even once he'd gotten to the Baltics, helping those small, devastated towns try to rebuild after the turmoil, he thought about Art and the way he had supported their whole community

Elaine Fox

as a general practitioner. Art Curry was a linchpin, a stalwart, a town elder.

He laughed to himself, knowing how Art would roll his eyes at the description, but it was true. And Davis, after his two years overseas and two months in a practice in Charlotte, now knew that what he wanted was that sense of community, that feeling of belonging, of being needed by an entire town.

And with Art's retirement, the town was going to need a new doctor. . . .

A gentle breeze fluttered the bows on the table-cloths and rustled the tent overhead. Gwyn brushed a lock of hair from her face and pushed it behind her ear.

"I've had a couple of shows," she explained to Mrs. Witherspoon, loudly, into her good right ear, "but it's difficult in New York. There's so much competition, you know."

"What's that?" Mrs. Witherspoon demanded.

"There's a lot of competition," Gwyn repeated, darting looks around to see how far her pathetic story was traveling.

"Ah, but the cream always rises to the top!" Mrs. Witherspoon crowed, raising one bony finger into the air. "Competition is a good thing, if you're really serious about your art. It will only make you better. Success attained too easily is always taken for granted."

Gwyn pasted a smile on her face. "Of course you're right. But I don't think I'm in any danger of attaining success too easily."

"What's that?"

Gwyn cleared her throat and bent closer. "Success isn't coming too easily!"

"But you waltzed up to New York and got a job in a gallery right away, didn't you?"

"Well—"

"Yes, I remember Bernice telling me about it. So surely those people you worked for made it easier for you to get a show or two, didn't they?"

Gwyn sighed. "No, they hired me to hang other people's art. Not my own." Then, seeing Mrs. Witherspoon inhale deeply, no doubt for another *What's that?*, she repeated, "I hang other people's art!"

The breeze blew again and the hem of Gwyn's dress fluttered against her legs. Mrs. Witherspoon's netted hat tilted slightly to one side.

"You hang other people's art?" she bellowed.

Gwyn shifted and glanced around. "That's right."

"Well, what is there to that? You just put a nail in the wall and hang it up!"

"There's a little more to it than that. There's the lighting, and placement. Sometimes the pieces need to be reframed—"

"Well, my goodness, Harry does that all the time at our house. He got this little kit, down at the five and dime, and he framed all our pictures of the grandchildren. That's sixteen, now, you know. So he was at it a while." She cackled merrily and Gwyn smiled with her, with effort.

That was about the size of it. Her great stab at success had amounted to hanging other people's art. While she knew it was a little more complicated than Harry Witherspoon's efforts to frame and hang pictures of his grandchildren, it certainly wasn't worth trying to explain to Mrs. Witherspoon. Especially now that she'd been laid off.

She glanced beyond Mrs. Witherspoon's hat to the groups of well-dressed people mingling on the lawn. White-coated servers floated through the crowd with silver trays of champagne as the sun made long angled shadows and the breeze made sails of the ladies' skirts.

Mrs. Witherspoon rambled on about Harry's photographic efforts with the grandchildren while Gwyn tried to catch the eye of one of the waiters. She was just about to raise her hand to flag one down when her eye traveled across the lawn to the patio steps. There, at the top of the stone staircase, stood a tall man in a blue blazer and khaki pants, shaking hands with her grandfather.

Her heart turned over in her chest.

"But it was Kelly's picture that gave him the most trouble," Mrs. Witherspoon continued. "It was one of those five by sevens, you know. Or no . . . not a five by seven . . . what's the other size? The one they give you now instead of the little prints you used to get at the grocery store?"

"Four by six," Gwyn murmured.

"What's that?"

Gwyn's eyes shot back to Mrs. Witherspoon. "Four by six!" she said loudly, but the expression on her face must have been startling because Mrs. Witherspoon hesitated a moment, staring at her.

"Yes," the older woman said after a pause. Then, "Yes, that's it. Four by six. That's what Kelly had, but of course Harry had made all the frames the same size—"

"Excuse me, please, Mrs. Witherspoon." Like a sleepwalker, Gwyn circled the old lady, barely hearing her "Well, I *never!*" She took a full glass from a passing server and sidled to the edge of the tent. Her eyes didn't leave the man on the patio steps.

Her heart thundered, her cheeks burned, her hands felt clammy, and she felt slightly nauseated. It was him, all right. Dr. Davis Hilliard. For a long uncomfortable moment, she had the feeling that everyone's eyes must surely be on her. They must all be as shocked to see him as she was. And their first thought would naturally be: Weren't *they* planning to get married on this date, too?

But no. Gwyn shook her head and took a long swallow of champagne. No one knew about their wedding plans. No one knew anything except that they used to date, and now they didn't. And all of that was so far in the past anyway, nobody probably even remembered except herself. Maybe not even Davis . . .

She crept around the tent pole, careful to keep groups of people between her and Davis's sight line, and meandered to the hors d'oeuvre table. He was still talking to her grandfather, white teeth flashing when he smiled, his dark hair ruffled by the breeze. His sunglasses made him look like a movie star. When he spread his hands outward, apparently to illustrate a point, his sleeve pulled back and Gwyn caught the gold flash of a watch glinting in the sun.

He looked handsome. And prosperous. And happy.

21

"My, my, but he's looking sharp," a voice said beside her.

Gwyn jerked her eyes from Davis to see Leslie Jacobson spear a strawberry with a toothpick and put it contemplatively into her mouth. Gwyn and Leslie had gone to school together, though Leslie was a couple of years older. These days they only saw each other when Gwyn came home for parties like this one.

Leslie was very tan, slightly overweight, and bedecked with gold jewelry. She wore red lipstick and had two hard lines on either side of her mouth. She, too, watched Davis Hilliard. He might as well be on a stage, Gwyn thought. She had no doubt that all the single women at the party were looking at him, and more than a few of the married ones.

"Leslie. How *are* you?" Gwyn turned to her with a bright expression.

"I'm all right." Leslie poked another piece of fruit and popped it into her mouth, her eyes not straying from Davis. "Better now. I didn't think he was ever going to come back to this place, he was so hot to globe-trot a few years back. Did you?"

"Think he would come back?" Gwyn's gaze was drawn back to Davis. "No. No, I didn't think he'd be back." How lean his face was compared to the last time she'd seen him.

"You two used to date, didn't you?" Leslie, chewing, turned her full attention on Gwyn.

Gwyn's cheeks heated. "Yes. We did."

She and Davis used to joke about how things would be if they ever broke up, how if they ran into each other at the grocery store or something it would be impossible to make small talk, not after all they'd been to each other. But now here they were, virtual strangers, and she had no doubt that their conversation would be every bit as bland and inconsequential as they'd sworn it could never be.

"But I haven't seen him for a long time." She took what she hoped looked like an unconcerned breath and wrestled a grape from its bunch.

Leslie swallowed and perused the cheeses in front of her. "Me either. Unfortunately."

What on earth was she going to say to him? Gwyn thought. And had he just popped in as a surprise? Didn't he know he wasn't expected? How rude was that?

Once again her eyes strayed to the patio. Blindly, she reached out to grab something else to put in her mouth, keeping her eyes on Davis. Cheese, she realized with a grimace when she chewed. Swiss cheese. Sweaty from sitting out in the heat. She looked down at the food in front of her and picked up another handful of grapes.

This was ridiculous. She was acting like a junior high school student at her first dance. As if the boy she had a crush on had just entered the room. No, she reminded herself. She didn't have a crush on Davis. Certainly not. She'd been hurt by him, but that was a long time ago. They'd had a relationship and it was over now. Finished. That was all. They should be able to be friends.

She swallowed the cheese with some difficulty, washed it down with some champagne, and waved her grape-filled hand to Leslie.

"See you later," she mumbled. Then she edged

around the food table to cross the lawn toward the patio.

Hello, Davis, how've you been? she rehearsed mentally, sliding a grape into her mouth. *Nice to see you again. Yes, I'm still in New York. I've been working at a gallery*—not a lie, she told herself vigorously—*why yes, I've had a few shows . . . nothing spectacular, of course, but . . .* She would let that hang with a mysterious, self-deprecating smile, and with any luck at all he'd think she was being modest.

She could do this. She could have a casual conversation with this man. It had been two years.

Chapter Two

She couldn't do this. What in the world had she been thinking? Gwyn spotted her grandmother near the bandstand. Bernice's apricot scarf fluttered in the breeze, and her soft white hair looked as lush as a teenager's. She stood tall and strong, looking every inch the emotional refuge Gwyn needed.

Gwyn changed course away from Davis and started in her grandmother's direction. As she had many a time, Gwyn hoped age and experience would someday help her become the rock that her grandmother was. But in the meantime, she reflected grimly, she had to muddle along as best she could, sorting through the mess that was her life and figuring out how to find some peace. It was unfortunate that *now* of all times she had run into Davis. Now, when her life was more unsettled than ever. Now, when she was trying to come to terms with the idea that he might have been right all those years ago, that ambition was the key to a happy life.

Well, she could do one thing for her peace of mind, she decided. She could settle where she was going to live for the next year.

"Darling," Bernice said as Gwyn approached. The older woman extended a ring-laden hand to brush her grandchild's hair affectionately. "Have you seen Swordfish? He was just looking for you. Apparently someone called."

"For me?" Gwyn couldn't quell the rising dread in her chest. It could only have been John Paulson, the Southwalk Academy's headmaster, calling to let her know about the job. She hoped he hadn't let it slip that she'd applied or there might be some embarrassing confusion. She hadn't yet mentioned moving to her grandmother.

"He was going to ask whoever it was to call back if he couldn't find you."

"I was probably hiding behind the fruit," Gwyn said with an internal grimace. "Did he say who it was?"

"John somebody or other. Why on earth were you hiding behind the fruit?"

Gwyn sighed and pushed her hair back from her face. "No good reason. Gran, listen, I'm sorry to bring this up right now, but I would feel so much better if I could get something off my chest. Can we talk for a minute?"

Inexplicably, Gwyn felt a sudden urge to cry. Stress, she told herself. Seeing Davis had been the final straw in an already bad month.

"My goodness, darling, of course. Let's talk." Bernice put an arm around her shoulders and turned her toward the peony garden that bordered the fence. "I had the feeling you were unhappy when you arrived yesterday, but I didn't want to push. Now, tell me what's wrong."

Gwyn swallowed hard, more irritated than upset with the lump in her throat. She brushed a finger under her damp lashes. She couldn't mention Davis, that seeing him had been the catalyst for this agitation. If she tried to talk about him now, she'd go completely over the edge. But she could ask her grandmother about the cottage.

"I'm sorry to get so emotional on you. I've just had a bad couple of weeks." She laughed wryly. "Okay, a bad couple of months. But don't worry, I've got a plan to make things better. The only trouble is, I need your help."

She slowed, then stopped and lowered her eyes as her grandmother's consoling face turned toward her.

"You know all you need to do is ask."

Gwyn took a deep breath. "I want to leave New York and come back. Here. To Southwalk. Just for a year or so, and live in the guest house. I thought since Grampa's retired now—" She lifted her brows in question. "Maybe it wouldn't be such an intrusion? Just until I get my life back on track?"

With a quick, welcoming hug, her grandmother laughed, and Gwyn felt as if the sun had burst through a cloudy day to bathe her in warmth. "Well, of *course* you can come back, sweetheart. Intrusion, my foot! In fact, it would be a dream come true for me, and your grandfather too. What

27

on earth were you so worried about?"

Gwyn smiled, brushing away tears of relief before her grandmother could see them. "I guess I was afraid you might be disappointed in me. Because I'm giving up, you know, on New York."

"But you're not giving up your painting, are you?" Bernice said, obviously scandalized at the thought. Her grandmother had always been her biggest champion.

Gwyn shook her head. "No. In fact I think coming back will help my painting more than anything. And my agent in New York, Jenny Rogers, is still working to get me shows up there. She's actually pretty confident."

"Well, of course she is. My goodness, anyone with half a brain can see you've got talent."

"Well . . ." Gwyn squelched an automatic desire to set her grandmother straight. Jenny was always after her to work on her self-esteem. *Artists need big egos,* she always said.

"I've also applied to teach art here at the South-walk Academy," Gwyn continued. "I think that might have been John Paulson who called, the headmaster."

Her grandmother looked at her in surprise. "Have you interviewed already?"

Gwyn nodded. "Twice over the phone. And I stopped there for a couple hours yesterday before I came here."

Her grandmother looked at her, nonplussed, a smile on her lips.

"Well, look at you! You've gotten *everything* sorted out and haven't left me with a thing to do to help you. Do you think he was calling to tell you you've gotten the job?"

"I don't know. It seems strange that he'd do it on a Saturday, but—"

"Well, strange or not, let's get him back on the phone." Bernice swirled toward the patio and raised a hand. "Swordfish? Swordfish!"

The butler, his portly frame buttoned into a dark suit and vest, stood close enough to hear, bowing slightly over a tray of canapes offered to Mrs. Dalrymple. The matron perused them as if she studied a tray of diamonds.

Bernice pursed her lips and shook her head impatiently. "He *hears* me, I know he does. Well, no matter, come along. We'll get the portable and call Mr. Paulson right back."

Gwyn and Bernice left the study, Gwyn's heart bursting with optimism over her new job, at the same moment that Davis and Art emerged from the library.

Gwyn saw them first and her elation immediately gave way to panic. Davis laughed at something her grandfather said, and she knew, without a doubt, that she did not have the strength to try to speak with him right now. It was too familiar, that laugh. Too close and companionable. She could almost hear it sounding softly in her ear, as if he chuckled beside her in bed.

But of course she had no choice about speaking to him. Her grandmother was already calling across the foyer to them. Taking a deep breath, Gwyn glanced over. Davis glanced up. And for a second the world stopped. Outside, Gwyn heard

29

voices, saw from the corner of her eye waiters carrying glasses, felt the breeze through the open French doors, but in that hallway time stood still.

How could she have forgotten *those eyes?* she thought as her stomach hit the floor. Golden brown, framed with decadently lush lashes and lean, dashing brows. *God help me,* she moaned to herself, *I'm going to make a fool of myself.*

"Gwyn?"

Was it her imagination or did his voice sound just the slightest bit unsteady?

"Davis." She managed a smile but knew that *her* voice was unsteady. Gritting her teeth against the back flips her heart was doing, she held out a clammy hand and said, an octave lower than normal, "What a pleasant surprise."

"Yes, it certainly is." The honey-brown eyes glanced at her grandfather, who beamed at the two of them.

Gwyn noted the closely shaved plane of Davis's cheek and the muscular cords in his neck as he turned.

He was *better* looking, damn him, she thought, trying to muster something within herself besides this abject, paralyzing nervousness. Even anger would be preferable. But really, what was there to be angry about? Relationships end. He'd said those very words to her before he'd left for Latvia for two years.

There it was. Anger. She felt her cheeks heat at the memory.

"Davis, darling, you made it after all." Bernice enveloped him in a hug before he had a chance to respond. "How was the trip down?"

"Not bad," he said, looking at her quizzically. "I know I told you that I'd be leaving later, but I wanted to avoid the traffic—"

"Of course. Wonderful. That's excellent," Bernice enthused, taking his arm. "Let's go out on the patio, shall we? I notice that none of us has any champagne, and this is supposed to be a *celebration!* We must celebrate everything—especially old friends. Isn't that right, dear?"

Bernice turned and looped her other arm through Gwyn's, so that she escorted both of them through the doors onto the hot stone surface of the patio.

"Isn't it wonderful to see old friends after so long?" her grandmother insisted, squeezing Gwyn's hand and looking at her pointedly.

"Yes, of course," Gwyn murmured. Something about this scenario seemed awfully fishy, she thought. Examining her grandmother's over-bright smile from the corners of her eyes, she felt certain Bernice had known Davis was coming all along. The fact that she'd lied to Gwyn about it meant she was definitely up to something.

"How is Charlotte these days, Davis?" Bernice continued buoyantly. "That practice of yours still going great guns?"

Gwyn craned her neck to see around her grandmother, curious to see if he would reveal more about how much they'd really been in contact. The perplexed expression he wore told her that he, at any rate, was not involved in the deception about whether or not he was coming to the party. Her grandmother had apparently perpetrated that alone.

31

"Yes, it's doing well, though it's not my practice, as I told you on the phone. I'm just an underling, working my shift for a paycheck."

"Well, you'll have your own soon enough," Bernice said confidently, waving and actually catching the butler's eye this time. She beamed as he came toward them. "Swordfish, champagne for the four of us, please. We have such celebrating to do. When was the last time we were all together, hmm? *Years* ago, I vow."

Swordfish floated off to do her bidding.

"I believe," Davis said slowly, gazing at the ground, "it was your forty-eighth anniversary party."

Gwyn squelched the automatic twisting in her heart. *He* probably hadn't thought twice about it.

"*That's* right." Bernice commandeered a passing waitress. "Dear, why don't you get us some of those chocolate-covered strawberries, that's a good girl."

The girl scurried off.

"I didn't expect to see you here, Gwyn," Davis said, finally turning his gaze upon her. "I thought you were still in New York."

Bingo, Gwyn thought. Her grandmother had masterminded the whole awkward reunion. But it wouldn't work, Gwyn thought sourly. There was far too much water under this bridge. But as their eyes met, her blood seemed to stall in her veins.

"I am." She nodded. "I just came back for the"— She waved a hand and looked out over the lawn— "party."

His eyes lingered on her and she kept hers averted. Of all the wretched things for her grandmother to bring up—the last time they were all together. That *other* anniversary when she and Davis had made the ill-fated decision to marry. *To marry on this very day.* God, didn't he remember? she wondered. Did this date not make him as sad as it did her?

She swallowed. "I'm so glad I could make it. It's a beautiful day for a party."

"Yes. It's great you could come down for it," Davis said, studying her. After a pause, he added, "It's good to see you. Here. Again."

"Yeah." She barely squeezed the word out over the emotion in her chest. Was she truly upset, or did she just think she was supposed to be? In any case, her uncertainty prevented her from going on and uttering the requisite "You too." She had no desire to appear emotional in front of him. If anything, she needed to look strong, as if she'd gotten on with her life without him. She wondered briefly what Jenny would do, and then acknowledged that her agent would never find herself in a ridiculous situation like this.

Why, Gwyn lamented again pointlessly, why did she have to run into Davis *today* of all days?

Swordfish appeared with the drinks and Bernice swept them up in her hands and distributed them, first to Gwyn and Davis, then to Art and herself.

"To old friends," Bernice said, lifting her glass with a beatific smile. "May we not be parted for so long next time."

"Hear, hear," Art said, chiming his glass with Gwyn's and winking at her.

"Absolutely," Davis murmured, the bedroom

33

voice sending ripples of painful pleasure down Gwyn's spine.

"Mmm," Gwyn said, with a nod that she hoped looked sincere. She clinked her glass against Bernice's, paused, and then held her glass out toward Davis's.

She kept her eyes on his hand as the two glasses clinked. His square, long-fingered, surgeon's hand clasped the delicate crystal deftly. As she brought the glass to her lips, her eyes rose and found his honey-brown gaze on her.

He was *laughing* at her! Well, not laughing outright, but she could see a glimmer of amusement in his eyes. She felt the knot of emotion fall from her throat and her chin rose indignantly.

She searched her mind for something to say that might give her back some self-control. "So I hear you're quite the financial wizard these days, Davis. Playing the stock market and what not."

The amusement in his eyes reached his lips and he grinned. "Been keeping tabs, Gwyn?"

She scoffed. "Hardly. But people talk, you know. I was happy to hear it, actually. It seemed perfect for you, dating a stockbroker."

His eyes narrowed. "Did it, now?"

He knew what she meant. There was some triumph in that. "Yes, there's nothing like the harmony of matching aspirations in a relationship."

"Whoa, hold on there," Gwyn's grandfather interjected with a laugh. "I would hardly call stockbrokering and medicine matching aspirations."

"Yes, I've always thought of medicine as something of an *art*," Bernice contributed with an innocent smile at her granddaughter.

"I meant in terms of lifestyle, Gramps," Gwyn said, slanting a knowing glance at her grandmother. If she'd had any doubt before, she knew now that her grandmother had orchestrated this whole thing. "But I was joking," she added, reluctant to appear bitter. Nothing so pathetic as a scorned ex-girlfriend still angry after *two years*.

"No, you weren't," Davis said, with characteristic candor. "You think I'm a gold-digging, money-grubbing leech. Come on, Gwyn, you've as much as said so."

His eyes glittered with challenge, his words thrown out like a gauntlet.

Ten spiteful comebacks darted through her head, but she let them pass.

"I don't know, Davis," she said. "You may have changed."

He chuckled, eyeing her. "That I have, darlin'."

She rolled her eyes. "*Darling*," she repeated. "I'd forgotten the way endearments roll off the tongues of southern men."

Her grandparents exchanged a look.

Davis grinned at her, exaggerating the southern drawl that tinged his speech. "You've been up north too long, then, missy. How long's it been?"

"Two years," she said pointedly, unable to keep the ire from either her tone or her expression. Since shortly after he'd left for Europe. She recalled with a pain the dreadful days before she'd left, packing the truck, throwing out any and all reminders of Davis Hilliard. The trash can had been full—holding years of gifts and mementos.

Davis's lashes dropped and he swirled the champagne in his glass. How sweet it would taste on his lips, she thought suddenly and remembered all too well the last time she'd tasted it—that forty-eighth anniversary party when she'd gotten, so briefly, engaged.

"Ah," he said after a minute. "Long time."

"And we've been trying to get her to come back ever since," her grandfather said. "You came back, Davis. Got that world traveling out of your system and came back to Carolina. Why do you suppose my own flesh and blood won't return?"

"I don't know, Art. Maybe her memories of the place aren't as fond as mine." He lifted a brow in her direction.

Was he trying to say she hadn't appreciated what she'd had? Or maybe that she didn't know what she'd had. The fact that she'd only just recently discovered that very thing made the comment sting.

"As a matter of fact, I have many fond memories." She looped her arm through her grandfather's. "Most of them from growing up in this very house. In fact," she said, seizing the moment, "I'm coming back to stay for a while." She turned a beaming smile on her grandfather.

"Why, that's wonderful!" he exclaimed. "When did you make this decision?"

"I've been thinking about it for a while. And I've just spoken to Gran about it, haven't I, Gran? I'm going to live in the guest house, over your old office."

At this her grandfather really did look struck, turning his gaze swiftly to her grandmother.

"Is that right?" he said, obviously at a loss.

Davis chuckled and shook his head, his gaze

dropping once again to the glass in his hand.

Gwyn looked anxiously from her grandfather to her grandmother. Maybe it *wouldn't* be all right with Grampa, she thought. Maybe he felt that she was swooping in too quickly, taking over his space before he'd even had time to leave it. Maybe he thought she was kicking him out. The fact that Davis was laughing at her didn't help matters either. What did he know that she didn't?

"Is that all right, Gramps?" she asked. "I mean, if you still wanted to practice, I wouldn't be in your way upstairs. I don't need the downstairs at all." She felt a momentary pang for the studio she'd envisioned, but let it pass. Her grandfather was far more important. "And I'd be quiet. In fact, I'd be gone most of every day."

"Goodness, of *course* it's no bother. He's not going to be using the place," Bernice said, exasperated. "He's as excited as I am about your return, aren't you, Art?"

"Well—well, of course," her grandfather said, his cheeks reddening. "Couldn't be happier, dear." He squeezed her arm with his. "It's just that, well, I've just been talking to Davis here."

Gwyn turned her gaze to Davis, who still looked at his drink, a small smile on his lips.

"And I've agreed to let *him* use the office. You see, he's coming back, too. He's going to be Southwalk's new general practitioner."

"That's it. I'm going back," Gwyn said to her grandmother as she dragged her from the porch back to the study. "I can't live with him there."

"Well, he wouldn't be *living* there, dear." Bernice closed the door quietly behind them.

"Yes, he would. Practically. He'd be down there, every day, all day, working."

"Yes, and you'd be at the academy, teaching. By the time you got home he'd most likely be gone. You'll probably never see each other."

Gwyn ground her teeth together and pushed her hands back through her hair. "But he'll *be* there. All his things, his work, his life. God, he'll probably want to *work late,* if I know him." She felt anger grip her and shook her head vehemently. "And I *do* know him. I don't care how long it's been. He actually thought it was *funny* that we both planned to use the guest house. Did you see his face? He could barely contain his smile. God, I'd forgotten about that smugness of his. Always in control. Always getting exactly what he wants." She paced toward the window and gripped the sill with both hands.

"And so you think he's getting exactly what he wants now?"

Gwyn turned to face her grandmother. "You can just wipe that smile off your face, too, Gran. I know you set this whole thing up—"

"Don't be ridiculous." Bernice waved the suggestion away with a manicured hand. "I had no idea you planned to come back here to stay. Or that he did, for that matter."

"No, I mean this party. You *knew* he was coming. Admit it."

Her grandmother smiled, and Gwyn wanted to throttle her.

"Well, yes, all right. I'll admit that much. I knew he was coming to the party. But it had been so long since I'd seen you, darling, I didn't want to risk your not coming."

Gwyn closed her eyes. And of course she wouldn't have come. It was hard to fault someone for wanting to see you so badly that they perpetrated what they probably thought was nothing more than a little white lie.

But still, her grandmother *had* to have known how painful this meeting would be. Maybe not, Gwyn thought sadly. Her engagement to Davis had been so brief, no one had known about it except the two of them. And Gwyn had never seen her way to confessing to Bernice how thoroughly she'd been dumped. She'd presented it as a difference of opinion, of goals, a simple parting of the ways. Davis had wanted to experience emergency medicine in eastern Europe, and Gwyn had had her first show in New York. The two goals were incompatible.

So for Gwyn, what had started as a short trip to New York for an opening had turned into a move. She'd had no reason to stay in North Carolina. She would only have been tortured by memories.

"Well, I don't know what to do now," Gwyn sighed finally.

"Don't go back, dear," her grandmother said, coming forward and taking her hand. "It might not be so bad. Maybe you two could be friends."

Gwyn laughed, a dry, hollow sound. "I don't know who I'm kidding. I *can't* go back." She didn't have a job and she was two months behind on her rent. "I've already told John Paulson I'd take the teaching position," she elaborated at her grandmother's questioning look.

Elaine Fox

"Well, of course, you only just told him that an hour ago," her grandmother said philosophically. "You should stay because you want to, not because you feel backed into a corner."

Gwyn smiled. She couldn't be in more of a corner. But the truly irksome part of it was she *wanted* to come back. This was a town she loved and she'd missed it terribly while she was gone. Despite her dire straits in New York, love for this place was her biggest motivation for the move.

But to come back and have to face her biggest failure day in and day out in the form of Davis Hilliard would take quite a bit of nerve.

"I do want to stay," she said finally. "And I will."

Her grandmother let out an unladylike whoop of triumph.

"But I'm warning you, Gran, no dinners together. No socials. No happy hours." She leveled a hard look at her willful grandmother. "I only intend to see Davis Hilliard when I absolutely have to."

Chapter Three

Davis heard a bump from overhead and knew Gwyn was awake. Sitting amid boxes in his empty waiting room, he had little else to do but listen to the groggy movements of Gwyndolyn Curry. And groggy they would be, he remembered with a private smile. If he remembered anything about her, it was that she was not a morning person.

He sipped coffee from one of the chipped mugs left in the kitchenette and listened to the quiet rush of the tap going on upstairs. Brushing her teeth, he thought and pictured her tousled hair and sleep-puffed eyes. For an instant he remembered the feel of their legs tangled together under the sheets. She'd always been so warm in sleep. Like a little generator in wintertime, heating up the bed with her soft, pliant body. He remembered how good her body had felt on his when he circled her waist with an arm and curled up next to her. Constant and calm and safe. She was permanence, a kind of anchor to reality.

But then, that had not been what he'd wanted at the time. He'd wanted action, achievement, maybe some small bit of notoriety. He'd wanted the unexpected, never knowing how harrowing the unexpected could be. And he'd been single-minded about it, unable to take his eyes from the prize long enough to appreciate what he already held in his hands.

But she had known.

How can you just throw this away? He could still hear the break in her voice as she said the words, could see the way her eyes pooled with tears. He couldn't think of it now without agony, without feeling something uncomfortably close to shame at the betrayal she must have felt at his hands.

Of course it had hurt him, too, at the time. He loved her enough that he couldn't watch her suffer without feeling pain. But he couldn't have stopped himself. Not then. Back then he couldn't see beyond his own drive to succeed.

He took a sip of coffee and pulled a book from the box in front of him. But he didn't look at it. Instead his gaze focused inward.

She had always known what she wanted, he reflected. She'd followed her desires with a blind, vigorous trust in her own instincts. Every step she took—from the time he'd met her when she was fourteen years old—seemed to lead inexorably toward the artistic life; her entire character reflected it. But Davis's course had been different, less sure, more forced, and composed of dramatic twists that were completely at odds with the steady step-by-step construction of her life.

Now, years later, he wondered how she'd managed to possess such surety, such *wisdom* really, at such a young age. For he'd traveled all over the globe only to find himself wanting what he'd left behind. Wanting what she had tried to hold onto so long ago.

The tap thunked off. A moment passed and the creak of faucet handles heralded the onset of the shower. Davis rose and sauntered to the tiny kitchenette where there was a coffee pot, a small refrigerator, and a microwave. He poured himself another cup of coffee and leaned back against the counter.

She must have just returned yesterday, because he'd spent most of the last week moving his equipment into the office and the upstairs had been empty. Art told him Gwyn had gone back to New York for her things. Davis wondered if there was someone there she needed to say good-bye to.

Half an hour later, as he finished unpacking the box of reference books, he heard her light step on the upstairs landing. Picking up his third cup of coffee, he went to the back door, opened it, and leaned against the doorjamb. After a second of listening to jingling keys, he saw her legs through the stair slats as she trotted down toward her car. A yellow sundress feathered around her pretty calves. Her feet looked tan in leather sandals.

He watched as she fumbled with the car keys while trying to keep a large portfolio tucked under one arm.

"First day of work?" he asked.

She jumped, dropped the keys, and turned on him with that little line of frustration he'd forgotten about between her thin dark brows.

"Yes, and I don't want to be late." She placed the portfolio on the ground and bent to pick up her keys. Rising, she pushed one into the car's door lock.

He glanced at his watch. "It's only eight-fifteen. This is summer school, isn't it? What time do you have to be there?"

"Nine." She opened the back door and pushed the portfolio into the back seat.

He liked the way she flipped her curly hair off her face, only to have it tumble right back. She leaned in, moving something so the portfolio could sit on the floor and allow her to shut the door, and he shamelessly watched her backside. Good shape, he thought. She hadn't changed much in two years. Not that it would have mattered if she had.

"You're only about ten minutes away. Can I get you a cup of coffee before you go?"

She glared at him over her shoulder, then backed out of the rear seat. Straightening, she drilled him with a hard look and seemed about to say something. But she only pressed her lips together.

"It's fresh," he added.

"No. Thank you." She turned, looked around at the ground as if she had dropped something, then glanced into the front seat. With a muttered comment he didn't quite hear, she turned back toward the stairs.

"Forget something?" he asked.

"Yes." She kept moving, traipsing up the stairs with a heavy tread.

"Can I help you carry anything?" he called.

"*No.*"

He smiled at the irritation in her reply. Keys jingled again, the door squeaked open, her footfalls sounded hollow on what he knew was the kitchen floor. A second later she stepped again onto the landing, locked the door, and came quickly down the stairs.

"Say, I was just wondering," he said as she threw her purse onto the front seat of the car. She paused and looked at him as if he were someone selling unwanted magazines at her front door. "You and I are both kind of new back here, and I was wondering if maybe you'd like to go out for dinner sometime. You know, see how the town's changed and all. Or see how it hasn't changed. I heard The Supply House is still selling great seafood down at the docks."

She was silent for a long minute, looking at him inscrutably through dark, lively eyes. The silence lengthened, and he began to think she planned never to reply when she took a deep breath and let it out in a huff.

"You're kidding, right?" She crossed her arms over her chest and leaned her weight on one hip.

He shrugged and shook his head. "No. Why would I kid about something like that?"

"So you're asking me on a *date?*"

Her tone was disgusted, and he laughed once, feeling stung. "You don't have to say it like that, Gwyn. It's not as if I asked you to do my laundry."

"I'd rather do that."

He straightened and swept a hand through the door behind him. "Well, there's plenty of it, darlin'. You just name the day."

She shook her head and turned abruptly to the car. "You're unbelievable."

"What do you mean?" He came toward her as she hopped in the car and slammed the door. He motioned with his hand for her to roll down the window.

She complied with obvious reluctance. "What."

He leaned his forearms on the car door, his coffee cup clasped between them, and ducked his head to see her through the window. "Why am I unbelievable?"

She sighed. "Davis . . ." She took a deep breath and sighed again, then glanced at him sideways. "You're doing this on purpose, aren't you?"

"Doing what? All I did was ask if you wanted to go to dinner sometime. If it's that important to you, we can go dutch. That way it won't be a date." He cocked his head. "Come on. It'll be fun, I promise."

She blew air through her cheeks. "No, that's not all. You're goading me and you know it. All I want to do is go to work, do my job, and come home. Alone. I don't want to see you, I don't want to go to dinner with you, I don't really want to be neighbors with you but I don't have much choice about that. At the moment, anyway."

"I'm getting the feeling you want me to leave you alone."

She smiled with exaggerated pleasure. "*Exactly.*"

He frowned. "Can't I even be neighborly and say

hello to you? Maybe offer you a cup of coffee in the morning? Or maybe you get up early and make yourself a pot before you go?"

She flushed and he grinned.

"I don't drink coffee in the morning," she said.

"I didn't think you did. But maybe that's not because you don't want any."

She leaned her head against the headrest and looked over at him. "Davis, you know what I'm saying."

"Well, Gwyn, I guess I know what you're *trying* to say. I just don't understand why."

Her mouth turned down at the corners and she suddenly looked not just annoyed, but sad. He felt a pang of remorse for teasing her. But the fact was, when he'd caught sight of her at the party, he'd felt so happy to see her, and had experienced such a breathtaking renewal of the effect of her charm, that he hadn't considered the idea that his presence might distress her.

It was possible, he realized all of a sudden, that even after so much time she might not have forgiven him.

"I have to go," she said, leaning forward and turning the key in the ignition. The already running engine let out an ear-splitting shriek, and she swore under her breath.

He looked at her closed eyes and wanted to reach out and cup her face with his hand. But he didn't.

"Whaddya say, eight o'clock?" he said instead, backing a step away from the door. "I can make reservations. It gets crowded down there this time of year."

She shoved the gearshift into reverse. "I'm busy." She let go of the clutch. The front wheels spun, spewing gravel onto his legs, and she whipped the little car out of the driveway.

He watched her go, and then slowly dumped the remaining coffee from his cup into the dirt. "Ah, Gwyn," he said softly, and watched the dust her car kicked up settle on the driveway.

He was sitting on the back stoop when she pulled in, just as she'd feared he might be. Despite herself, she felt a flutter of excitement trill through her at the sight of him, followed quickly by anger.

All she'd wanted in coming back home to Southwalk was some *peace*, dammit. But with Davis Hilliard constantly underfoot—*literally*—she felt more unsettled than she had even in those last couple of months in New York. Of course she also felt more alive, a demon part of her mind pointed out. She countered this by deciding it was illogical to consider nervous anticipation a good thing.

He was dressed in a white polo shirt and jeans, and he rose when her car crunched onto the gravel drive. Warily, she shut off the engine and opened the door.

"Now, before you say anything," he said, coming toward her with his hands up in surrender, "I've been thinking about this all day and I think we should go to dinner, if for no other reason than to discuss why we shouldn't go out for dinner. I've made reservations at The Supply House for seven and it's going to be a perfect sunset—remember the view over the river from there? If we leave right away we can have a drink on the pier first."

Gwyn locked the car door and tried to still the tremors that rattled her nerves before facing him.

"I thought I told you I was busy," she said, walking toward the stairs to her apartment.

"You did. I didn't think you meant it." He followed her toward the steps, kicking pieces of gravel before them with well-worn loafers.

"Well, I did."

"Washing your hair?" he asked wryly.

She turned after mounting the first step and looked down on him. "Davis, don't you understand? You and I have a long history together. One that doesn't lend itself to casual renewal. You're just going to have to trust me when I tell you that being friends isn't in the cards for us."

There. She'd said it. There was nothing he could say to that, she was sure.

"We don't have to be friends. In fact, I don't want to be friends either."

It was not a comeback she'd expected. She looked at him, confused.

"I just want to go out for dinner." He grinned and cocked his head. "Come on, Gwyn. We might have fun."

She shook her head and gazed into his beach-warm eyes, laughter glinting in them like the sun on the sea. His smile was loose and easy, like the clean white shirt he wore and the breeze that ruffled his hair.

He'd changed clothes since this morning, she noted. He'd dressed nicely for her and he looked freshly shaved. She caught a slight hint of cologne and told herself that if she gave in to him now, his galling presumptuousness would never stop.

49

She'd wind up having coffee with him in the morning, drinks with him in the evening, and he'd probably end up breaking her heart all over again.

But as the breeze kicked up and her skirt waved softly around her legs, she let her eyes drift skyward. The sunset would be gorgeous along the pier. In the blink of an eye, she saw herself with a glass of wine, sitting across from this vibrant, intelligent man, and she knew she would feel more excited and attractive than she'd felt in years.

"You're impossible."

His smile broadened, and she frowned.

"That's better than unbelievable, right? Impossible's an improvement, I'm sure of it."

She didn't want him to win this easily. She'd spent *years* feeling bad about him; to cave in this quickly would make her feel like a fool.

"I don't know . . ."

"Let me tell you, then, it is. I know. And you're going anyway." His smile shone on her with the intensity of a desert sun. "I promise you'll have a good time."

"That's just what I'm worried about," she muttered, turning to climb the stairs.

"Then I'll make sure you're not disappointed. I'll give you half an hour; then I'm coming up after you."

She pivoted on the top step and glared at him. "Don't you dare."

He raised his hands again. "Kidding!"

"I'll be down in forty-five minutes," she said. Then she added, to appease her kicking conscience, "Maybe."

* * *

They drove the short distance to the restaurant in silence, Davis figuring he'd let her get used to her decision to accompany him by putting the top down and letting the warm evening air wash over her. With a little Louis Armstrong, one of her favorites, on the tape deck, she'd loosen up in no time.

He parked the car and came around to her side to let her out, but she'd done it herself by the time he got there. He offered her his arm, but she merely grimaced at it and walked toward the restaurant unaided.

The sun was dropping slowly from the sky and the breeze off the river bounced the curls on her shoulders. She hadn't changed her dress, which was pretty, he thought, but she'd refreshed her makeup and put on some jewelry.

She might not want to call it a date, he thought with some satisfaction, but as his father used to say, if it walked like a duck, and talked like a duck . . . most likely it was a duck.

The Supply House looked exactly as he remembered it—open air out the back with brightly colored Christmas lights strung around the ceiling and up the adjacent pier. A bar formed a horseshoe in the center, around which were small red lights shaped like chili peppers.

They were seated next to one of the windows flung upward to let in the breeze, with an unobstructed view of the water and the great orange globe of the sun sinking toward it. From the harbor nearby they could hear the tinkle of sailboat riggings hitting masts and the slurp of the water against boat hulls. If he looked down, Davis re-

51

membered, he would see water through the dining room floorboards.

"I like a place with a sense of danger about it," he said as they were seated. "One good wake from a passing boat and we'll have water splashing up to our knees."

"That never happens," Gwyn said, draping a sweater around her shoulders.

He watched creamy skin disappear under white cotton. "Are you cold? We could ask to sit inside."

"No. I'm fine." She shook her head. "This is— it's nice out here."

He smiled. She was trying so hard not to have a good time. "Good. What would you like? Chardonnay?"

She glanced up at him, clearly wishing she wanted something else just to contradict him, but after a moment she nodded. "That's fine." She turned her gaze to the river.

He motioned for the waitress. "Chardonnay and a beer. And how about an order of oysters to start?" He raised his brows at Gwyn.

She shrugged. "Whatever you want."

He nodded to the waitress. "Six on the half shell."

"You know, you shouldn't be trying so hard," Gwyn said when the waitress had left. "I'm not going to change my mind about you."

"Why not?" he asked, his tone scandalized. "Even if I get you a chocolate soufflé for dessert?"

At that a reluctant smile curved her lips. It was her favorite dessert, he remembered well.

"They don't have them here," she said.

"Lucky for you, darlin'. Or you'd have no defense against my charm."

"Oh, I don't know." She brushed a couple of dark windblown curls from her face. "I have at least one defense."

"Oh? And what's that?"

"A long memory."

He was quiet for a moment, and then he gave in to the impulse to say, "Long enough to remember the good times too, Gwyn?" The second he said it, however, he knew he'd abandoned his good-natured bravado too early.

Her face closed up, her eyes turned away, and her lips pursed into a frown of pure gloom.

"I'm sorry," he said quickly.

She shook her head, her eyes hard. "You think you can just jolly me out of remembering what you did, Davis," she said in a throaty voice. He could hear the suppressed emotion behind it. "And maybe you can for a minute or two at a time. But I'll never be able to completely forget, and that's why we'll never be friends. I can't believe you'd even be cruel enough to expect it of me."

Her words hit him like a slap in the face, and he felt the bottom drop out of his stomach. It was like a dream he'd had once, in which he woke thinking he'd forgotten an entire semester of classes and he simply couldn't fathom what could have made him do something so stupid. Only, in this scenario, he suddenly realized that her reluctance was not an act, and her rejection of him was not punishment for something that had happened two years ago. Her hurt was real and present and undiminished. Her desire not to see him was genuine.

What an idiot he was. He felt like smacking himself in the head. She was right. It *was* cruel to do this to her. To pop back into her life and "jolly" her into going out for dinner. To tease her and entice her by remembering all of her favorite things. If he'd planned to torture her, he couldn't have fashioned a meaner method.

The waitress came and deposited their drinks. Gwyn stared out at the water and Davis sat stewing in self-recrimination, wondering what to do next.

"Gwyn, I'm sorry," he said finally. For a second he thought she hadn't heard him. Then her head turned slowly back toward him. "I guess I—wasn't thinking."

A seagull squawked its rusty-wheel call nearby. A group of diners near the back burst into muted laughter.

"I certainly didn't intend to be cruel."

A flush crept slowly up her neck to her cheeks. God, what else could he say? He had no idea, and yet he knew something else was required. Should they leave? How awkward would that be? Should he offer to take her home, or would she take that as a further insult?

The bottom line was, of course, that he didn't *want* to leave. Not yet. Not like this. He wanted to make it better—all of it, the past, the now, the future—but he knew that was impossible.

"I know you didn't mean to be cruel," she said finally. "It's not your fault.'"

He laughed once, incredulously. Of course it

was his fault. *He* was the one who'd proposed to *her* and then left her almost immediately thereafter. *He* was the one who'd decided their lives were incompatible. *He* was the one who'd lured her to him and then sent her away when his goals changed.

He was the cad.

"It's not my fault?" he repeated dryly.

One corner of her mouth rose, a quirky, half-amused look he remembered. "Well, it *is*. But it's not."

A small thread of relief trickled through his veins. If she could joke about it . . .

"Gwyn . . ." He leaned across the table to take her hand. "I promise you, I have no intention of hurting you again."

Her fingers closed so he was holding her fist, and she looked down at the table in front of her.

"That's a pretty arrogant thing to say," she said finally. "What makes you think you could?"

Her eyes rose to his, and he could see in them a resolve he'd missed earlier.

"Nothing," he said, feeling foolish again. He let go of her hand and leaned back. "I just wanted you to know that that's the last thing I want. And the last thing I'd ever do again."

Amazingly, she laughed. "You've got that right," she said firmly, rising to her feet.

He watched her gather her purse and push in her chair, a sinking feeling in his chest.

"If anything," she said, leaning toward him with one hand on the table. "This time *I'm* going to hurt *you*."

Chapter Four

He watched her weave through the tables, her slim back straight, dark curls bouncing lightly on her shoulders. She passed their waitress, carrying six oysters on the half shell toward Davis, without even glancing at her. She flung open the screen door to the dining room as if she were bursting from a cake and strode across the threshold.

Davis scratched his chin and stared at the doorway through which she'd passed, the wooden slam of the screen door echoing in his head.

The waitress set the plate down in front of him and picked up his empty beer bottle, looking quizzically at the empty seat across from him.

"I suppose it would be too much to hope," he said slowly, "that she's just gone to the ladies' room."

The waitress glanced back at the door through which Gwyn had departed, obviously remembering the shotgun *smack* of the door slamming.

She sighed and looked back at him with a sympathetic frown. "Want another one?" She waved his beer bottle slightly with two fingers.

He shook his head. "You may as well take that one, too." He glanced at Gwyn's place across from him and motioned toward the chardonnay.

"You're pretty sure she's not coming back, then." She stopped waving the bottle.

Davis bit the inside of his lip thoughtfully. "I don't think so."

She paused, then picked up the wine glass. "Let me bring you another beer. On the house." She smiled.

He tried to smile back but could get no further than a wry grimace. "No. Thank you. I appreciate the thought, though." He got to his feet, pulled a twenty from his wallet and handed it to her.

"You sure?" The waitress hesitated before taking the bill.

"I'm sure," he said. He knew what he had to do.

"Jenny, walking out of that restaurant, I never felt more powerful in my life," Gwyn said to her agent on the phone the next morning.

"That's wonderful!"

"Or more awful."

"What?"

"I know it was the right thing to do, but I just didn't feel good about it," she explained, trying unsuccessfully to fathom the reason herself. When it occurred to her to leave, to get up and stride out of the restaurant like a woman with a spine, a woman with a life, a woman without useless unrequited feelings, she thought she'd feel liberated, finally free of the emotions that had haunted her since Davis had left. But she hadn't.

"It just made me feel sad," she admitted. Then, knowing how that would sound to her feisty and self-righteous friend, she added, "Plus it was immature. Bitchy even, to be brutally honest with myself."

"Gwyn," Jenny said with exaggerated patience, "get some perspective here. It's not like *you* left *him* for a career in a foreign country."

For a moment, Gwyn felt stung by the words. She didn't need to be reminded of how unceremoniously she'd been dumped. But Jenny had a point.

"You know, you're right," she said, mustering what self-righteousness she could. "I was sitting there feeling bad about myself for caving in to his desires and going to dinner with him, so I should feel good about walking out, right?"

"Absolutely. You don't need to let him manipulate his way back into your life after he pushed you out of his."

"That's right." Gwyn lowered a fist onto the arm of the chair she sat in. He *had* pushed her out of his life. "If I'm going to deal with him, I'm going to do it on my own terms. When and *if* I want to."

"Gwyn, you don't have to deal with him at all. Remember that. You moved back there for a reason, remember? You wanted to get back to your art. Don't let him disrupt that."

"I know . . ."

"Speaking of which," Jenny added, excitement

tingeing her voice, "the *real* reason I called, aside from seeing how you were dealing with the devil in your midst, was to tell you that *you*, Ms. Curry, are on the short list at the Rutherford."

Gwyn's heart flipped over in her chest. "What?"

The Rutherford was one of the most exclusive galleries in New York. A showing there would put her on the map as nothing else could.

"The Rutherford, my love. Home of the masters of the future."

"My God," Gwyn breathed. "When do we find out?"

"Well, there are three other artists being considered. But frankly, my dear, I think you are their favorite. Remember Gin Jones, the curator you met last year at Kim's party, who liked your work so much? Guess where her new job is."

"*No! She* got the job at the Rutherford?"

"And she's in your corner, honey. They're supposed to let me know this week. Hopefully before Friday, because I'm going out of town until Monday."

Gwyn's mind raced with possibilities. If they really liked her work, she could probably have more done by the end of the summer, now that she was down here with a saner schedule. And if any of that sold, she could possibly teach part-time next year and have even more time for painting.

She glanced at the clock. "Oh, my God, Jenny, I've got to go. Call me *as soon as you hear anything!*"

"Of course. And stay away from Mr. Wrong, all

right? I can tell already he's sapping your creative energy."

Gwyn sat in her classroom, before a small sea of heads bent to the task of contour drawings, and watched herself walk out of the restaurant again. The screen door slamming behind her had sounded like a starter's pistol. *Annnd, they're off!* she'd imagined. Just like at the racetrack. She couldn't get out of there fast enough.

There'd even been an empty cab in front of the restaurant, as if the whole thing had been preordained.

But then there was that part of her that was not so sure she'd done the right thing. As she'd told Jenny, walking out was a bitchy thing to do. But if, as she'd also told Jenny, she was being brutally honest with herself, she also had to admit that she did not want it to be the last she saw of Davis. And that was what made it all so confusing. She didn't know what to do now.

She kept thinking how nice dinner could have been. What a beautiful evening it was. How easy it had been, on one level, to be with him. And how charismatic he'd looked with the lowering sun glancing off his dark hair and hazel eyes.

But Jenny was right. He *was* sapping her creative energy. Good Lord, she was on the short list at the Rutherford! Success could be right around the corner. And here she was meditating on a disastrous date with an ex-boyfriend.

She glanced at her watch and rapped the wooden end of a paintbrush gently on the table. "All right, class. That's all for today."

The Anniversary That Never Was

Pencils clattered to desktops and chairs screeched abruptly backward. "Bye, Miss Curry" wafted over the noise of gathered backpacks, and before she could count to ten, the classroom was empty.

She didn't blame them. It was summer, and this was another glorious day. She stood up and moved down the aisle of desks, glancing at each student's work in progress. She had a talented group this time. They were doing well.

She got to the back of the room and looked toward the front, remembering her own schooling at Southwalk. She'd come here as a freshman, alone in the world after the death of her parents. Fortunately, she'd been close to her grandparents so living with them was not as strange as it might have been. But still, it was difficult moving to a new town, being the new kid in class, and being orphaned, to boot.

Davis had saved her then. He'd been two years older, the most popular boy in school, and he'd taken a shine to her. Why, she didn't know. She hadn't been pretty, not the way high school girls wanted to be pretty anyway. Her hair was too curly, her clothes unassuming; she wore glasses; and she'd never mastered make-up, so she didn't wear any. But he'd singled her out anyway, because he'd lost his parents too, and they'd become fast, deep friends.

Gwyn sighed and leaned on the radiator, remembering how amazed and proud she'd been to walk the halls with him. He'd never seemed to notice how good-looking or popular he was. He didn't think it unusual that a boy like him would be talking to her, a nobody. But she'd never lost sight of it. She'd felt thankful every day he'd said good morning to her. Thankful that he hadn't forgotten overnight that he liked her.

As she sat in the quiet classroom, she heard the outside door open and footsteps echo down the hallway. At first she thought one of the students must have forgotten something, but no, a student would have been running. And it didn't sound like tennis shoes. It sounded like the steady footsteps of an adult.

She sat still, her eyes on the door, still wrapped up in the memory of Davis in high school. In many ways, the memory was so much more familiar than the Davis she'd seen last night. He was still confident, still charming, but was he still kind? She didn't know. She didn't know him anymore.

She was not surprised when the footsteps slowed outside her room and Davis appeared in the doorway.

She couldn't help it; she smiled when she saw him. "Where's your letter jacket?"

He pushed his hands into the pockets of his jeans and smiled back. His eyes were still kind, she thought.

"It's a little warm for it."

She crossed her arms over her chest and regarded him across the rows of desks. "I was just thinking about high school, and how nice you were to me when I first moved here."

He leaned against the door frame. "I'm glad you were thinking nice thoughts. After last night, I was afraid there were no good memories left."

She shrugged and felt a lump grow in her

throat. If only things were as simple as they'd been in high school. If only being nice to one another was enough to make a strong relationship.

"Not that I don't deserve to be remembered for the bad ones," he added quietly.

She swallowed. "I have all kinds of memories of you, Davis," she said. "Mostly positive, if you must know. And you deserve them all."

He looked down and chewed the inside of his cheek.

"I'm sorry I left you last night," she added. "When I sit here in this school, it seems strange to feel so at odds with you. You were my best friend. For a long time."

"You don't need to apologize for last night. *I* do." His voiced sounded lower than normal, constrained. "I want you to know, it's not that I was ignoring what I did, or how you must have felt. I just—I guess it just felt so good to see you, I wanted to pretend that all that other stuff hadn't happened. I wanted *my* best friend back, but I didn't deserve you. I *don't* deserve you."

She took a deep breath. "We went in different directions, Davis. You just saw yours first. You knew what you needed to do. That's all."

He smiled, a small, knowing smile she'd forgotten about. And she felt her stomach give a little leap at the familiar sight of it.

"I went halfway around the world, Gwyn, only to find that what I really wanted I had left behind."

Gwyn felt suddenly as if every nerve had been set on fire. "Sometimes it just seems that way, when you leave everything you're familiar with behind."

He shook his head. "I knew you'd say that. That's not what I'm saying."

"What are you saying?"

"I'm saying that I made a terrible mistake in leaving. I'm saying that from the day I landed in Latvia, I knew that I'd lost the one thing that was really important. You, Gwyn."

Her thoughts spun in her head, too numerous and confused to untangle. "From the day you landed in Latvia?" An intense desire to believe what he said warred with an old, half-buried anger. "Well, what in the world took you so long to let me know?" She laughed cynically.

"I know what you're thinking. And you should be mad. I have no right to pop up now, over two years later, and tell you these things. But believe me when I tell you I'm not expecting anything from you; you don't need to respond. I wasn't thinking you'd come running back into my arms or anything."

She laughed again, and had to stand and turn away from him to gather her thoughts. "This is crazy," she said, mostly to herself. After a minute she turned back. "You're telling me that as soon as you left, you knew it was a mistake. So why didn't you call me? Or write? Or let me know *somehow* that that's how you felt? Why did it take you *two years* to come back?" She scoffed at the absurdity of it.

He exhaled heavily. "I had made a commitment. I felt that if I called you, I'd want to come back too much, which I couldn't do. I'd signed on for two years, and two years was what I'd give them."

"And the commitment you'd made to me? The

engagement? That was less important?" Her stomach knotted with the old frustration.

He shook his head. "I didn't break off the engagement, Gwyn. *You* did that."

"As if I had any choice. You were leaving for two years! What in the world did you expect?"

He was silent a moment, looking at his feet. "I guess," he began slowly, feeling his way with the words, "I didn't *expect* anything. I was just going. Doing something. Trying to move forward, toward my goal. And when you got so upset, I guess it felt like you were trying to stop me from achieving something I felt was important. You made me make a choice, and I didn't know what to do. It wasn't until I'd made it irrevocable that I realized I'd made the wrong one."

Yes, she knew that. She had given him an ultimatum. And since she was being so brutally honest with herself today, she would admit that if he *had* called, she would have written it off as homesickness, not a real commitment to their engagement. Especially not if he'd told her all that and then told her he still wasn't coming back.

"And I knew if I called you," he continued, watching her face, "and told you how I felt, you would have just told me I was using you to ease my homesickness."

She glanced at him quickly, unnerved that he could still read her mind so accurately. That sort of thing used to happen between them all the time. She'd have a thought and he'd know it. She could never hide anything from him.

Now she wondered if he could read her other thoughts as clearly, the ones that wanted her to make a complete fool out of herself by running across the room and throwing herself into his arms. She wanted to kiss him so badly, she had to clench her teeth against the desire. Most of all, she wanted to know how badly he had missed her, and that he still loved her after all these years.

Stupid, weak thoughts, she chastised herself.

"Then," he continued, "time went by and the life there was so hard, all I could think about was the next moment, the next patient, the next starving victim. Not to be melodramatic, Gwyn, but I started just being thankful that I was alive and in one piece, and able to return to a country where starvation and want are not accepted daily occurrences. It wasn't until I got back to Charlotte that I realized what my life was missing. That may sound convenient to you, but once you're not living amidst total social and political upheaval, it takes you a while to remember what normal life is like."

"So you returned to Charlotte and realized that your life was missing me, so you started dating the stockbroker." She hated the way her voice sounded, petulant and bitter. He started to respond and she held up her hand. "No, wait. Don't explain. You don't owe me any explanation. You and I broke up. Both of us were free to do whatever we wanted after that."

"No." His voice was angry and he straightened from his leaning pose against the door frame. He took several steps toward her and stopped, one finger outstretched. "That's what I'm trying to explain to you. I was not free once we broke up. I was *never* free from you. It hit me over and over again, stronger and stronger the more time passed, that I was *never* going to be free of you. And I didn't even want to be."

Gwyn swallowed, staring at the emotion in his face, the way his throat worked when he stopped talking, as if he had the same lump in his that she had in hers.

"And you've never been free of me, either," he said quietly. "I can tell." He lowered his hand.

At that the tears she felt behind her eyes welled up and spilled over her lashes.

"You have no idea how many times I wanted to come back and find you," he said. "But I told myself it wasn't fair. Not to you. I heard you were doing well, a great success in New York." He flung his hands out and laughed. "I just couldn't see myself showing up after all that time and saying, 'Hey, here I am. Want me back?'"

You don't have any trouble doing it now, though, do you? she thought, wishing she could say the words aloud but not trusting her voice.

"Which is not what I'm doing now," he added with that small smile. He moved closer and raised his hand. Gently, with his thumb, he wiped away a tear. "I just wanted to apologize for last night. For not considering your feelings. And I wanted to explain a little about mine."

She sat for a long moment unable to speak. He was so close. And his touch was so tender.

Finally, she said, "I don't know what I'm supposed to do with this information."

He shook his head. "Nothing."

"No." She looked up at him, her eyes hard and direct. "You can't just come here and dump this all on me and then tell me I don't have to do anything with it. What were your *real* intentions here, Davis? At least be honest with me. What were you hoping for?"

She studied him to be sure it was an actual blush that flooded his cheeks.

He cleared his throat. "I came back to this town, Gwyn, because this was where I was happiest. I told myself that to come live here would make me as content as I was growing up. But what drew me here, what I was *really* looking for, was you. You are in every memory I have of this place. You represent happiness to me. I knew it when I was driving back here. And I was sure of it when I saw you again. I made a mistake, Gwyn. I made a mistake letting you go. And I just can't tell you how sorry I am."

He was close enough for her to see his chest rise and fall as he breathed. He was close enough that she could smell the soap from his shower. He was close enough that she could reach out and touch him, if she wanted.

He was too close.

"I'm sorry, too," she said. But the words emerged in a whisper. She took a breath, steeled herself, and added, "I've been sorry for two years. I've been sorry, upset, lonely, and heartbroken. But you know what, Davis? I'm better now. It took me two years, but I'm better. And I just don't think I can allow myself to jump back into the exact same situation that hurt me. Do you understand?"

He dropped his gaze. "Of course I do."

She noted the way his tan faded along the side of his neck where his dark hair fell.

"Do you understand that I've gotten on with my life? And that you're not a part of it anymore?"

He hunched his shoulders. "Yes. Yes, I do."

Her eyes dropped to where his thumbs looped inside his front pockets, to where the waistband of his jeans dipped slightly with the pressure, to where lean hips met muscular legs.

"And do you understand now that seeing you on a casual basis would be impossible?"

He nodded and expelled a long breath. "Yes."

She remembered clearly how powerful his chest felt against her hands, how the flat skin of his stomach felt on her palms, how the muscles of his abdomen rippled under her fingers. She remembered clearly how it felt to grasp the zipper of his faded jeans and lower it slowly.

She closed her eyes. "Oh, God."

"Tell me," he responded.

She remembered the feel of their bodies coming together, skin against skin, and she felt her knees go soft. She sat down hard on the radiator and licked her dry lips.

"Tell me," he repeated.

She opened her eyes and let her gaze travel up his chest, envisioning the polo shirt pulled over his head and off, picturing the solid chest and the dark hair scattered across it. She swallowed hard and raised her eyes.

Heat emanated from his gaze and scorched her with the look he gave. His expression was contrite no more, and the intensity in his face took her breath away.

"Gwyn," he murmured.

She wanted to protest, to move away, to say no

or even just to shake her head, but she was paralyzed. Her body had sold her out and would no longer do as she bade. Instead it throbbed for his touch, reaching out to him with every nerve ending, every ounce of desire she'd ever felt.

But he didn't move. He didn't come toward her, didn't touch her, didn't give an inch. He stood less than a foot away and pinned her with molten eyes while her whole body cried out for him.

She felt as if she were becoming liquid from the inside out, and if he didn't touch her soon, she would melt at his feet.

"Davis," she said, her own voice a whisper again.

"What do you want?" The low words sent waves of desire crashing through her body.

Her hands were slick against the radiator.

"I don't—"

I don't know, her mind screamed, but a very conscious part of her knew that if she said that, he would leave. And she didn't want him to go. She wanted him to touch her again. She wanted all of him again so badly that she couldn't move.

"You don't what?"

Had he gotten closer? She felt as if they were gravitating toward each other, as if without either of them moving, they had gotten closer together. His mouth was firm, his eyes unyielding, and she knew that if she wanted him, she would have to make the first move.

Trembling, she pushed herself to her feet. They *were* closer together now, their shirts almost touching, and part of her did go liquid inside.

"I don't want you to go," she said.

"I'm not going anywhere." His breath touched her hair.

She gazed at him steadily. "I want you, Davis."

He inhaled at the words, and she thought she heard a little catch in his breath. Briefly, he closed his eyes. Then he raised his hands to her bare arms.

Her nerves were so alive, she flinched at the touch. His hands were hot, his fingers gentle, as they slid up her arms to her neck. He cupped her face and, with great care, lowered his mouth to hers. Their breath mingled and his lips touched hers with infinite tenderness.

Gwyn opened her mouth under his. Her body was on fire and her hands rose to his rib cage. Her fingers grasped his muscled sides and pulled him closer.

His tongue plunged into her mouth. He dropped his hands to her waist and pulled her tightly against him. She rose on tiptoe and wrapped her arms around his neck. Their mouths fused, their bodies flattened against each other, and she felt him grow hard against her almost instantly.

Holding her to him, he moved her to one side, away from the radiator. She felt her back touch the cool, painted cinder block, and his hands flattened on the wall on either side of her, his hips pressed into hers. Her own rose up to meet them, and she brought her hands to the waistband of his jeans. With only a moment's hesitation, she popped the button.

His lips were everywhere then. On her mouth, her cheeks, down her neck, nuzzling her skin and nipping her with gentle teeth. His right hand came between them and undid the buttons of her shirt.

She lowered the zipper of his jeans and slid her fingers into the waistband of his boxers. Then she reached down to touch him, hot and hard.

He moaned into her mouth.

He pushed her shirt back, lowered her bra straps, and bent his head to her peaked nipples. Gwyn inhaled sharply and arched her back. Her fingers gripped him lightly.

Abruptly, he pulled back. Gwyn nearly gasped at the sudden abatement.

"What is it?" she breathed.

He gave her a brief, intense look, then strode to the door and shut it. Flipping the lock, he turned and pulled the polo shirt over his head.

His chest was lean and strong, just as she remembered it, and she longed to lay her hands on it.

She pushed her shirt off and unhooked her bra, dropping both as he pulled her into his arms again.

"God, you're beautiful," he murmured just before capturing her mouth again with his.

Gwyn broke away briefly, pushed her pants off, and watched him do the same. Then they met skin to skin, Gwyn's heart swooping with pleasure at the sudden total contact. He pulled one of her legs up his side and ran his fingers along her moistened heat. She quivered at the touch and reached for him.

"I want you, Davis," she whispered. "I want you inside of me."

She pulled him toward her hot center, rubbing him lightly against her first.

"Do you really want this, Gwyn?" he asked quietly.

She chuckled low. "Fine time to ask." She smiled against his lips and kissed him, her tongue tracing his mouth and then plunging inside in obvious rhythm.

He took over then, taking himself in hand and guiding himself to her. Bending his knees he pushed upward, and with a low groan he slid deep inside.

Gwyn gasped with pleasure and raised her other leg. He grabbed it and pinned her against the wall. With his arms supporting her, he pushed himself further inside.

"I've missed you," he breathed into her ear. "I missed you so much."

Her heart pumped blood through her so rapidly, it was a roar in her ears. She felt deaf and blind with desire, and leaned her head back against the wall.

Davis bent his head, trailed his lips along her neck and thrust deeply inside of her, again and again, until she peaked and cried out. A second later he thrust one last time and shuddered, laying his forehead against the wall beside her.

She clung to him, their bodies slick with sweat, and felt his heart thundering against his chest and into her own. She breathed in the clean smell of his exertion and drew a small circle with her tongue on his shoulder, then kissed him. Her skin tingled with satisfaction.

"Gwyn, you're incredible," he whispered. "I remembered it being good, but *this* . . ."

She laid her head on his shoulder and exhaled.

Slowly, without her consent, reality slipped back over her like cool dusk after a scorching day.

It *was* incredible. But who was to say it would last this time?

Chapter Five

Davis turned into the gravel drive whistling to the sound of Louis Armstrong's trumpet blaring from his car stereo. He had more than enough time to settle in and make some coffee before Gwyn had to leave, he figured, so he was surprised to see that her car was gone.

He slowed to a stop, pulled up the emergency brake, and looked around the little parking area, as if he might have somehow overlooked her car. After a moment, he turned down the radio. Then he turned off the ignition.

Could be an early meeting, he told himself. Maybe there were things—projects to grade or something—that she hadn't done yesterday afternoon. Things she had to finish before the students showed up. Maybe she had to take her car to the shop. Maybe aliens had landed and abducted her.

Or maybe she was avoiding him.

He sat in his car and stared up at her back door. She wasn't home, he knew it. He knew with every fiber of his being that she had left early because she did not want to see him. And she did not want to see him because she regretted what had happened yesterday.

"*Dammit!*" He hit the steering wheel with the heel of his hand. "Dammit, dammit, dammit," he muttered, shaking his head and staring at her apartment. He laid his head back against the headrest and stared at the sky.

She hadn't forgiven him. And if she hadn't forgiven him after yesterday, he didn't know when she ever would. He'd poured his heart out to her, and she'd responded. He felt as if their souls had touched.

And today she was avoiding him.

Anger stirred in his gut. Don't be ridiculous, he told himself. It's probably just a breakfast meeting. But he knew better. He knew her so well.

The trill of a bird wafted over the silent morning air. How peaceful it would have been to sit on the front porch with her. He'd even bought croissants. A moment passed, and the bird trilled again.

He lifted his head.

It trilled again.

It wasn't a bird, he realized. It was a phone. But it was coming from outside.

He got out of the car and walked toward the house. The phone trilled again, and he raised his head.

It was on the landing, upstairs. From where he stood, he could just make out the small black body of Gwyn's portable phone on the railing. She should have an answering machine, he thought absently, and listened for the ring.

Nothing came. Whoever it was had given up. He moved to the back door of his office and unlocked it.

He was just starting to make coffee when he heard the phone ring again. He scooped the grounds into the filter and listened to it ring. If it stopped after four rings, he'd know she had a machine. But the phone kept ringing. And ringing. At ten rings he decided he should answer it. Obviously somebody needed to get hold of her and he could at least take a message. Which might even give him an excuse to go see her this evening, not that he needed more of an excuse than to ask her why she was avoiding him.

He had just reached the steps when the ringing stopped. He paused with one foot on the first stair and sighed, looking up at the landing. When he was about to turn around, the phone rang again.

Somebody was definitely trying to get hold of her. He had a momentary panicked thought that it might be Art or Bernice, that something might have happened to one of them, but realized immediately that either of them would have called his office, too.

He reached the phone, picked it up, and found the talk button. He hit it with his thumb and said, "Hello."

A pause. "Hello?" A woman's voice.

"Yes, hello?" he said.

"Ah, did I dial seven-oh-four—"

"Are you looking for Gwyn?"

Another pause, then a slow intake of breath. "Actually, yes. Is she there?"

"No. Can I take a message?"

"A message? You take messages for her?"

The woman's voice was marked by a distinct New York accent and laced with something he could only define as suspicion.

"Look, I have an office right under her apartment and I heard her phone ringing. If you want to leave a message, I'll make sure she gets it."

"So you're the doctor," she said, as if it confirmed something tragic.

"That's right. Davis Hilliard." So Gwyn had mentioned him to this person. He wondered in what context. Reflecting on the woman's tone of voice, he decided she probably knew their whole sordid history. "Do you want me to take a message?"

"Davis Hilliard," the woman mused. "Hmm. Ah, yeah. You know, in fact, yes. Yes, you can take a message."

Well, hallelujah, he said to himself, deciding he couldn't be rude until he found out how important this person might be to Gwyn.

"This is Jenny Rogers, Gwyn's agent?"

"Okay." He started back down the steps, thinking he might need a pen.

"Tell her she got the show at the Rutherford."

"Okay, wait, hang on. Let me get a pen." He jogged the rest of the way in to his desk and grabbed a pen and paper. "All right. She got the show at the Rutherford . . ."

"Yeah, and this is a *really* big deal, Hilliard. I'm telling you her career will *take off* after this."

"That's great." He underlined Rutherford.

"No, you don't understand. She will be *hot*. And if I could get her to move back up here, there's no telling what she could do. You know how personable she is; she'd have these people *begging* to show her stuff."

"Really?" He underlined Rutherford again and frowned.

"Oh, God, yes. In fact, the reason she got this show is because she met Gin Jones at a party and Gin fell in love with her."

Davis didn't like the idea of anyone, let alone someone named after an alcoholic beverage, falling in love with Gwyn. Especially not someone who could have such control over her career.

"And does—uh, *Gin* want her to move back too?"

"Of course! Everyone does. So you tell her about the Rutherford and that if she comes back I can probably get her into the Severne and Claybrooke's both within six months. With the Rutherford on her resume, there's no place she can't go now. And Gin knows everyone, too. You tell her that. Gin will get her shown wherever she wants."

"Oh, you bet. I'll let her know." He made three more black lines under *The Rutherford*, then drew a line through the whole thing entirely.

"Have you got all that, Hilliard?" The woman was starting to grate on his nerves.

"Got it." He obliterated the word *Rutherford* with the pen.

"Thanks. And tell her to call me back on Monday. I'm going to be gone for the weekend, but I'll expect to hear from her first thing Monday morning."

"Yeah. Right. Okay."

"Good."

The woman hung up, and Davis lowered the phone from his ear. This was the worst news possible. For him, he amended quickly. How could Gwyn not go back to New York with success like that waiting for her? For God's sake, she'd probably go back for a whole lot less now that she was so determined to avoid him. If only he had more time. He knew he could have brought her around if he'd had a week or two. Even four or five days would have been better than this. A weekend. How could he convince her to stay in two days after news like this? She'd probably pack her bags and go up this weekend.

He could not give her the message, the devil whispered in his ear. Maybe if the woman didn't hear from Gwyn, she wouldn't call back on Monday. Maybe she would think Gwyn had to think about it, make up her mind and give her a decision later. That might buy him a few days.

But that would be bad. That would be truly despicable. This was the most wonderful news Gwyn could probably receive. How much could he love her if he didn't want to make her happy with it immediately?

The coffee pot gurgled the last of its water through the filter and he stared at it.

How much could he love her? he asked himself again. He lifted his eyes and looked around the office, at the books he'd finally gotten unpacked, at the instruments in their glass-fronted cabinets and the jars on the counter. He even had a stack of magazines in the waiting room.

How much could he love her?

Gwyn stared out the window of her classroom after the students had gone and forced herself to be objective.

He had come back to this town without knowing she would be here. He'd come back, in fact, thinking she was still in New York. So he hadn't made any concerted effort to find her again. He'd just happened upon her.

As much as she might wish his actions yesterday meant he still truly loved her, in the cold light of day they just seemed the actions of a healthy, red-blooded, American male in response to the obvious invitation of a red-blooded, American female.

She turned from the window and gazed at the spot where they'd made love just yesterday. Her knees felt weak thinking about it. Nobody had ever touched her the way Davis did. He brought out feelings in her she had never felt with anyone at any other time. He was her soul mate.

But that was just the sort of thinking that had broken her heart before, she reminded herself fiercely. Two years ago she'd thought nothing could separate them; she'd been completely confident in their future, and then he'd told her he was leaving. She was taking nothing for granted now.

She turned her back on the place where they had made love and moved purposefully to the front of the room. She would pack up her things and go to the river to paint. She wanted to paint The Supply House, and in the late afternoon light it would be perfect. She would go and create something, and she would forget about Davis Hilliard for the moment. Later, after she'd exorcised her demons through her art, she'd figure out what on earth to say to him.

She picked up her portfolio and unzipped it. Plenty of paper. She walked to the back of the room to pick out some brushes. She should work in oils, she decided. Watercolors were redundant in a river scene. She grabbed a small canvas she'd stretched and prepped yesterday and picked through the tubes of paint in a box. She'd do a little one first. A study.

Down the hall the doorway creaked open and banged shut. Footsteps sounded on the linoleum. Soft, leather-soled shoes. Well-worn.

She spun as the steps slowed outside her room. A second later, Davis appeared.

They stared at each other for a long minute. Finally, he smiled, a little sadly, she thought.

"Hi," he said.

"Hi." She clutched the paint tubes so hard they started to conform to her hand. She loosened her grip.

He pushed his hands down in his pockets and walked slowly into the room, stopping at the desk. He leaned back against it.

"How're you doing?" he asked.

"I'm fine."

Sure, fine. She was surprised he didn't roll his eyes. He knew something was wrong. He'd have to be an idiot not to, and he was a far cry from an idiot.

"Early meeting this morning?" The corner of his mouth lifted wryly.

She looked at her feet, then placed the brushes and paint back on the counter, turning slightly away from him. "No. I just wanted to get an early start."

"I see."

Yes, he most likely did see, she thought. She should have known he would show up here. She should have prepared something to say to him. But what did she *want* to say? Should she ask him how he felt about her? What his intentions were? If he was still in love with her?

The problem was, she couldn't imagine what *he* could say to make her ever believe in their future again. If, of course, that was what he wanted to do.

He took a deep breath and looked at her, really studying her face, as if he were curious about something he thought he'd seen there.

"Is something wrong?" she asked finally.

"No." He shook his head. "No, in fact I think I have some good news for you."

She drew her brows together. "For me? What?"

"Well, I hope you don't mind, but I answered your phone for you this morning. . . ."

"My phone? How did you get in?"

He chuckled softly. "You'd left it out on the landing. And even then I wouldn't have answered it except that it was ringing off the hook. Somebody really wanted to get hold of you."

Her heart beat picked up. "Who was it?"

"Somebody named Jenny."

"Jenny Rogers. My agent." She clasped her hands together and brought them to her chin. Could it be? The Rutherford?

"That's the name. Jenny Rogers. She said to be sure to tell you, you got the show—"

"At the Rutherford?" Gwyn's eyes widened and her breath stopped.

He nodded, smiling, and she laughed.

"Oh my God! Do you know what this *means?*" She covered her mouth with her hands and looked at him over her fingers.

"She explained it to me pretty well, I think. For some reason she really wanted me to understand that this means your career could be on easy street now."

Gwyn shrugged and dropped her hands, but could not quell the smile on her lips. "Well, I wouldn't say easy street, but it sure will make a difference." She leaned back against the counter and hugged her arms to her middle. "I really didn't think it would happen. She told me I was on the short list, but I really didn't think it would happen. Oh, my God," she repeated as the reality of it hit her again. "It's really happening."

"Congratulations," he said sincerely.

"Thank you. And thank you for answering the phone."

He lifted his arms out to the sides. "Anytime."

"I've got to call Jenny." She pushed both hands through her hair and looked around as if there might be a phone nearby.

"Don't bother. She's out of town until Monday. But she expects to hear from you first thing."

Gwyn laughed. "Oh, she'll hear from me, all right. Wow." She sighed. "I can't believe it."

"Believe it."

"You're not just making this up to make me feel good about myself?" She looked at him sideways.

"Now what good would that do? Eventually you'd feel even worse."

She shook her head again. "I just can't believe it."

He looked thoughtful and gazed down at his shoes, his arms crossed over his chest.

There was something more, she could feel it. She knew he was happy for her success; she knew him too well to believe that he wouldn't be. Yet, there was something in his stance, something in the somber set of his face, that made her uneasy. His downcast eyes were somehow vulnerable. Looking at him, she felt her heart swell with potent, old emotions.

"Davis . . ."

He lifted his head.

Uncertainty colored her tone, but she had to ask. "Is there something else? Is something wrong?"

He took a deep breath. "Gwyn, your agent . . . she sounded pretty positive that if you came back to New York, she could do even more for you. She mentioned two other places . . . ah, Severne and . . . damn." He searched his pockets. "I wrote it down. Claymore? Clayton?"

"Claybrooke's?" she couldn't keep the surprise from her voice.

"That's it. She really seemed to think you should be back in New York."

Gwyn scoffed.

"No, listen, Gwyn, I was thinking. This is too good an opportunity for you to pass up. You could build your future right now—"

"I don't want to go back to New York—"

"*Listen* to me, Gwyn. I have a plan."

She looked at him, curious. The expression on his face was so intense.

"I know you were struggling up there; it's an expensive place for an artist. And believe me I know how draining that can be. But suppose you had some help? Suppose . . ."

Dread curled her stomach. "Davis, you're *not* going to offer to lend me money," she said ominously. "Please tell me that's *not* what you had in mind."

He looked up at her and chuckled. "Don't you think I know you better than that?"

His soft voice sent a ribbon of excitement through her.

"My plan was . . . that is, I thought, if you *wanted*, that we could both go. It could be purely platonic," he offered quickly. "I got some job offers up there—one that was really good. I—I was thinking about taking it anyway."

She gave him a heavily skeptical look, but he kept on.

"And I've got some savings. It would make the move a whole lot easier on both of us."

"Davis—"

"No, really."

"Davis, I know you're lying. You hate the city. You've always hated the city."

He looked abashed, but still he did not let go.

Her heart swelled even further for him, for this gallant, misguided effort.

"Gwyn, I want to help you. Please let me do this for you."

She looked at him, suddenly unsure of what, exactly, he was proposing. Did he..? Could he..? She wasn't sure she could ask why he wanted to help her so badly.

"Davis, this is nice of you—"

"No, it's not," he cut her off. "It's totally self-centered. You see . . . I feel like I've just found my heart, Gwyn. Please don't make me rip it out again." His voice was soft, but perfectly audible, his eyes direct. He was not mumbling false words of sentiment. "I just don't think I could take losing you all over again."

She opened her mouth to speak but nothing emerged.

After a second, he smiled mildly. "I see I've stumped you."

Logic jammed in her head. "But—but what about your practice? You just got here. This was your dream, your own place."

He shrugged. "I told you, there was that job offer. Besides, there'll be time for being a country doctor later. And Dr. Walker over in Crescent Beach wanted the practice here if I didn't, your grandfather told me. I'm sure he'd be more than willing to take it over now. And I'm also sure the school can find another teacher, too, so don't let that stop you."

Gwyn's heart accelerated. "You'd do this," she asked, her voice nearly a whisper, "for me?"

"This and more, darlin'," he said softly.

Her heart hammered in her chest. She could see in his eyes that he meant it.

"This is your chance," he continued, "just like I thought Europe was mine. Only now I understand how painful it is to lose someone to pursue an ambition. And how pointless." He hesitated, and then smiled wickedly. "I don't want to put you through that. So I'm going with you."

Against her will, she laughed. "Davis—"

"No, no." He held up his hands. "There's no talking me out of it. I've got my heart set on New York."

"Then you'll be going alone," she said with a smile. "Because I'm not leaving here."

"What?" He frowned. "Why not?"

"Davis, I came back here not just because New York was hard, but because I was losing touch with that part of me that wanted to create. The last six months I was there, I couldn't paint. I was so stressed out, my life was no longer making sense."

"So you came back here to relax, and found me. Doing nothing but complicating things."

"Yes." She nodded. "That threw me for a loop. But you know what? I think it's also clarified something for me. Part of me thought coming back here was a defeat, like I was giving up on myself. But it wasn't. In fact, this was the one thing I could do to help myself. New York wasn't right for me. New York will *never* be right for me. And maybe . . . maybe whatever it was that drove you to Latvia drove me up there to try to succeed. But maybe we've both learned from our mistakes, Davis. I know I've learned that I belong here."

"And I," he said, coming toward her, "I've learned that I belong with you, Gwyn, and nowhere else."

Gwyn's heart threatened to burst from her chest at his words. "You . . . you were willing to move for me. You were willing to give up your brand-new practice and go to a place that you hate."

He looked at her steadily. "That's right. And I'll do it the moment you say the word."

Gwyn felt tears prick her eyes. "Oh, Davis . . ."

He didn't relinquish her gaze.

"I won't be saying the word," she said softly, thinking it was amazing. He'd found the one thing he could say to make her believe in their future again. A smile trembled on her lips. "I'll be staying here."

"With me?" he asked, his whispered voice breaking over the words.

She smiled and reached out a hand. "With you, Davis."

Chapter Six

"To Gwyn and Davis," Bernice Curry announced, lifting her champagne glass high. "On their first anniversary. May there be many more!"

"Hear, hear!" The cheer went up from the crowd of people strewn across the manicured lawn. White-coated servers moved soundlessly through the group distributing flutes of champagne with white monogrammed napkins.

"And to Bernice and Art," Davis added, when the noise had abated a little, "On their *fifty-second* anniversary!"

The crowd was even louder this time, and the clinking of glasses sounded on the May breeze like miniature church bells.

Gwyn and Davis exchanged a smile over their champagne, Gwyn taking just the barest sip of hers before turning to her grandparents.

"That cake is fabulous," Gwyn said, meeting her grandmother's glass with her own and then moving to her grandfather's.

"Isn't it divine?" Bernice agreed, her long white scarf billowing out behind her in the breeze. "You'll never believe it, but Swordfish's *sister* made that. Turns out she's a caterer in Wilmington. We're going to use her for the opening of the new Curry wing at the hospital."

"Really? That's wonderful." Gwyn looked at the extravagantly tall confection, unable to imagine anyone related to Swordfish creating something so festive looking. "But I hope I won't have to wait so long to have that cake again. December's too far off."

"Not to mention that you won't be there anyway," Davis said, snaking an arm around her waist. "Remember that's the same weekend as your opening at Claybrooke's. I can't believe I even have to remind you."

"That's right, dear," her grandmother said, looking at her quizzically. "Don't go getting as forgetful as your old grandmother, now."

"Old, my foot," Gwyn scoffed.

"I hope you at least remember how sorry we are to be missing your opening, darling. But these people were so particular about our being there."

"Of course they were," Gwyn said, laughing. "You gave them several million dollars."

Bernice waved the fact off with a hand. "Yes, but we didn't intend for them to throw a *party* with it, for crying out loud. It was for the hospital."

"I hardly think a cake and some champagne are going to break the budget," Davis said. "It's just too bad it's all happening on the same weekend."

"Yes, isn't it," Gwyn murmured.

They all sipped their champagne, letting companionable silence reign briefly.

"But you know," Gwyn said after a minute, "I'm thinking it might be best for us to go to the hospital in December, after all, Davis. There'll be other openings, and we were just in New York last month."

Davis pivoted so that he looked her square in the face, his hand resting on her waist. "What are you talking about, Gwyn? This is Claybrooke's. The 'ultimate triumph,' according to your alter-ego Jenny."

Gwyn took a breath and pretended to think a minute, keeping the smile from her face with some effort. "Well, yes, there is that."

Bernice studied her with narrowed eyes. "Gwyndolyn . . ."

"It's just that I thought," Gwyn said to Davis, "that it might be good for you to go meet some of the doctors there. You know how you've been talking about expanding the practice here. Maybe someone there would be interested."

"But I can do that anytime."

"But it's an obstetrics wing, so there will be a lot of obstetricians there." She smiled up at him.

"Well, obviously, sweetheart." He laughed and shook his head at her grandparents. "But even if I do decide to expand, I'm not going to get a specialist. Just another GP, like me." He reached out and pushed a lock of hair behind her ear.

Bernice hooted with laughter beside them.

Davis's brows drew together and he glanced over at her. "What's so funny?"

"Trust me, Davis," Gwyn said, drawing his attention back to herself. "I think you should meet some obstetricians. Especially in December. Good timing." She shrugged nonchalantly and nodded with her grandmother.

"Gwyn, honey, I told you—"

Davis stopped. His mouth dropped open.

"Are you—?" His gaze flew from a smiling Gwyn to Bernice, whose eyes streamed with tears of laughter, to Art, who chuckled along with her.

Davis took Gwyn by the shoulders and turned her to face him. "Stop playing around now, Gwyn, and tell me straight out. Are you..?"

She gave him an exaggeratedly expectant look, waiting for the rest of the sentence, and then slowly supplied, ". . . pregnant?"

He stared at her, blood rushing to his cheeks.

She laughed and nodded. "Yes. I am pregnant."

He straightened, his grip on her shoulders tightening slightly, and glared at Art and Bernice over her shoulder. "Did you know this?" he demanded.

They shook their heads, laughing.

Davis again focused on Gwyn. "How long have you known?"

"About three weeks. I'll be due in December, in case you didn't catch that part."

Finally, a broad smile broke across his face. "Pregnant."

Gwyn nodded.

"My God. I'm going to be a father."

Gwyn smiled.

"I'm going to be a father!" He looked down on

her in wonderment, then bent, scooped her up and twirled her around, capturing her mouth with his.

"Hey, everyone!" Art bellowed out, ringing a fork against the side of his glass. "Listen up!"

The crowd quieted again and turned to face them. Davis could not take his eyes off Gwyn as he set her back on the ground.

"We have another toast," Art said. "To the parents-to-be!" He raised his glass high, and the guests cheered again.

Davis pulled his wife close to him with one arm around her waist and kissed her soundly on the mouth.

"I love you," he said against her ear, to the accompaniment of the crowd's applause. "I love you so much."

"And I love you," Gwyn replied, her arms around his neck. "More than anything on earth."

Ever
a
Bridesmaid
Kathleen Nance

*For Grady, Sara, Carl, and David. For your patience,
support, surrendering the computer, and willingness
to eat a lot of pizza.*

Chapter One

Kristen Lucas had been a flower girl twice, a bridesmaid four times, and a maid of honor three times, but she'd never been the best man. Nine trips down the aisle, but being best man for her friend Ross would be a first.

What did one call a female best man? Kris pondered the question as her airplane pulled into the gate at New Orleans International Airport. Best woman? Groomsmaid? Primary attendant? She picked up her purse and the portfolio holding her wedding present to Ross and Olivia and shrugged her duffel over her shoulder. She had a week before the wedding; she'd think of something. Until then, best man would have to do.

At least with this wedding, there was one complication she wouldn't have to worry about. Ross would never try to pair her off with one of the groomsmen—unlike all her other stints as an attendant, excepting the two as flower girl, when the brides invariably tried to match her up with someone.

What was it about weddings that brought out that two-by-two urge in everyone but her? Ever a bridesmaid, never a bride, was just the way she liked it. And Ross knew it.

Once deplaned, she headed toward the taxi stand, striding past the Mardi Gras posters, the mobile daiquiri cart, and the Lucky Dog vendor. She paused, eyeing the giant hot dog cart. Lunch had been a long time ago.

"Kristen Lucas?"

The deep masculine voice startled her. Kris pivoted, and her glance caught on a broad chest encased in a pin-striped shirt and navy linen jacket. When she looked up—a rare event, since she was five-ten—her lungs forgot to breathe and her stomach decided it was still airborne.

Dark had always attracted her, and this stranger's short-cropped hair, thick brows, and eyes were all as dark as a starless midnight. Only the shadow of a beard saved his finely chiseled face from masculine perfection. Two small silver cuffs on his left ear added a piratical air.

Kris forced herself to drag in a deep breath. This man radiated pure sex, in its most elegant and powerful guise.

"Kristen Lucas?" the man repeated, sending shivers of awareness through her.

"Yes."

He was lean, polished, and staring at her with an intensity that gave her freedom to stare right back. His eyes narrowed—with disapproval?—as his gaze swept down her tie-dyed tunic, gold nail polish, white tights, and oft-worn boots before returning to her face. "I'm Alex Devereaux, Olivia's brother. Ross asked me to pick you up."

This was Alex Devereaux? Buttoned-down, shined-shoes, grilled-Ross-about-his-intentions-toward-his-sister Alex Devereaux? This walking inducement to carnal thoughts?

In a daze, she shook his hand. "Call me Kris."

It was a good thing she already knew Alex wasn't her type; they were as different as a New York subway was from a New Orleans streetcar. Otherwise she'd be tempted to renounce her anti-wedding-match-up vow without a whimper.

He glanced at his watch. "You're late. You were supposed to be here two hours ago." He reached for her duffel bag.

She hesitated—she'd been carrying her own bags since she could walk—and then handed it to him. "Last-minute delays. I took a different flight. Didn't know anyone would be here. Have you waited long?"

He grunted an answer.

Kris winced. "Sorry. Do we have time for a Lucky Dog?"

Shaking his head, he headed down the walkway. "We're having dinner with the family tonight at Commander's."

As Kris kept pace with his long strides back to the main terminal, she surreptitiously wiped her sweating palms on her tights. She hated walking into strange groups, although she never let anyone know it.

He glanced over at her, his face unreadable. "Ross said you're an artist."

"I decorate cakes."

Alex lifted one brow. "Didn't you do the caricature he has hanging in his living room? It's good."

"I did that a long time ago." She hadn't realized Alex had seen that.

"Do you like living in New York City?"

"There's a lot I love about it, but it's not New Orleans." Even after three years, she still missed her hometown. She was ready for the move back.

At the lower level of the airport, Alex nodded toward the baggage carousel. "I'll get the car while you claim your luggage."

She gestured toward the duffel he carried. "That's it."

He lifted that dark, full brow again, sending her stomach into a tailspin; then he glanced at his watch and frowned. "We should have time to stop at home and let you change before we have to meet Ross and Olivia and the family at Commander's. It'll be close, since traffic is heavy this time of day, but we'll be going toward the city."

"I flew as fast as I could," she said innocently, then stuck out one booted foot. "Won't this do at Commander's?"

"No," was his single answer, but his gaze lingered on her leg.

Kris regretted teasing him. After all, he'd had a long wait. "I am sorry you had to wait for me. I wasn't expecting anyone to pick me up or I'd have called."

"Forget it."

"Really, you didn't have to wait."

"I told Ross I'd pick you up. It would have been a waste of time to leave and come back."

"How did you know which flight I'd be on?"

"There was only one more flight from New York tonight, and I figured you'd be on it. I had my briefcase and cell phone. I didn't waste the time."

Kris tilted her head to look up at him. His firm lips would be a lot more attractive if they were smiling. "Do you ever?" she muttered, remembering snatches of Ross's conversations about Alex. He was a clock-watcher; she often forgot to wear a watch. He wore ties; she wore tie-dyed.

So why did he have to be the first man she'd met who turned her insides to quivering crème brûlée?

Outside, the April heat of New Orleans enveloped her like an enthusiastic but fickle friend, who sent beads of sweat to mar her make-up and tighten the curl in her hair. Kris lifted the red mass off the nape of her neck, wishing she'd fastened it up. Or shaved it off.

Alex stowed her luggage in the trunk of his car, then held the door open for her. After three years of cabbies, the gesture was a startling, but strangely pleasant, change of attitude.

"It was kind of you to agree to stay with my parents this week," he said, bracing one arm along the edge of the door. "I know Olivia's caught up in wedding frenzy, insisting the out-of-town attendants stay nearby, but if you have friends or family you'd prefer to stay with, I'll talk to her."

"I won't have time to socialize with other friends this week," Kris answered, settling into the front seat. "I appreciated the invitation."

Appreciated? The invitation to stay with the

Devereaux family had been a godsend, but she was unwilling to explain the deep-seated reasons why she wouldn't stay with her father and stepmother.

Once seated, she leaned back, closed her eyes, and tried to relax. She'd gotten little sleep the past two weeks, trying to get ahead with her work so she could take time off for the wedding; the lack of rest was starting to catch up to her.

However, Alex's presence filled the confined interior, and the faint spice of his lime aftershave teased her senses.

So much for relaxation.

"Ross said you were a lawyer," she commented while Alex maneuvered toward I-10. "What kind of law do you practice?"

"Environmental law."

"On the side of the pelicans or the pencil pushers?"

"The pelicans."

Kris opened one eye to reassess him. With the trim fit of his jacket and the elegant line of his loose-cut slacks, she'd pegged him as corporate all the way. "Don't environmentalists wear red plaid flannel?"

"I prefer suits. Besides, if I wear the corporate uniform and understand the corporate jargon, company officials and legislators are more willing to listen to me. I'm more effective." He flashed her a piratical grin that sent electric butterflies across her nerves. "And it surprises them more when I go for the jugular."

She should have paid closer attention to the two earrings.

The blare of horns from rush-hour traffic, the stifling southern humidity, and the nauseating exhaust barely penetrated the quiet cocoon of the Lexus. Alex put a CD in the player, and Kris tapped her fingers to the earthy jazz vocals of Irma Thomas.

"Ross said you were an Irma Thomas fan," Alex commented.

Sudden suspicion pounced on her. Ross's many conversations about his soon-to-be brother-in-law, Alex Devereaux, usually ended with, "You have to meet him. I think you'd like him."

That was one reason she'd tuned out a lot of the time.

Don't tell me Ross has the wedding match-making bug, too.

"Are you one of the groomsmen?" she asked.

"Yes, and you're the . . ." He faltered.

Oh, rats, and here she thought she was safe this time.

To cover her annoyance, Kris grinned at her companion. "A difficult concept, isn't it?"

"An inappropriate one," he muttered, but didn't elaborate.

Inappropriate? Alex was as proper as he was elegant and sexy. Definitely not her type. So, why oh why did he make her heart pound double time, like Charlie Brown on the verge of winning his first baseball game?

She took a deep breath. Her life had enough turmoil, enough changes going on right now, without adding a fling with a groomsman. She was here to help Ross McMain, her best friend since kindergarten, get married, and she was not the least bit interested in anything but being his . . . right-hand woman?

Best man? Whoever heard of a woman being a best man?

Alex looked away from the woman beside him, toward the burgeoning traffic. His hands tightened on the steering wheel.

Why couldn't Kris Lucas have been as ugly as sin? Or even mildly unattractive? Why did she have to have fresh green eyes, a ready grin, and freckles she didn't bother to conceal? Why did she have to have rose-gold hair that curled halfway down her back and made a man think of tousled sheets and satisfying nights?

Every time he stood in a wedding, someone tried to match him with one of the attendants, and he'd bet Olivia and Ross were matching him with Kris. He'd thought his sister knew him better.

Being a groom wasn't on his life's agenda. The shell dredgers were active in Lake Pontchartrain again, and he was readying an important action against chemical dumping in the Mississippi. He would not divide his energy between professional and personal demands, shortchanging both.

Right now, the last thing he needed was a woman who dressed like a Bohemian and didn't wear a watch. A woman with a man's handshake and kiss-me lips.

He pulled into a narrow, dead-end street. Old oak trees marked the edges of Audubon Park in Uptown New Orleans on one side; large houses lined the other. His parents' residence was about halfway down the block. Alex opened the wrought-iron gate in the fence surrounding the house and drove into the driveway.

Kris gave a low whistle. "My dad took me to Audubon Park and Zoo when I was a kid. I always wondered what these places looked like from the inside." Her glance caught on a car pulled farther into the driveway. "Oh, good, Ross is here. I can't wait to see him. It's been months."

She bounded out before he could open her door and waited at the trunk for her luggage. Alex hefted her duffel, wondering idly how she had managed to pack an entire week's worth of clothes in one soft-sided bag. Olivia took at least three suitcases, even for just a weekend. He ushered her up the steps and into the formal entryway.

Ross, a big blond man, hurried from the parlor and opened his arms. "Luke!"

In two steps, Kris was in his embrace. He twirled her around and then set her down, planting a smacking kiss on her cheek.

There was nothing loverlike in their hug, Alex noted. *That's not how I'd greet her, if I hadn't seen her in months.*

Her trim derriere peeked beneath the hiked-up hem of her top, and Alex gripped the duffel handles. Maybe Ross hadn't patted her there, but his palms itched to do just that.

Kris looked up at the face of her best friend. She didn't ever remember him looking so happy.

Ross squeezed her shoulder. "It's great to see you."

"Welcome, Kris. We're so glad you're here," added a well-modulated voice.

Kris looked over Ross's shoulder. She'd met Olivia once before. During the trip down, she'd wondered if her memory had overrefined the lady's grace and charm.

Nope. No wonder Ross had fallen hard. Olivia was petite, glossy, every strand of her sleek blond hair in place, not a wrinkle or a smudge on her white silk suit. And those earrings were diamond, not zirconium. She personified a style unknown in the neighborhood where Kris and Ross grew up.

Kris shoved her hair back again, mentally cursing the unruly mass, and greeted her. The smile Olivia gave Kris was genuinely warm, and when she followed it with a gentle hug, Kris felt truly welcomed.

Olivia knit her brow. "Why does Ross always call you Luke?"

"If you want to see her red hair in action you could call her Luke-A—" Ross began.

Kris punched him in the arm. "It's an evil myth that redheads have a temper, but if you tell anyone that name, I swear, my retaliation won't be pretty."

Ross laughed and playfully rubbed his arm. "You did that the first time, too."

Alex came up behind her. He didn't touch her, she didn't see him, but she instantly sensed his presence. Heat radiated from him, igniting a fire deep in her belly.

"We need to go, darling," Olivia said, glancing from Ross to Alex to Kris. "Kris, would you prefer to freshen up first?"

Ross looked from Kris to Alex. "Alex," he said,

"will you bring Kris when she's ready?"

A heavy rock dropped into the pit of her stomach. Oh, rats—she'd guessed right. Ross had been her best friend for twenty-two years, and she could read him like a comic strip. He was pairing her up with Alex.

"I'll bring her," Alex said drily.

She didn't want to be encased in the shadowed, intimate confines of his car again, listening to the sultry voices of Irma Thomas and Allen Toussaint. Not with this disturbing man who set her breathing awhack and started her hormones singing "Hallelujah!" But, apparently the decision was out of her hands. Kris picked up her belongings. "If someone will show me my room, I'll get changed."

Alex had known Kris for about an hour, but he'd listened to enough of Ross's stories about the woman to believe he knew her better than that short acquaintance. He shoved his hands into his pockets, not liking the insistent restlessness that urged him to get to know her much, much better.

Kris Lucas was a bubbly cauldron of emotions. She moved quickly and talked faster. Not his type at all, not even for a casual, no-strings-attached affair.

Alex swore softly. So why did he keep wondering how all that emotion, all that energy would be in bed? With him.

He wasn't looking for attachments, didn't want to be a groom like Ross. He just had to keep reminding himself of that.

"I'm ready."

Hearing Kris's husky voice from the top of the stairs, Alex glanced up. And stared.

Damn. No wonder she didn't need a big suitcase. That dress could be packed into a space of about three inches.

Judging from her outfit on the plane, he'd expected her to change into something loose and flowing. He should have remembered that she lived in New York City, home of high glamour and high fashion. He should have remembered Ross's comment once about her chameleon exterior, her uncanny ability to blend into any situation.

She wore sexy, high, black heels that emphasized the delicate bones of her feet. His gaze traveled up her shapely calves and thighs, up the long, long length of her legs, for she was tall and the dress she wore was short. It was black, a slip of a dress held up only by her generous curves and some nearly useless black straps. She had a narrow waist, he noticed, under that glittery belt.

His breath deepened, and the simmering arousal in him threatened to boil.

His lingering, appreciative survey brought a flush to her cheeks. She hesitated at the top of the stairs, smoothed her hand down the mane of hair she'd attempted to tame with sparkling clips at the sides of her face, then glided down the steps to his side.

"You look nice," he said, his voice husky.

"Shall we go?" she asked, rubbing her palms against the dress.

Never before at a loss for words, Alex simply nodded. He ushered her to the door, using the polite gesture of a hand at the small of her back as an excuse to touch her. Beneath the dress, her back felt warm and firm.

He fumbled for a topic of conversation. "We've been having some hot weather lately." *Great opener, Devereaux.*

"It's been hot in New York, too."

"What was Ross about to call you when you broke him off?" *Smooth, real smooth.*

The red on her cheeks surpassed the color in her hair. "Don't ask."

"I'm curious," he urged, handing her into the car.

When he settled himself into the driver's seat, she sighed. "I first met Ross in kindergarten. Lucas came right before McMain in the alphabet, so I sat in front of him. Ross had a rather advanced street vocabulary for a five-year-old, and he promptly started calling me, 'Luke-*ass.*'"

Her voice sounded so disgusted, Alex couldn't help laughing. "What did you do?"

"Hauled off and socked him in the eye. Got sent to the principal's office my first day of school." She shook her head and laughed. "It wasn't the last time either. That name made me so mad. Later, Ross told me he kept it up because he liked to see my face turn as red as my hair. Eventually, he shortened it to Luke."

Stunned by the way her husky laugh shot through him, Alex's hands tightened around the steering wheel. "You've been friends a long time." *Have you ever been lovers?* he suddenly wanted to ask.

"Twenty-two years. Since we were five," she said fondly, then shifted in her seat to face him. "I copied a list of best-man responsibilities from a wedding book so I wouldn't forget something. Have you ever been a best man?"

Apparently the discussion of her past was over. "Twice."

"Groomsman?"

"This will be my fourth."

"Usher?"

He held up two fingers.

"Ring bearer?"

Alex rubbed the back of his neck. "Once."

Kris laughed. "Then we're tied. This will be my ninth trip down the aisle, too."

He gave her a startled look.

"As an attendant," she assured him, then tilted her head. "Ever want to be the groom?"

His shoulders stiffened. Oh, no, not another one who got starry-eyed and mushy-thinking at weddings.

She twirled a lock of hair around her finger. "We need to get one thing straight. I don't want to be a bride."

"Then we're even. I don't want to be a groom."

"Good, because every wedding I'm in, my friends try to set me up with their groomsmen. I spent one wedding alternately dancing with an usher who talked about his tropical fish tank and a ring bearer half my height who'd developed a crush on me. By the end of the evening, I had a crick in my neck and a new aversion to filet of sole."

Alex glanced away from the traffic, saw the amusement hovering on her lips, and laughed, a hearty laugh he hadn't shared with anyone in a long time.

"Oh, no, not you, too?" He could envision the scene, since he'd once been stalked by a smitten flower girl. "Have you ever been paired with someone who, every time the bride and groom kissed, thought it meant the attendants should kiss, too?"

Kris gave a snort of laughter. "She *didn't*."

"She did. It was at a sit-down dinner and by the end, she'd decided I had serious intestinal problems, since I got up so many times. She never did figure out I was trying to escape."

They shared wedding war stories, laughing together, until Alex pulled up to the valet parking in front of the restaurant. The maître d' led them toward the back of the restaurant and the private dining area bordering a secluded garden.

Alex saw Olivia look out toward them. A brief glance only, before she returned to her conversation, but it was enough to reinforce what he'd already suspected. His sister was matchmaking. "Damn," he muttered.

Kris stopped abruptly. "Ross and Olivia. They're trying to make us a couple, aren't they?"

"You got it."

"What is it about married people that they can't stand to see someone remain single?" Kris shook her head.

"Envy?" Alex suggested.

Kris laughed. "More likely some primal throwback to Noah's Ark. If I'm not interested in you, they'll probably start lining up the alternative candidates." She tilted her head to look at him. "There are others, aren't there?"

His cousin Larry was about the right age and considered handsome. Alex frowned. This particular cousin was noted for his love-em-and-leave-em attitude. He wouldn't do at all. Or maybe the guy who worked with Ross? No, he was all hands.

Alex didn't want anyone *else's* hands on Kris. His were another story, however.

An intriguing idea grabbed hold of him. Used to making quick decisions, he studied it from different angles, turned it around, tried it out in his mind.

It would be short-term, not long enough for their basic differences to become annoyances. They'd gotten along fine in the car, no arguments or disagreements. He couldn't remember feeling so light-hearted with a woman before.

And it had been a long, long time since he'd felt this thrumming excitement, this prelude to arousal.

His plan could work.

He turned to Kris. "We're both tired of fending off matchmaking attempts and attendants who think a wedding is an occasion for everyone to pair up, right?"

"Right."

"And we're both agreed that we don't want entanglements or commitments, right?"

"Right."

"So, let's pretend."

"What?"

"Pretend we're an item, that the matchmaking worked. Lust at first sight. No one else will bother us, and Ross and Olivia will be happy. We'll spend the week together, have a few laughs, then go our separate ways."

A slow grin lit her face, and Alex felt himself grow hot. The lust part wouldn't be any trouble at all.

"Sounds perfect," she drawled. "What could go wrong?"

"Wrong? Nothing, absolutely nothing."

Chapter Two

"You're the *what?*" Alex's grandmother peered at Kris over half-glasses rimmed with diamonds.

Again? Kris had lost count of how many times she'd answered that question and been met with incredulity, amusement, or shock.

"She's the best man, Mama," answered Alex's mother, Mary Eulalie.

The older woman studied Kris from head to toe and then shook her head. "No, she's not. The best man can't be a woman." Grandmother Desirée tapped her cane on the floor. "Why didn't you tell me Alex was getting married?"

"Alex isn't getting married, Olivia Elizabeth is. Kris lives in New York City. She's a . . . What is it you do, dear?"

"I design greeting cards."

"Well, it should be Alex getting married."

Grandmother Desirée fumbled in her purse and pulled out a pack of cigarettes.

"Mama! You can't smoke here."

"What are they going to do about it? Put me in jail?" She tapped out a cigarette.

Mary Eulalie plucked the cigarette from between her mother's lips. "Smoking turns your lungs black, yellows your teeth, and gives you bad breath."

Kris watched the exchange, torn between amazement and amusement. When she'd first walked into the room and seen the glitter of diamonds, heard the whisper of silk, and tasted the sparkle of expensive champagne, her palms had started to sweat with familiar panic. Events like this always brought out the old fears, the old insecurities—not that she ever let anyone know.

All her life, she'd been told she was different, outside the mainstream, unconventional, and a few less-flattering adjectives. She didn't belong; she was tolerated, not accepted.

Grandmother Desirée, however, made her feel right at home.

Mary Eulalie's attention focused across the room. "Oh dear! *What* is he bringing out?"

Why would a lone waiter setting out bowls of soup cause that reaction? Kris's fingers curled around an imaginary pencil. If she were to draw Mary Eulalie right now, she'd have a good visual model for alarm.

"This will never do. I'm sure I ordered spring rolls, not vichyssoise." Mary Eulalie patted Kris on the arm. "Details are so important," she advised and then hurried off.

113

"Always a crisis when Mary Eulalie's around," commented the older woman.

"Did you meet the best man, Grandmother Desirée?" Alex joined them and laid a proprietary hand on Kris's waist. The light touch started a tingling cascade that fed a strange yearning for more. His fingers flexed slightly when he kissed his grandmother on the cheek. "You've been smoking again."

"Everyone needs vices, and at eighty-seven there are few left to me." She tapped Alex with the cane. "You're nearly thirty. In my day, you'd be married and have four children by now. Why aren't you getting married, boy?"

"Because I've never met a woman who held a candle to you," Alex answered smoothly.

Grandmother Desirée gave a snort. "Never met a woman who could fit into one of your schedules, you mean." She leaned over to Kris. "The boy means well, but he overcompensates for his mother's perpetual state of crisis."

Kris cleared her throat, trying to think of an intelligent response, but Alex's nearness, his faint touch, scrambled her thoughts.

Grandmother Desirée, however, required only an awake audience, not a verbal one. She poked Alex again with the cane. "All my friends ask me why aren't you married, as though it's my fault. I did my part; I introduced you to their granddaughters. How can I explain that you're not interested? I'm still trying to explain why Olivia Elizabeth is named after a dictionary."

Kris's eyes widened. *A dictionary?* she mouthed to Alex.

Mary Eulalie, crisis handled, hurried back. "I remember now. I couldn't decide, so I ordered both vichyssoise and spring rolls. They'll serve the hot dish when we sit down. Alex, make sure the final bill includes both items."

Alex sighed. "I doubt the restaurant will forget."

"One must follow up on the details."

"All right. I'll verify the bill later, Mama."

Over her eyeglasses, Grandmother Desirée eyed Kris's body. "Good hips—she'll be a good breeder. Good choice for a bride, Alex. I knew you wouldn't disappoint me."

Kris's cheeks flamed, and Alex's hand dropped away.

"Mama," said Mary Eulalie, "It's *Olivia Elizabeth's* wedding."

"Will you excuse us?" Alex asked. "I think Kris should meet more of the family."

"Kris? Kris who?" asked Grandmother Desirée.

"Her mind sometimes wanders," whispered Mary Eulalie.

Thump went the cane. "I heard that. It does not."

Hardly able to contain her laughter, Kris accompanied Alex across the room, his arm draped across her shoulders.

"Drop it, Devereaux," she whispered. "No one's watching."

"You never know. Besides, to make our deception believable, we need to get used to touching."

Truth be told, she enjoyed the feel of Alex so close, his casual touches. It was like a roller coaster ride: fun, a bit scary, could set your stomach flipping, yet, all along, you knew you were safe and protected. Alex gave her a tiny kiss on the cheek. Over in an instant, it still set her senses reeling.

These feelings aren't part of the bargain.

This was only a charade, Kris sternly reminded herself, a convenience for them both. She wouldn't embarrass Alex, or herself, by reading more into the way he hovered near, or the way he sometimes brushed against her, or the way she could always tell when he stood behind her.

Alex dropped his arm and introduced her to his mother's sister's son's father-in-law. Or some such convoluted relationship. Alex claimed a lot of relatives.

Listening to him chat with the in-law, apparently unaffected by that short kiss, Kris had to admit their masquerade was working. She'd seen the satisfied look Ross and Olivia exchanged when she'd walked in with Alex, and when she'd talked to them earlier, not one sentence began with phrases like "You should meet . . ." or "I think you'd like . . ."

Because of Alex, this was one wedding where she could relax and do her attendant thing without added, unwanted pressures.

Alex's jacket brushed against her bare shoulder, and her muscles tightened in expectation, while her heart thudded against her chest.

Because of Alex, this was one wedding where she was going to spend the week with her hormones clicking and her libido crackling.

"What do you do in New York?"

Kris realized the in-law—Bradley something—

was addressing her. "I arrange flowers," she answered.

"I wish I'd had a best man like you." Bradley's gaze brushed across her breasts, then up to her face. "I've been in a few myself—weddings, that is. Perhaps we could meet for drinks, discuss your responsibilities."

Oh, rats, the guy was hitting on her. Veteran of numerous cocktail parties and peruser of a dozen body language books, she recognized the signs.

Alex crowded closer to her and caught her hand in a firm grip. As body language, it was decidedly unsubtle—male establishing his territory. While Kris appreciated the gesture, she had no trouble handling this kind of situation herself.

It was the dignified, elegant ones that tied her in knots.

She flashed the smile she saved for business contacts who thought cartooning was a simple art form, the smile that exuded confidence and welcome and was totally insincere. "I sure do appreciate that invitation, but I'll be so busy with the wedding. A best man has so much to do. And"— she turned to Alex, her smile warming to a real one—"Alex and I have discovered a few things we'd like to do together."

Alex brought her fingers to his mouth for a kiss, his eyes never leaving hers. "More than a few," he murmured, his voice low and deep. "What's your first choice?"

Her active imagination conjured several salacious choices in a nanosecond, and Kris felt a flush spread across her cheeks. To cover her reaction, she fanned herself with her free hand.

"Why, I do declare, this room has suddenly gotten very warm."

Alex leaned closer. "This is New Orleans, not Atlanta, Scarlet," he breathed.

"Sorry," she whispered from the side of her mouth. "I got carried away."

Hint taken, Bradley departed. From a circulating waiter, Alex snared a stuffed mushroom cap. He held it out and she took a bite, her lips grazing his fingers, and then he popped the rest into his own mouth.

"Good?" he asked.

"Mmmmm," she mumbled, her lips zinging from the tastes of Tabasco, butter, and Alex.

Kris sought an acceptable explanation for her reaction to this totally unsuitable man. She was tired from the grueling pace she'd worked to meet the unexpected, but critical, deadlines that meant a boon to her career. She hadn't had anyone special in her life for more months than she cared to count, and now she was partnered with a man whose looks fulfilled every one of her fantasies, including the more explicit ones. Physical lust, that's all it was.

That's all it could be. She had friends, lots of friends, but inside she was alone, and she'd learned long ago that to expect more was to invite heartache.

Her career was at a critical juncture; the next few months were too important to risk the tempting distraction and emotional upheaval represented by Alex Devereaux.

And Alex didn't want even the lust. He'd started

this deception to avoid women with those thoughts.

So why did he look and touch with such warmth, with the hint of male hunger simmering below the surface? A dangerous question that knotted her stomach and heightened her sense of longing.

She needed to think about something else. "Tell me about your sister, the dictionary."

Alex grabbed two glasses of champagne from a passing waiter and handed her one. "It was the one moment of true crisis in my mother's life. While she was pregnant with Olivia, a petty thief broke into the house. She became an instant heroine by dropping an Oxford English Dictionary on him. Poor man never knew what hit him; he was unconscious for two hours afterward. Mother claimed that dictionary saved her life and decided her child's name would be a tribute to the heroic book. Oxford English Dictionary. OED. Olivia Elizabeth Devereaux." Alex held out his hands. "My mother isn't exactly the logical sort."

"Maybe not, but I like her."

"I love her, but most people find her exhausting."

Kris shook her head. "Involving. So, where do you get your practical nature?"

"From me," interrupted a man.

Kris faced him. Well-cut suit, Harvard-striped tie, shiny wing tips. This had to be Alex's father.

"Just get here, Dad?"

"I had to work late. You understand how it is."

"The way it has always been." The muscles in

Alex's jaw tightened, despite the impeccable formality between the men.

Alex's father smoothed a hand across his silver-and-black hair and tightened the knot of his tie, then bowed over her hand. "Claude Devereaux. I hear you're the best man."

"That's right."

Mary Eulalie scurried up. "Alex, your uncle Richard has had too much champagne, and he's asking the trio to play 'Hernando's Hideaway.' They claim they've never heard of it, and Richard is getting quite huffy." Her gaze shifted to Claude, and she blinked. "Oh, hello, dear. I didn't realize you were going to make the party." Her attention returned to Alex. "I just know the band is going to quit. Come, do something before everything falls apart."

"In a minute, Mama," he answered. "Maybe Dad could handle it?"

Mary Eulalie blinked again, as though surprised by the suggestion. "Claude?"

Alex crossed his arms. "Uncle Richard is his brother."

" 'Hernando's Hideaway!' " A bellow echoed across the room.

Mary Eulalie wrung her hands. "Oh, dear! And we need to sit for dinner."

Alex wrapped an arm around his mother's shoulders. "You and Dad get your guests seated, Mama. I'll talk to Uncle Richard."

Claude gave a long sigh. "I'll handle Richard. You help your mother, Alex." He made a beeline for the band.

Grandmother Desirée thumped over to Alex and

Kris. She prodded Kris with the cane. "Go on, girl, the bride should sit."

Unfortunately, the room quieted at that moment, and Grandmother Desirée spoke in the tones of the slightly deaf. Her voice rang out clearly, startling the other guests. All eyes turned to Kris.

"*Olivia Elizabeth* is the bride," said Mary Eulalie between clenched teeth.

Kris burst out laughing. It was a good thing she'd agreed to this deception with Alex. Otherwise, there was no telling who Grandmother Desirée would have her married to by the end of the week.

Alex enjoyed his relatives, but he preferred them in small doses. A roomful of Devereaux and LeBlancs, loud and chaotic, gave him a headache.

Kris, however, seemed to thrive on the confusion. She'd danced an impromptu tango with Uncle Richard, entertained them with a story of her first job—this time she claimed to be a waitress—and switched conversational topics with lightning ease. Now she was trading jokes with his cousin, love-em-and-leave-em Larry. Larry scooted his chair forward, closer to Kris.

Much too close in Alex's estimation. He laid a hand on her shoulder, interrupting the tête-à-tête. She turned toward him, puzzled.

She had beautiful skin, he decided, seeing it up close and personal. With that red hair, she wouldn't tan, but she had a dusting of freckles on her cheeks. Did she have freckles elsewhere?

121

Lightly, he grazed one finger across the soft skin of her neck.

Where had this urge to touch her, to lay a masculine stamp of claim on her, come from? Swiftly, he dropped his hand, but not before he saw the pulse beat in Kris's neck.

Perhaps her responses to him weren't all for show?

"Are you ready to go, Kris?"

"It's been a long day." She nodded to Larry and rose.

As they said their good-byes to Ross and Olivia, Alex noticed the droop of fatigue in her shoulders, watched her shove back her hair with a grimace of annoyance and rub a hand across her eyes. She was exhausted, but he'd bet no one else here, besides him, saw that behind her brilliant smile.

They walked out through the garden to the street, the night air enclosing them in thick heat and carrying with it the essence of Kris's perfume, seductive and feminine. Candlelight from the restaurant's interior flickered across the stone path and the broad palm leaves. Her hair seemed a torch in the wavering darkness. The sultry, sensuous evening worked its magic on him, quickening his pulse, building the hum of anticipation.

His car arrived, and Alex settled her into the seat, taking a moment to admire the view of her leg when she swung it inside.

"I think our little masquerade worked well tonight," Kris said as he pulled away from the curb.

It had worked fine, if you discounted the fact that her musky perfume had lingered in his senses all night, that he'd traced every lithe movement of her hips, that her husky voice had reverberated deep inside him.

Did she feel the same excitement?

It was a possibility worth exploring.

He didn't want commitments and neither did Kris. She'd been adamant about that. One evening had shifted some of his preconceptions about Kris Lucas, but she was still too mercurial. Too undependable. Too chaotic.

She'd drive him crazy in a matter of weeks, but that didn't mean a short-term liaison couldn't be highly pleasurable for them both. She'd be going back to New York after the wedding, so any affair would die a natural death.

Yes, definitely promising.

"Why don't you want to get married?" he asked. Most women of his acquaintance had just the opposite goal.

She chewed her lip a moment. "I'm not sure I want to make the adjustments. I've been alone most of my life."

"No family?"

"Mom skipped out when I was a baby—guess I was too much for her to handle—and Dad worked a lot of odd hours. He's with the police department. He remarried when I was thirteen, but I was a real brat at that age and my stepmother and I have never been close." She gave a small laugh, then flashed that impudent grin at him, perhaps regretting her moment of open introspection. "Married? Who could put up with me for long? Way I figure it, a dog's a better bet."

Alex pulled into the driveway, opened the windows, stopped the engine, and turned to study her in the night. "A dog?"

"Yeah. They're warm when it's cold out, they like to jog with you, they're easy to cook for, they listen when you talk."

She glanced up at him. They sat in shadow except for a yellow sliver of light from the streetlamps. The light flickered, sending a beam across her face. Honeysuckle, rich and fragrant, filled the shadows with its perfume.

A rush of predatory awareness energized him, sending his blood and breath into overdrive. He wanted this woman, and he didn't bother to hide the telltale expression beneath his customary courtroom poker face.

"All the advantages of a husband without . . . the drawbacks. . . ." Her words faltered as she gazed into his face, and she licked her lips.

Alex followed the motion. "Perhaps there are a few things a husband would be good for," he murmured. He shifted, imperceptibly pressing his leg against her thigh.

"Like what?" The husky note in her voice told him she was as aware of his desire as he was of hers. She brushed against his sleeve. A surge of heat, as potent as though there were no clothing between them, radiated throughout him from the brief contact.

He bent forward. Her musky perfume raised primal needs, but he didn't touch her, except for his breath across her neck. "Moving heavy furniture."

"I can hire that done," she whispered back.

"Reaching the top shelf." He shifted, until she

looked directly into his face, her lips scant inches away.

"I'm five-ten."

"Mowing the lawn."

"I live in the city."

The absurdity of the conversation, so at odds with the very dangerous feelings stirring inside him, struck a chord in Alex, and amusement spiced the emotional cauldron.

"Changing a flat on the car?" He deliberately lightened his voice.

Lines of laughter crinkled around Kris's eyes. "Been there, done that."

"Taking out the garbage."

"Oh, puh-leeze."

Alex leaned back, his arm spread across the top of the seat. "You've convinced me."

For a moment, Kris regretted the retreat from intimacies shared and the promise of intimacies to come. *No, this slower way is better. Remember, this is just a convenience. Keep things light, if not cool.*

No words of wisdom could banish the wondering, however. How would his lips taste against hers? Did he laugh in bed as well and as often as he'd laughed tonight? Would he move against a woman with that slow, deceptively lazy way he had when he walked?

"Why don't you want to be a groom?" she asked, ignoring the more troublesome questions.

"Usual reasons," he answered with a noncommittal shrug.

"There are no 'usual reasons.' Everyone has their own motives, their own slant. What are yours? C'mon, I confessed about the dog."

He stared forward, toward his parents' house. "I work for the Clean Water Foundation, and I believe in their goals. I'm good at my job because I'm ambitious, work hard, and don't accept half measures. I don't want to be torn between obligations. A family demands so much of you." The tendons in his neck tightened, then relaxed. He turned to her and flashed a grin. "I'll bet you don't have a house key."

She tapped the heel of her hand against her forehead. "Didn't even occur to me."

"I'll let you in."

In the foyer, Alex leaned one shoulder against the wall. "I think we need to set a schedule for the week."

"A *what?*"

"A schedule. Make sure we fit in enough time together to make our masquerade believable."

Kris wrinkled her nose. "I'm not good with schedules. Why don't we take it as it falls? See what happens."

Alex folded his arms. "Because we can't leave this to chance. The details are important." His head dropped back against the wall, and he groaned. "I can't believe I said that." He opened one eye. "I jog in Audubon Park every morning. Would you like to go with me?"

"Sure." The answer slipped out so easily.

Alex straightened. He took a step toward the door, then switched directions. In two strides, he stood before her. "There's something I've wanted to do all evening, ever since I saw you in that slinky dress," he murmured. With thumb and forefinger, he tilted her chin up. "Do you mind?"

"Mind? Uh . . . no." Her sense of self-preservation deserted her.

He kissed her, slowly, thoroughly, without leaving an inch of her lips unstimulated, though he touched nowhere else. A languid kiss that burned her insides.

"I like a man with an aptitude for details," she breathed, when he drew back.

She felt his smile against her cheek. "And I like a woman with a happy mouth."

"It's very happy right now," she confessed.

He moved away. "I'm glad, although I meant that you have a lot of smiles for everyone."

On his way out the door, Alex paused and cocked a finger at her. "See you tomorrow morning. Six sharp."

Without waiting for an answer, he left.

Kris stared in horror at the door. Six? A.M.? Oh, rats, she should have guessed.

He was a morning person.

Kris opened one eye, peered at the bedroom clock, and groaned. In a flash, she shoved herself out of bed, yanked her hair into a pony tail, pulled on shorts, T-shirt with the sleeves ripped out, and holey sneakers, then let herself out of the house, leaving it unlocked because she didn't have a key. As fast as possible, she ran over to Audubon Park.

Alex waited at the parking area, holding the leash of a frisky golden retriever who wound around his legs and leaped at the chirping birds.

Dang, the man looked good in a tank top and running shorts. Firm muscles, interesting bulges, a feathering of dark hair on his arms and legs.

She'd always been partial to black hair.

Too bad he was staring pointedly at his watch. "You're late."

"Sorry. You have a dog!" Kris crouched down and patted the dog's furry head. "Why didn't you tell me?"

"Your arguments last night convinced me. Went out and bought her this morning."

The dog licked her face. Kris ruffled its fur. "You did not. What's her name?"

"Sunny."

"Hello, Sunny." Kris pursed her lips and made smacking sounds. The dog licked her again, and Kris laughed, then stood. "Ready for a jog?"

Alex's gaze traveled the length of her, and Kris felt her cheeks grow hot, though the morning still retained a hint of the marginally cooler evening. "More than ready," he answered, a heated promise in his voice.

Sunny kept them moving around the track. Alex, Kris noticed, moved easily with the dog, his run as effortless and loose-limbed as his walk. When Sunny barked at a squirrel, straining at her leash, Alex brought her to heel with a whistle. When Sunny needed to run, Alex stretched his stride until Kris had trouble keeping up.

Just bought the dog, my eye. The two of them were a team.

Alex and Kris reached the end of the jog, panting and coated with sweat. The last of the morning chill had burned off in the rising sun, and another steamy day threatened.

Kris walked in a circle, cooling down after the run. "I enjoyed that. Tomorrow?"

"How about every morning this week?" Alex suggested. "If you can make six o'clock."

"Sure." Well, she'd be close.

"I'll walk you back to the house. Sunny and I need to cool down, too."

It was a short walk back. Alex picked up the newspaper from the porch and then paused, one foot on the bottom step. "Would you like to have dinner with me tonight?"

"Unless there's something I need to do for the wedding."

He shook his head, then glanced at his watch. "I'll pick you up at seven-thirty."

"Sharp."

He looked up at that. "Sharp. I know we should spend today together, to make our masquerade more believable, but I can't take the time from work."

"No problem. I planned on spending time with Ross today."

A muscle twitched in his jaw, but he said nothing.

She held out her hand. "Can I have the paper? I never start my day without the funnies."

Kris sat down on the top step and slipped the paper out of its plastic sleeve. Eagerly, she turned to the comics in the Living section.

Alex dropped beside her. "Which is your favorite strip?"

"I like them all."

He read over her shoulder, then suddenly laughed, a deep full laugh. Sunny barked and pulled at her leash, eyeing a mourning dove with doggy intent. "All right, girl," Alex said to the dog. "Read 'Byrde's Eye View,'" he told Kris, pointing to one of the comic strips. "Do the New York papers get it?"

She shook her head. "Not yet." Her voice sounded faint, breathy.

"It's new, just started in the *Times-Picayune* this week, about a fuzzy, one-eyed alien who tries to understand the insanities of everyday life. I bet you'll like it." He rose with masculine grace and jogged off, Sunny in the lead.

Filled with a sense of pride, Kris traced the figures in the strip in question, not needing to read the captions. "Byrde's Eye View" was her baby, and every mother likes to hear that her baby is beautiful.

Kris met Ross at the tuxedo shop for a final fitting later that morning. The proprietor fussed and fumed, protesting that he did not have clothes to fit a woman, but Kris insisted on an outfit identical to those of the rest of the groom's attendants.

"Do you mind, Ross?" she asked. "If you'd prefer, I could wear a long skirt."

Affectionately, Ross tousled her hair. "I don't mind a bit. You have your own style, and I've always liked it. You'll look fine and feminine, even in a tux."

"I'll make sure everything's picked up before the wedding and returned afterward," she told him as they walked together down St. Charles Avenue.

"Thanks, Luke. I knew I could count on you."

Kris patted the pocket of her shorts. "I've got my list."

He laughed. "I'm glad you're here. All the other attendants are Olivia's relatives or guys from work. They're friends; you're family."

She and Ross always told people they'd been friends since kindergarten, but it went much deeper than that. Her mother had abandoned her physically, and her father had done the same emotionally. Both of Ross's parents were drinkers before they died, and he'd been lucky on the days they hadn't noticed him.

She and Ross were more than friends; they were family, as Ross said, in the best meaning of the word. Together they had survived and nurtured each other. Together they had had the courage to dream lofty dreams and to hope for the future. Together they had succeeded.

"I saw Dad today," Kris told him. "Thanks for sending him the wedding invitation."

"I've known your father for a lot of years, although I never agreed with the way he tried to make you into someone you're not. Is he coming?"

She shook her head. "He said he didn't want to if I'm going to make a spectacle of myself."

"That's his loss then. What else did he criticize?"

"My hair. My wild ways. I'm not 'toeing the line.' My frivolous career." She deepened her voice in imitation of her father's deep tones. "And oh, by the way, am I ever going to get married and settle down? I'm his only child, and I'm disappointing him." She laughed, a brittle sound in the soft, hot morning.

"Ah, Kris, when are you going to learn? You

don't need to hide behind that carefree shell; you're lovable the way you are."

"Is that the way Olivia loves you? Just the way you are?"

Ross nodded. "And I love her."

"Then I am truly happy for you. I hope Olivia realizes what a lucky woman she is." Kris laid her head against him and wrapped an arm around his waist. His hand rested on her shoulder. They walked down the street that way, words unnecessary.

"You and Alex seemed to hit it off the other night," Ross began.

She couldn't lie to him. "I enjoy being with him, but it's only for this week, so back off, Ross."

"It doesn't have to be. You're moving back to New Orleans next month."

"And I'll be very busy. My career's on the verge of something big, now that 'Byrde's Eye View' is syndicated and half a dozen newspapers have picked it up. I like my life the way it is, Ross."

"You have friends, but you deserve someone special."

"I'm content with my idiosyncrasies, but I don't ask anyone else to be. I don't want to have to cater to a man's whims."

"You indulge me all the time, Luke-ass," he teased.

She elbowed him. "You're different."

"So's Alex."

Kris sighed. "You saw him last night. He's elegant, smooth. He wears linen; I wear wrinkled cotton. He moved through those people with ease because he was born to it; I was there on sufferance. He wears a digital watch that tells the time in six countries, has dozens of alarms, and can probably do your taxes. Clocks give me hives."

He shook a finger at her in mock admonition. "Did you lose that Oscar the Grouch watch I bought you?"

Kris winced. "I wear it when I have to."

Ross nudged her down a side street. "I want to show you something. Alex is all you said, but that doesn't define him." He pointed to a small brick building, institutional in its plainness except for two small brass plates at the door. "That's the home of the Clean Water Foundation and Alex's office."

Kris gaped at the drab building.

"You were imagining green leather, perfectly-coiffed secretaries, and hushed corridors, weren't you, Kris?"

That had been exactly what she'd thought. Kris closed her mouth.

"Alex could have that if he wanted, but he chooses to work here, at a lower salary, because he believes in what the foundation does. Want to go inside? It's just as functional."

Kris shook her head.

Ross pointed to a playground across the street, where a toddler squealed as he shot down a shiny red slide and a baby practiced its unsteady steps on the thick grass under the watchful eyes of their mothers. "This neighborhood had no play area until Alex raised the money for that lot to be cleared and landscaped and the equipment purchased. He painted most of the equipment himself."

There was more to Alex Devereaux, Kris admitted, than she had been willing to acknowledge.

"Point taken." She gave Ross a chaste kiss on the cheek, then rested her head against his shoulder. "That doesn't change the fact that I'm bridesmaid—or best man—material, not bridal."

Ross's arm went around her again, and he rested a hand on her head. "You could be," he said softly, "but until you believe you deserve it, you won't take the risk." He squeezed her tight.

Resolutely, she stepped away, then linked her arm through Ross's and turned her back on the building and the playground.

Alex Devereaux was pure temptation. She didn't need reminders that she could like him, too.

From the vantage point of his office window, Alex watched Ross and Kris kiss, hug, and then walk down the street, arm in arm.

Had they been lovers? How long ago? Were all the old feelings gone? A stab that felt uncomfortably like jealousy pierced him. He didn't like it, knew he had no right, but it persisted nonetheless.

His fist clenched against the sill. He didn't like these out-of-control, chaotic feelings that being near Kris Lucas engendered.

Yet he stared, motionless, until they disappeared around the corner. His sister's fiancé and the woman he wanted in his bed.

Chapter Three

"Are you always late?"

Kris raised her eyebrows at Alex's irritated question. "It's a failing of mine." She glanced at the car clock. "Only seven minutes this time."

"We'll be late for our dinner reservation."

She could almost hear the grinding of his teeth as he pulled the car into traffic. Her hands folded around her purse as she resisted the urge to pull out her sketchpad and capture the set of his jaw. "Won't they hold it for seven minutes?"

His hands relaxed on the wheel. "I suppose they will."

And she would bet he'd built in a safety factor when he'd told her what time to meet him. "Where are we going?"

"Antoine's. I reserved a private room for us."

Private room? Kris swallowed around her dry

throat. *Oh, my.* Alex had the connections to reserve, last minute, an intimate parlor in one of New Orleans's premier restaurants. Her palms started to sweat.

Why couldn't they have gone someplace where the tables were crowded together and a piano or harp made private conversation difficult?

Her body longed for Alex's touch, and her preconceived ideas about him had taken flight. Now, she'd spend the evening in a hushed room, with attentive and discreet waiters serving exquisite food and Alex's focused attention on her from across a narrow table graced by candles and flowers.

She didn't know if she could survive. The bliss or the danger.

It was one thing to be with Alex in a crowd of relatives. It was quite something else to be alone with him in an atmosphere of intimacy and romance. All day she'd struggled against the faint, confusing tinges of regret at her never-date-a-groomsman vow. Now this. It made their masquerade too real, too much like the first dance in a night-long ball.

But the stroke of midnight, and the return of reality, always banished Cinderella.

Kris clenched her fists. She didn't handle these situations well. She often said and did things she regretted.

"Let's go to the Hard Rock Cafe," she blurted out, picking the noisiest, most crowded spot she could think of.

"That's chaos."

"Invigorating."

His fingers tightened on the steering wheel. "Fine. I'll cancel our reservations, and we can stand in line for an hour."

Kris stared out the window. The shops on St. Charles blurred before the rapid pace of the car. Who was she kidding? This evening she didn't want to share him with a gaggle of relatives or a nameless crowd. "I'm sorry. No, Antoine's is perfect."

"Make up your mind."

"I did. Antoine's."

"Fine."

Kris rested her head against the headrest. Alex was surly; she was panicked. The way this evening had started, she might regret not going for the buffering crowd.

Silence dragged between them, and Kris rarely met a silence she didn't hate.

The streetcar rumbled past them on the St. Charles neutral ground. "I love the streetcar," Kris said. "I think I'll look for a new home near it. Either that or in the Quarter."

"What?!" The car swerved, nearly sideswiping a Jeep. To the blare of horns and the screech of tires, Alex pulled back into his lane. "A home? Whose home?"

Alex, Kris noted, asked a lot of questions. Must be the lawyer in him. "My home."

"You live in New York."

"For one more month. Then I'm moving back here."

"You can't."

Kris tilted her head to eye him. "I can't?"

Alex rubbed the side of his neck. "I mean, you seem so at home in New York."

"I'm a southern girl at heart, and I can . . ." She wasn't ready to tell him she drew cartoons for a living. People she told tended to feel either faintly superior or very ill-at-ease, thinking she observed their every foible. Maybe Alex would be different, but she wasn't about to bet the farm—or her heart—on it. "I can work anywhere."

Alex's knuckles turned white on the steering wheel. "Great," he said faintly. "You'll be living in New Orleans."

For an evening he'd been looking forward to with unusual anticipation, things had gone downhill quickly. Alex blamed himself for most of it.

To put it bluntly, he'd been an ass. He stabbed the last bite of fish on his plate.

The chemical dumping case was at a critical juncture, yet, for the first time, he'd had trouble concentrating on it. Instead he'd thought about this evening, about that kiss he'd seen Ross and Kris share.

He'd told himself the kiss was merely a kiss between friends. There had been no sign of passion, yet the image had made him dizzy, like dangling from a broken trapeze.

Learning Kris was moving back to New Orleans had knocked the safety net from under the trapeze. He'd counted on her leaving after the wedding. This week was supposed to be a masquerade, a convenience for them both. A dinner or two, some pleasant conversation, scorching kisses, maybe something more intimate, nothing serious.

Now, it appeared the charade didn't have to end, didn't have to stay a charade. She would be living in New Orleans.

That wasn't in the plan, and Alex didn't like having his plans adjusted without his prior consent. It was too unsettling.

Absently, he swiped his bit of fish through the remaining hollandaise sauce. Unsettling? Kris defined unsettling. An optimist would call her a breath of fresh air, but to a cautious man she was a tempest, tossing all his plans, his good intentions, and his logic into a jumbled heap.

Because of her, he'd gone around in a state of semi-arousal for two days. Because of her, he'd adopted a regimen of cold showers.

So why did he look forward to their jogs, to seeing her first thing in the morning? He hadn't asked for and didn't understand the exhilaration he felt with her. She made him yearn for something elusive, something that he'd long since turned his back on.

And why couldn't he get the picture of Kris kissing another man out of his mind?

Fish finished, Alex dropped his fork to his plate with a clatter. His disordered thoughts had plagued him throughout dinner, and the quieter he got, the more voluble Kris became.

Abruptly, she sat back in her chair and crossed her arms. "Let's go, Alex."

"We haven't had dessert or coffee."

"You obviously don't want to be here with me." The statement ripped him from his self-absorption. He wanted to be with her. He wanted it too much.

How could he explain? Ask her if she was over Ross? Find out if she was as confused as he, Alex, was? Suggest they couldn't leave things between them as they were, hot and unfulfilled? Definitely not here. "You're right."

"Then I won't bother you any longer." She tossed some bills on the table. "That's for my half. I'll catch a cab."

Damn! She'd misinterpreted his answer. He thrust the money back at her. "I asked you out. I pay. I take you home."

She slid it back across the table. "This wasn't a date. It was a smoke screen."

He stuffed the bills in her purse. "Then you pay the next time."

"There won't be a next time." Kris rose to her feet and stalked from the room.

Quickly, he paid the bill and followed her into the streets of the French Quarter. Weeknights were slower than weekends, but not by much. Crowds still thronged, carrying plastic go-cups from bar to bar, and curio shops did a brisk business. Alex wanted to lay a hand at her waist to keep her close and safe in the crowd, but he didn't think Kris would appreciate the gesture.

After a few silent moments of following a determined Kris, Alex said mildly, "My car's the other way."

"I'm going to The Sporting Edge."

"Why? The place is a dive."

"That's where I'm hosting Ross's bachelor party, and I wanted to—"

Ross again. *"You're* giving the bachelor party?"

She blinked at him, apparently surprised by his vehemence. "Of course. It's my responsibility as best man. The Sporting Edge is a perfectly respectable restaurant."

"Not anymore. You can't have it there."

"I can't?" she said very softly.

Oops. Kris, he'd learned, didn't respond well to commands.

Alex raked a hand through his hair. Ross had asked several friends, including him, to keep Thursday night open, but he hadn't mentioned any details—apparently because Ross didn't know those details. Otherwise he would have nixed this whole crazy idea. And some of the guys were planning their own surprises, surprises he didn't think Kris would appreciate.

"Aren't you taking this best man thing too far?"

Kris halted in front of The Sporting Edge and glared at him. "All I've heard the past two days is how a woman can't be a best man, and I'm sick of it. I thought you understood."

"Hell, no."

She put her hands on her hips. "What is it with you tonight, Alex? You've been rotten company."

Rotten company? He knew he had been, but perversely he didn't like her confronting him with the fact. He lashed out defensively. "I saw you kiss Ross today, and I think it's shabby of him to foist an ex-lover on the wedding party."

Her face flared until the red surpassed her hair; then her eyes narrowed to brilliant green slits. "What makes you think we're *ex*-lovers?"

He leaned forward until their faces were inches

apart. He touched the pulse at her throat and was gratified to feel the heartbeat quicken beneath the pad of his finger. "Because you wouldn't have kissed me like you did last night."

"I like variety."

Despite his unreasoning frustration, a thrill raced through Alex. She hadn't backed down; she was going, literally, nose to nose with him.

"What is Ross McMain to you?"

"The best I ever had."

"Then you should withdraw from the wedding."

"No." She said it very deliberately. A shadow darkened her eyes; then she straightened. "I know what you think of me. Have you always had this low an opinion of Ross?" She punctuated the question by slapping her hand against the door and stomping into the nightclub.

One thing that made him a very good lawyer was his ability to read people, to assess small hints for a clearer picture of the inside and draw rapid conclusions. Alex stared at the swinging door.

Kris and Ross had never been lovers.

Kris was right. Ross would never do that to Olivia. And neither would Kris. They were very good friends, just as they claimed, and nothing more.

He owed her an apology. Big time. Remembering the rotten companion comment, Alex winced. Would Kris bother to listen?

His eye caught on the posters outside The Sporting Edge, and he smiled. He'd bet Kris had been too angry to notice. Alex followed her inside. She'd stopped short a few feet in, and stood, staring at the stage.

Alex crossed his arms and leaned against one

wall. The stage show had just reached the finale. Marilyn Monroe, Diana Ross, and Carol Channing sang and danced to a sultry tune.

He had to admit the make-up was superb. If it wasn't for the posters out front, you'd never know this was an all-male revue.

Kris rotated to face him. "Maybe I should re-think the location."

When Kris entered the Devereaux home later that evening with Alex, she found Olivia and Ross opening wedding presents.

Olivia caught sight of them and held up a shiny, four-inch, silver object. It had a flat paddle about two inches square and when she squeezed the handle a thin bar swept across the square. "What do you think this is for?"

"You're opening Aunt Heloise's gift," Alex said.

"No-brainer guess," answered Olivia.

Alex flopped into a love seat opposite his sister and propped his feet on a coffee table. He patted the cushion beside him; Kris settled herself onto the floor, kicking off her heels in the process. He grinned at her; she glared back.

She didn't hold grudges—her temper flared and then fizzled—but Alex deserved to sweat for his behavior tonight. Traces of the hurt his accusations had caused still lingered.

Unfortunately, he made it difficult to keep a smile away. He'd apologized most sincerely on the way home and had acted the perfect gentleman since, darn him. He'd been solicitous, agreeable, and hadn't looked at his watch once.

She leaned against the leg of the love seat. "I'll

143

bite. What's the story of Aunt Heloise?"

"Aunt Heloise believes every bride needs silver," Olivia said. "Unfortunately no one can ever figure out what her gifts are supposed to do. Any suggestions?"

Smiling, shaking her head, Kris picked it up. "It's a cookie scoop. You dip this into the dough"— she illustrated with the square paddle, then squeezed the handle—"and that scoots the dough off onto the cookie sheet to bake."

Alex stared at her. "How did you know that?"

"Antique and novelty shops. I love 'em."

He picked up her hand with a flourish. "Finally, someone who can interpret Aunt Heloise. Better watch out, Kris, or this family will never let you go."

Kris's breath caught in her throat, stilled by the rush of longing at his offhand words. Alex stared at her, motionless, her hand still clasped in his, as though frozen by the unexpected implications of his words. The paintings on the walls, Ross and Olivia's voices, the hardwood floor beneath her, all faded behind Alex's heated gaze on hers.

Kris blinked, then shook away her daze and handed Ross the cookie scoop. No, it could never be.

Spell broken, Alex turned to Olivia. "Have you opened Aunt Hilaire's gift? That's Heloise's twin sister," he told Kris.

Olivia pointed to a wrapped rectangle leaning against the fireplace. "I don't think I have to."

Alex clucked in sympathy. "The velvet Elvis."

"How do you know what's in it?" Ross asked.

"Because Aunt Hilaire always gives either a

painting of Elvis on velvet or a footstool shaped like an armadillo. She read an article once about southern tacky and is convinced one day these will become valuable collectors' items. She says she's giving the newlyweds an investment."

Kris heard the affection that tempered his explanation. Alex accepted his family, eccentricities and all. Did Aunt Hilaire realize how lucky she was? "You two have an interesting collection of relatives."

"Do you have a few black sheep hidden away?" asked Olivia.

"No zany relatives for me," Kris answered. Just a father and stepmother who rarely spoke with such fondness of her mistakes and weaknesses. Kris scrambled to her feet. "Let me get my present to you."

In her room, she took off her stockings, exchanged the dress for old shorts and an oversized shirt, and then fished her gift from the portfolio. Back downstairs, her gaze snagged with Alex's. He skimmed a look down her legs, and when he finally lifted his eyes to hers, smoldering desire had replaced the light of humor.

Okay, so maybe I'll forgive him this once.

It was hard to keep reminding herself this was all a sham between them. Not only because of the simmering excitement that bubbled inside her with Alex, but also because her opinions about him kept undergoing a one-eighty. He still drove her nuts with his watch-watching, his notions of propriety, his schedules, but she kept discovering things she liked about him: his humor, his belief in his work, his kiss.

145

His kiss. That man could do a lot more with his mouth than just ask questions! She found herself staring at his talented mouth and immediately heat rose in her cheeks. A knowing grin stole across the mouth in question.

She held out the thin package to Olivia. "Here."

Kris settled back on the floor and chewed on her lip while Olivia daintily undid each piece of tape. Maybe Olivia wouldn't appreciate it. Maybe Ross hadn't told her any Fitzelhugh stories.

Olivia studied the drawing she'd unveiled, and then looked up from her intent perusal. Her smile evaporated Kris's worry.

"Oh, Kris, thank you! It's Fitzelhugh!"

"It's what?" Alex asked.

Olivia turned the picture around so Alex could see. It was a framed pen-and-ink drawing of Ross and Olivia seated together on a bench, a shared book in their laps. Behind them was Fitzelhugh, the gnome, smiling in blessing.

"Fitzelhugh," Kris answered. "Ross used to tell stories about a gnome named Fitzelhugh who lived under the Mississippi River bridge." The stories had been his escape, and hers.

Olivia gave her fiancé a fond look. "He still tells them."

"Who drew the picture?" asked Alex.

"I did. Who knows, maybe it will be valuable someday." Kris's mouth shut abruptly. She'd just suggested it might be a collectible, like Aunt Hilaire and her velvet Elvis.

Alex leaned forward to study it. "You've got talent, Kris. Joy, love, longing—you've caught them all in the expressions."

With that praise, Alex returned to her good graces.

An alarm on his watch beeped. Alex got to his feet. "I have to get going. I have an early meeting tomorrow. Kris, will you walk with me to the door?"

"Sure." Did he want to apologize again? Maybe share another kiss? Heart pounding, Kris followed him into the hall.

Alex saw the anticipation inside him mirrored in Kris's face. She tilted her chin up, bringing her lips only a dip of his head away. For the moment, Alex resisted the invitation. That wasn't why he'd asked her out here. Or at least, not the only reason.

He didn't have a wedding present for Ross and Olivia. He'd planned to give them a check, but after seeing Kris's gift and the pleasure it brought, cash suddenly seemed a dull choice.

He remembered the year he'd asked for a new baseball mitt for his birthday. What he'd really wanted was the mitt and someone to play catch with. His father had given him a check and sent him with a maid to buy the glove. Claude hadn't even taken time to see Alex make a game-saving catch with that new mitt.

Alex had vowed he'd never disappoint his own family the way his father continually did. That was why he'd decided not to get married. He didn't want to become his father.

A check for a wedding present? Had he already turned into his father? Or was there still hope?

"Would you go with me tomorrow afternoon? Help me pick out a gift for Ross and Olivia?"

147

"A man *asking* to go shopping? I wouldn't pass this up for three sevens on a slot." Kris drew closer. "Anything else you wanted?" she drawled, slow and sultry.

The musky scent of her perfume washed across him, tightening his groin. "Kiss me," he commanded.

This was one command she didn't seem to mind. She wound her arms around his neck and settled against him. She had curves, curves aplenty, and each one nestled into a spot that seemed especially designed to fit her. Alex rested his hands on her buttocks and pulled her tight against his growing hardness.

She gave a small moan—of pleasure, he hoped. Slowly she rose to her toes and slid across him with a deliberate motion that felt so good, it was almost painful. He bent his head until their lips were even, and then waited.

Kris closed the tiny gap, resting her soft mouth on his.

Oh, damn, she felt good.

She sure kissed good, too. Her mouth was as friendly, as fiery, as kinetic as the rest of her.

Alex forgot they were standing in the foyer of the Devereaux ancestral digs, forgot everything but the woman he held in his arms. Kris. He wanted to strip her down and take her right here on the marble floor. He wanted her in his bed where they would be free to employ imagination and intellect. He wanted to keep her close by his side forever.

Whoa! Where had that last "wanted to" come from?

A rustle and a discreet cough penetrated the burning need.

Alex opened one eye to see Ross lounging in the doorway.

"Don't stop now," Ross said. "I'm taking notes."

The smell of brewing coffee drew Kris into the kitchen before her morning jog with Alex and Sunny. Olivia, dressed in a satin robe, stood gazing out the window, her hands cupping a coffee mug. Kris started to withdraw, to allow her this early morning peace, when Olivia turned.

"Come on in," she invited. "Coffee's ready."

"Would you prefer to be alone?"

Olivia shook her head and pulled a mug from a cupboard. "You're up early."

"Alex asked me to go jogging."

Olivia raised one brow. "My brother always said those jogs were sacred, that no one was even to think about coming with him. With this family and his job, I think he just needs an hour when no one makes demands on him."

Kris didn't know what to say. She sat down at the table and stared into the dark brew. Alex's anger last night at the closeness between her and Ross had started her thinking. Maybe others misinterpreted, as well. Most others she didn't care about, but Olivia she did.

"Ross and I have never been lovers," she said with blunt honesty, then groaned. *Real tactful, Kris.* "I thought you should know."

Olivia sat at the table. "I know Ross loves me as I love him, and I trust him completely. He doesn't harbor those kinds of feelings toward you now, I could tell, but"—she sighed—"I *had* wondered. He's told me some of his childhood, enough for me to know that you were the only good thing in it." Olivia looked at her directly. "Your friendship kept him from bitterness and despair, helped him develop into the man I love. I was grateful to you, and I figured anything past was past."

"We thought about it once, at my high school prom."

"Where did you go to school?"

Kris stifled a grin at the question. Where did you go to high school? was the second obligatory question in New Orleans society, the first being, of course, Who's your mama?

"Ursuline. Where'd you go?"

"Sacred Heart."

The niceties out of the way, Kris continued. "To make a long story very short, we got to the hotel room, we kissed, we fumbled at each other for a few minutes, then we both burst into embarrassed giggles. Like in that movie *Back to the Future*, when Marty McFly kisses his mother in the car. No sparks, only a sense that seeing each other like that was wrong. We spent the night playing poker. Ross is brother, not lover."

"Then can I be your sister?"

Kris looked at her over the rim of her coffee mug. "I'd like that."

Alex appeared in the doorway. "So this is why you're always late."

"First time, I swear," Kris countered.

"That's my cue that it's time to get dressed," said Olivia and left.

Alex held up the newspaper. "I come bearing morning funnies."

"Let me get my fix, and I promise I'll do an extra lap."

He handed her the paper, then straddled a chair beside her. "Read on, Macduff."

When Kris looked over her shoulder at him, he gave her a quick grin and a quicker kiss on the cheek. Her heart lifted and caught in her throat. With Alex, she felt appreciated, accepted. Perhaps he would respect what she truly did for a living.

Kris pointed to the Byrde's Eye View cartoon. "KK George, the artist, lives in my building."

Alex gave a low whistle. "Don't you worry about whether you'll appear in one of his cartoons? If I ever met him, I'd wonder if he was dissecting me."

The room receded, then returned in a dizzying rush, and the smile froze on Kris's face.

"She's not like that," she whispered. Carefully, she folded the paper and stood. "We're late for our jog."

Chapter Four

When he'd asked Kris to help him shop for a wedding present, Alex had expected a quick trip to Dillard's or Saks Fifth Avenue or an hour at the New Orleans Centre.

When would he learn?

"This is the last stop," he insisted, as Kris dragged him into another dusty shop on one of the side streets off Royal. Undiluted sunshine pounded the top of his head. Sweat stuck his shirt to his spine. His fingers felt grimy, and his eyes ached.

"But you don't have anything yet."

He looked around at the antiques, some polished, some dirty, some whole, some cracked. All . . . old. This was no more promising than the two art galleries, the poster shop, the leather-goods store, or the kitchen and bath boutique. "I won't find anything here."

"Just look," she insisted. "How about this?" She held up a lace tablecloth.

Alex shook his head, picked up a long-handled brass warming pan, set it down, and then browsed through a set of framed prints. "We passed this shop twice today. Why didn't we stop then? If we stopped at each place in order, instead of flitting back and forth, it would have taken half the time."

"Give me some credit. At least I made out a list of places to visit." Kris waved a paper in front of him.

"You could have put it in order."

She rolled her eyes. "Who organizes a list?"

"I do. It's called prioritizing."

Kris muttered something he didn't quite catch except for the words "anal-retentive." He didn't ask her to repeat it.

She leaned over to examine the contents of an old basket, her shorts pulling up her thighs and tight across her rear. Her long red hair, done up in a ponytail, swung free, as free as her unbound breasts. Alex paused in his rummaging to admire the view. Much more interesting than anything the store possessed.

The one bright spot in the frustrating afternoon had been Kris. With anyone else he'd have called it quits two hours ago, but Kris thoroughly enjoyed pawing through the laden stores, and he'd enjoyed her enthusiasm. They'd talked, finding a common love of Zephyrs baseball, George Lucas movies, and Mexican food, and a common dislike of coffee-table books and cigar bars.

Ashamed of his bout of ill temper, Alex crouched beside her. "Hey, I'm sorry. It's not your fault the day is hot and I'm picky."

She turned her head toward him. "That wasn't the word I used."

"I know." He laid a hand, palm up, on her leg. "I've enjoyed being with you today."

After a moment's hesitation, she covered his hand with hers, the first time she'd touched him voluntarily today. Ever since their morning jog, there'd been something missing in Kris. She was like a candelabra with one of the flames snuffed out. It still shone, but dimmer. It disturbed him that he didn't know what had changed and didn't know how to repair it.

His fingers closed about hers, and then he raised her to her feet. "Let's go back to Canal Street and the electronics stores there."

"Electronics?" she muttered, following him.

Outside, Alex squinted in the summer sunshine—a contrast to the cool, dark shop interior—and replaced his sunglasses over his eyes. Heat sat heavily on his skin and in his lungs. This was not a day to be roaming and shopping. This was a day for verandas and beer.

"I talked to a friend who manages a restaurant here in the Quarter," he said. "He'll let us have their back room for the bachelor party. I told him to hold it, until I talked to you."

"Thanks. That's nice of you, but I've already made other arrangements. Took care of it this morning. Started calling everyone. I meant to tell you, but it slipped my mind." Kris lifted her ponytail and fanned the back of her neck.

"This place is great. Top-notch food and atmosphere, and my friend will make sure we've got the best."

Kris looked directly at him. He wished she didn't wear such dark sunglasses, so he could see her eyes, but he recognized the faint tightening of her lips, and he didn't think the flush in her cheeks was due solely to the heat. "I've got it all set."

"Where?"

"Morten's. And I went there this morning to check it out."

"No more Sporting Edge surprises?"

"None."

Alex was surprised to find himself mildly irritated that she'd arranged everything herself. Used to handling his mother's perpetual crises, he'd assigned Kris a similar role and expected her to ask his help. This time, he'd wanted to help, and it was disconcerting to find he wasn't needed.

For all her disorganization, Kris was remarkably competent and self-sufficient. Another layer to her.

"Then I'll cancel with my friend."

Her lips relaxed, and they headed up Canal Street.

He gave her a sidelong glance. Her fiery hair swung in a short arc, and her breasts matched the rhythm of her stride. Suddenly, he was glad for the loose cut of his pants, which concealed his growing arousal. He noticed details about her: the fine sheen on her fair skin, the tinge of sunburn on her nose, the functional cut of her gold-painted nails, the ink and callus on her left middle finger. She was left-handed and sun-burned easily.

Somehow, those details seemed important. Details that took her beyond the stereotypes he'd saddled her with before he ever met her.

He'd been thinking short-term, a few hours of mutual pleasure. It was what Kris had insisted she wanted, what he had said he wanted. Ever a bridesmaid, always a groomsman.

It was what he still wanted, he hastily assured himself. He was too dedicated to his work to be husband material. But they didn't have to go the marriage aisle route to have something more. After all, she was going to be living here. Maybe she was as tired of the dating scene as he was. Maybe they could become . . . Alex floundered for a word, not sure how to describe what he wanted.

So, how did he tell Kris he'd like to peel a layer off the masquerade? How did he make it a shade more real?

"Maybe you'll find something here."

Alex blinked behind his sunglasses. "Huh?"

Kris gestured toward the glass store front. "Maybe you'll find something here. You said you wanted electronics." He must have continued to stare at her, for she added, "For Olivia. And Ross. You know, your sister. The wedding."

Alex shook his head, throwing off his confusion, then looked where she pointed.

It was an electronic dream. Micro tape recorders, VCRs that could be programmed for thirty shows, palm-sized video cameras, CD players that held a hundred disks. Alex gave a blissful sigh. This was where he'd find his wedding present.

He found it in under two minutes. He remembered Olivia saying she needed a camera to take on their honeymoon. This was the camera. Digital, so they could transfer pictures directly to the computer or a Web page, but with enhanced imaging, so prints would be as clear and sharp as with 35mm film. Maybe Ross could even use it to add illustrations to those gnome stories.

Kris looked at it askance. "A camera?"

"This isn't just any camera."

She glanced at the price tag, and her eyes widened. "What does it do? Dowse for gold?"

Alex started explaining the features, until he glanced at Kris and saw that her eyes were glazed over, though she pretended to listen.

"Not every gift has to be whimsical to be appreciated," he said, a trifle defensively.

Kris shook herself. "No, I'm sure it doesn't."

Alex gave a decisive nod. "Ross and Olivia will love this."

Two days later, Kris kicked back in a chair, her feet on another chair opposite, and surveyed the banquet room at Morten's. The bachelor party was in full swing, and everything seemed to be going smoothly. Ross was taking pictures with the camera Alex had given them. Alex had been right about that one; Ross and Olivia had waxed enthusiastic over the gift. Who'd have thought? A large-screen TV showed a basketball game. Several guys played pool. Steaks had been devoured and dessert was next. No one seemed on his way to an obnoxious drunk.

Everyone tonight had been friendly, but then,

she never had trouble talking to people. Oh, there'd been a few faintly crude remarks at the beginning about the "best man," but she'd handled those.

Kris rubbed her sweating palms on her tights. These were Alex's relatives, Ross's friends, yet she felt as nervous as she had at Commander's. More so. At least there'd been other women there.

However, the bridesmaid luncheon she'd attended yesterday with Olivia had been all women, and she'd felt even more out of place there. Charity fund-raisers, the latest Sacred Heart alumni event, lectures sponsored by the Junior League—she had little experience with any of it, not that that ever stopped her from talking. Kris closed her eyes as she remembered the way Jennifer, the maid of honor, had dismissed Kris's suggestion that they raise money for the SPCA with a beautiful mutt show. That luncheon had been among the longest three hours of her life.

All week she'd been surrounded by people, yet she'd never felt so alone.

Kris rummaged through her purse and plucked out her sketchpad, her solace. Idly, she drew, capturing the light on the pool table, the motion as someone knocked back a beer, a group of men intent on the NBA playoffs.

One of Ross's office friends plopped down beside her. What was his name? Relieved at the distraction, Kris searched for the mnemonic visualization that helped her remember. Big ears, Dumbo, five letters beginning with D. David? No, Duane.

"Nice party, Kris."

"Thanks, Duane."

He propped his feet up on the chair beside hers and peered at her sketch. "Hey, that's good."

"Thanks."

"You could do that for a living. Be one of those caricaturists in Jackson Square. I hear they make a mint."

Kris smiled. She'd done that in high school. "I'll think about it."

He took a drag from his beer, then eyed her over the rim. "Gossip has it that you and Alex Devereaux are sticking close these days."

Wrong news traveled fast. Kris gave a noncommittal shrug.

"So, where is Alex tonight?"

Good question. Where *was* Alex?

Alex snapped off his computer, looked at his watch, and swore. Ross's party had started an hour and a half ago, but he'd had to finish this brief. The chemical dumping case was too important—for Louisiana, for the people and their future—to lose because he'd stopped working to attend a bachelor party.

In a matter of moments, Alex was in his car, speeding toward Morten's.

His old man all over again. Working late, missing the family events. Always some important client or case. Always something more pressing than the family.

Alex snapped on the radio, needing a distraction from his thoughts, but he promptly forgot to listen.

He wouldn't do that to his family, because he

wouldn't have one. He wouldn't have to divide his attention to handle chaos and endless crises at home. He could focus on his work.

A red light stopped him. As Alex tapped a finger against the steering wheel, his gaze stopped on a man coming down the street. The man, dressed in a suit, wheeled a baby carriage with one hand. A toddler grasped his other hand. The man bent over, listening to something the tiny girl said, and then smiled. A wealth of love and caring filled that smile.

That man manages, whispered the insidious voice inside Alex. Ross will manage. You could, too. If you wanted to.

The light turned green. Alex shifted into gear and set off with a roar.

The party at Morten's was in full swing when Alex arrived. He paused, looking around the room, focusing only when he found what he sought. Kris.

She sat on a folding chair, her feet propped on another. She had on those eye-drawing white tights, black shoes that looked like ballet slippers, and a brilliant green top. Duane Rogers sat beside her, laughing.

The ache, the yearning, the doubts faded, replaced by calm, pleasure, desire, and a sense of coming home.

A woman—hair in a bun, glasses perched on the end of her nose, tweed skirt reaching below her knees, blouse buttoned to her chin though it didn't conceal her impressive chest—strolled into the room. She eyed him with a glance decidedly warmer than one might expect from her dowdy appearance. "Are you the groom-to-be?"

"No. The blond guy over there is."

"Thanks." She headed purposefully toward Ross.

Who was that? What did she want with Ross? Alex stared after her. She wasn't especially pretty, rather coarse actually, but with those attributes, it took a while for a man to raise his eyes long enough to realize it.

The woman lowered herself onto Ross's lap and played with his hair. "How could you do this to me, lover? Marry someone else in just two days?"

"Ah—" Ross seemed at a loss for words. "Who are you?"

Her lip extended to a pout; her hand trailed along his chest. As if on cue, the low-level music grew louder. Roy Orbison's sultry growl filled the room. With a dramatic motion, the woman pulled a pin from her hair, and her hair tumbled free. "That night in the library," she exclaimed with more drama than Liz Taylor. "How can you forget? Shall I remind you?"

Alex rested his head on his palm and groaned. He'd told the others not to do this. Ross wasn't the type, and Kris wouldn't appreciate it.

He opened one eye to look at Kris's reaction. She was sitting with her arms folded, staring at the woman, but whether she was angry, astounded, or fascinated, he couldn't tell.

The stripper stood and attacked her blouse. The men cheered. Ross smiled politely. Kris sat motionless.

Soon the music changed from Orbison to Robert Palmer's "Simply Irresistible." The woman was enthusiastic, Alex noted, almost keeping time with the driving beat. At the end, she wore more than a bather on the Riviera, but the guests didn't seem to mind. They hollered and clapped and tucked bills into her sequins. In the raunchy way of the male sex, they seemed as pleased with Ross's embarrassment as with the woman's dance. Soon the woman, apparently satisfied with the results, gathered her clothes and left.

"Wait'll you see what else we've got planned," said one of the guests.

Kris lowered her feet from the chair, moving slowly as though each muscle were stiff and sore. Catching sight of him, she came to his side.

"I'm sorry I was late," he said. "Work." It sounded like such a feeble excuse.

To his surprise, she wasn't upset. "That's okay. Ross said you had an important case to prepare. Something about chemical dumping? Is that what you were doing?"

"A firm upriver is dumping potentially carcinogenic chemicals directly into the river. I want to hit them so hard they'll never let even a whisper of an idea to do it again cross their minds. I had to finish up some things, and it's easier to concentrate after everyone leaves."

She nodded in understanding. "I like to work at night. Sometimes I get so caught up in what I'm doing I forget engagements. What you do is a lot more important."

Alex stuck his hands in his pockets. She understood? She didn't mind? She just went on and handled her affairs?

One of the guests started telling a seriously off-color joke, his voice boisterous until he glanced over, saw Kris, and the joke fizzled.

Kris grimaced. "Time for me to leave. The boys will have a better time without me. Could you act as host?"

Alex started to protest, but stopped. Something about the strain around her eyes, the sag in her shoulders, told him a lot more was going through her mind than offense at watching a stripper. "Sure," he said simply. "Do you have a ride home?"

This time her grin looked forced. "I live in New York. I take cabs." Her arms wrapped around her waist in an unconscious gesture. "The bill's taken care of."

She said a cheerful good-bye to Ross, laughed at something one of the guests said, kept a bright smile plastered to her face. Yet, loneliness seemed to hover above her. Watching her walk away, Alex was struck by a sudden realization.

Kris Lucas was a superb actress.

He'd seen hints of it before. At Commander's, the night of the family party, he'd seen her hide fatigue. At the male revue, there had been that flash of vulnerability and hurt, when he'd asked about her and Ross. She'd expected him to think the worst of her; that was why she'd thrown Ross's honor in his face, not her own. When they'd shopped for the gift, she'd hidden behind friendly conversation. Now, tonight, she covered up sadness.

Kris was so vivacious, so gregarious, so friendly. How much was a show to hide her vulnerability?

She blinded others to the fact that there was a

lot more to her beneath the surface. But not him, not anymore.

The urge to learn more, to see beneath the flashy exterior, stole across him, insidious and insistent, accompanied by a compelling urge to be alone with her.

Why had he promised to stay until Ross left?

Why had he told her he wanted nothing more than a camouflage to avoid any other entanglements?

They had two more days, two more nights. Tomorrow night was the rehearsal dinner. The following day was the wedding. Two more days and he'd lose the right to put his arm around her, to spend time with her, to claim her as his own.

A yearning, so powerful it made his bones ache, so strange he couldn't put a name to it, shook him. All he knew was that he wanted Kris Lucas, the Kris Lucas he'd discovered tonight. Before tomorrow night was over, he'd have her.

Kris sat on the front steps of the Devereaux house, her arms wrapped around her knees. She'd forgotten to ask for a key again, and the family was all out: Olivia with her bridesmaids, Claude at a dinner meeting, Mary Eulalie, in a dither, meeting with the florist and pastry chef despite the late hour. There was probably a housekeeper in back, but Kris didn't feel like seeking her out or pounding on the doorbell.

She rested her chin on her knees and listened to the rustle of the wind. Honeysuckle, a scent she'd forever associate with this week, drifted across the night. It was dark here, hot and humid and dark. She liked the night, liked the encompassing dark. Some of her best ideas came at night.

This night felt different. Tall oaks hid the streetlights, and at this hour the park across the street was empty. As empty as she felt. As alone as she felt.

Seeing Ross with his friends, in a camaraderie she couldn't share regardless of her claim of being the best man, had driven home how alone she'd always been. Ross had looked beneath the surface of her and didn't mind what he found there, but she'd learned not to give others the opportunity.

Most of the time she didn't mind, was truly content in her life, but sometimes . . . She sighed. Only recently, with Alex, had she been tempted to let down her guard.

She'd seen desire in his face, had felt him touch her beyond the simple needs of their deception, had tasted his kisses, but she hadn't felt compelled to warn him off with a friendly-but-that's-as-far-as-it-goes smile or a light joke. Because he was safe? Because she expected he wouldn't want to delve too deeply? Because a week—and maybe a bit more, she admitted to herself—was all he wanted?

Or because Alex touched something inside her, something that longed to be set free, even though she feared the consequences of exposure to light and to scrutiny?

Her hands started to sweat again. Kris dug her fingers into her palms until her nails made half-moons in her skin. No, that could never happen. She kept odd hours, was used to doing for herself,

being with herself. Her father had found her con-
trary ways frustrating; her last boyfriend had said
she was impossible to live with, that she was too
damn independent.

It must be the truth. She'd set her lone course a
long time ago.

Why couldn't Alex have felt differently about
KK George?

The sound of Alex, talking about his relatives
with fondness and affection, echoed inside her.

A lone course, or a lonely one? Tonight she
didn't have the answers.

Damp heat surrounded her with its familiar caress. New Orleans was her home; she had missed
even the hair-crimping humidity. Kris picked up
a stick and began drawing absently in the dirt.

The gate at the end of the driveway swung open.
Kris scratched out her drawing, and then watched
Alex's car drive in.

In a few moments, he sat beside her on the
steps. "No key?"

"Nope. How did the rest of the party go?"

"The stripper was the highlight. Ross said he'll
see you tomorrow, but to tell you thanks. A few
guys had a bit too much to drink, so I made sure
they went home in a cab."

"Thanks."

They sat for a moment in silence; then Alex
picked up a strand of her hair. He wound it
around his finger, released it, wound it up again.
"You have beautiful hair. It reminds me of
flames."

"Not carrots?" she joked.

Alex didn't smile. He seemed intent on studying

her hair in the faint moonlight. "On a night like this, I might even call it a beacon. You know, there's a lot of things I like about you."

Kris rested her elbows on the step behind her, unsure how to interpret Alex's pensive mood. "I'm fun to be with. I make you feel good. I listen well. I've got great legs."

He looked at her. The moonlight shone on his dark eyes, giving him the look of a night predator.

"That wasn't what I was going to say. I like your independence, that I'm always discovering something new about you. You aren't what I expected. I thought you were flaky, unorganized, and undependable."

"I am." Her heart thudded, filled her with its primal beat, as he said just the words she needed to hear tonight.

"One of the three maybe," he said, leaving her to guess which one he meant.

The night air, thick and humid, sat on her chest, making breathing difficult. Kris brushed her hair back, dragged in oxygen. "I thought you were snobby, elegant, and rigid."

"I am."

"Maybe one of the three." She echoed his assessment.

"Right now, rigid is definitely a word I would apply to myself."

Her eyes widened and, of its own accord, her glance flicked to below his waist, then back. Yes, he was definitely rigid, and he made no effort to hide the fact.

"Basically, though, we're incompatible," she said.

He shrugged, not answering. Or maybe his refusal to agree was answer enough. His glance flicked along her legs, and he pushed up the sleeves of his unstructured jacket.

"Two choices, Kris. I can use my key to let you in this house, or I can take you back to mine. I think maybe we've got something burning between us, something for tonight, maybe something for when you return."

She looked at his hand resting beside hers, but not touching. A strong, honest hand with blunt fingertips and a smattering of black hair on the back. Her hand moved over his, and her fingers tightened around him. She suspected she was letting herself in for heartache, but she rarely let fear of the consequences stop her. "I want you, too. Tonight."

With a single motion, he lifted her to her feet.

At Alex's house, however, Sunny's demands for a walk could not be ignored. Alex snapped on her leash and gave Kris a rueful grin. "You want to come along?"

"Sure."

Normally he loved his evening walks with Sunny. Since she was confined to the house much of the day, he usually took her to nearby Audubon Park and tossed a Frisbee or let her romp, then came home and tussled with her. Tonight, however, an eagerness to be back in his house, alone with Kris, had him feeling like he was the one straining at the leash.

They would turn off the air-conditioning, he decided, open the long windows to the night scents and sounds, let the whir of the ceiling fans cool them even as they came together in blazing heat. His blood drummed through his veins as the mere thought of Kris lying beside him, above him, beneath him, made him hard. Her wild red hair spread in a living forest fire, her green eyes snapping. How many places did she have freckles? He wanted to kiss each one.

She'd bring that incredible energy with her, that infectious laugh, and he would absorb it, savor it, return it to her many fold. He would chase away the aloneness that seemed so much a part of her.

Alex pursed his lips, but his throat was too dry to whistle for Sunny. "C'mon, Sunny. Time to go home, girl," he croaked and tugged at her leash.

"I think she wants to go to the park," Kris said as Sunny leaped toward the trees.

"She likes to play there."

"Maybe we should—"

"Not tonight."

Kris looked up at him, each freckle prominent against her skin, pale in the moonlit night. Her eyes widened.

"Not now," he added hoarsely.

"Were the Devereaux part of Jean Lafitte's pirate band?" Her hand traced the silver ear cuffs he wore. "In the moonlight, you are very dark and dangerous, Alex."

"Do I scare you?"

She shook her head. "I scare myself. I want you so badly."

He lifted her hand to his lips and kissed her fingers. A courtly gesture in times gone past, but tonight it was one of need and longing.

Sunny gave a leap. The unexpected jerk of the leash pulled Alex off balance, and he stumbled away from Kris, barely keeping his balance.

Kris gave a hoot of laughter. "I think Sunny has other ideas about losing her evening trip to the park. C'mon, Alex, let's take her." She cast him a sidelong glance, full of promise. "We'll wear her out. She'll be too tired even to bark."

Alex cast a baleful glance at his dog. "She'd better not wear us out first."

Kris linked an arm through his. "Oh, I think I can guarantee *we* won't be too tired to . . . bark."

Anticipation, Alex discovered, carried its own rewards, as long as it wasn't taken to the extreme. While they played with Sunny, Kris played with him. She brushed against him, her breasts creating a tingling that spread to his groin, her fingers in his hair starting a flush that warmed him to his toes, when he was already as hot as the night. Her low, husky laugh and her sultry perfume teased as they touched his other senses. He kissed her cheek, tasting the salt on her skin; then he kissed her mouth, tasting the chocolate she'd had for dessert.

By the time they got back to his house, Alex was about ready to explode. He gave Sunny a big bowl of water and some extra food, and shut her in the kitchen.

"Now, where were we?" His hands gripped Kiss at the hips, and he pulled her flush against him, letting her feel exactly what her teasing had wrought.

She wriggled, settling him more thoroughly

against her, and then wrapped her arms about his neck. "Here, I think."

Alex lowered his head to hers. He liked Kris's height. He didn't have very far to go to connect with her soft lips, which opened eagerly when he traced them with his tongue. She kissed him back, not shy or withdrawing, accepting his tongue mating with hers and her breath mingling with his.

Groaning, Alex pulled her hips closer. His hands tunneled beneath her green shirt, slid up the silk of her back, tracing each bump of her spine, unimpeded by any other scrap of clothing. *Dear Lord, she felt so good.*

Kris wound her fingers through his hair. Her fingertips gently massaged his scalp in a movement that did nothing to soothe and everything to excite.

Alex lifted his mouth from the drugging kiss and grabbed a fistful of her hair, not tugging, simply enjoying the feel of holding solid flames. His other hand slipped down, inside the band of her tights, to caress her more intimately.

"Is every place on you this silky and smooth?"

"I don't know."

"Shall I find out?"

"Mmmmm."

Alex took that for agreement. He had just bent his head when an insistent ringing intruded. Sunny, as always, started barking in accompaniment.

The telephone. Why hadn't he turned off the ringer? Alex swore under his breath, bent his head and tried to ignore the cacophony, hoping it would stop.

It didn't.

"Maybe you should answer that," Kris said against his lips, her voice trembling. "Could it be about your case?"

Maybe. He punched the speaker-phone button. "Devereaux," he snapped.

"Alex?"

Alex groaned and dropped his forehead against the wall. His mother. First thing tomorrow, he was going out and getting Caller ID.

"Alex, are you all right?"

"Fine, Mama." He fought to control his ragged breath. "I'm kind of busy right now."

Kris perched on the back of the chair next to the phone. Absently, Alex rubbed a hand along her arm. She shivered under his touch.

His mother dismissed his comment as inconsequential. "You must come over right away. Aunt Hilaire and Aunt Heloise just arrived, and they have everyone in an uproar. They should never have gotten that crazy notion to move across the lake. If they still had their house on Freret, this wouldn't be happening now."

"Why do you need me?"

"Because you're the only one who can calm them down. They're convinced New Orleans is a hotbed of crime, although why, if they think that, they came two nights early, I do not understand, but they say they will not sleep a wink unless there is a man in the house, and your father is out somewhere."

Of course.

Mary Eulalie paused to take a deep breath. "You have to come and wait here until your father gets home so they will settle down. Poor Olivia Elizabeth is fatigued, and I swear I am utterly *exhausted*, what with trying to get the florist to keep his promise to have only pink or pink-tinted in the bouquets and boutonnieres. Did you know they were trying to give me salmon-colored boutonnieres? Salmon!"

Alex glanced over at Kris. Her hand pressed against her mouth to stifle the giggles, but he saw her shoulders shaking and the humor in her eyes. He just shook his head.

"Do you think Kris will mind wearing a pink boutonniere, Alex, or should we get her a bouquet? No, a bouquet for a best man just doesn't work. Oh, and speaking of Kris, she isn't here. I need you to help me find her. Aunt Heloise and Aunt Hilaire are most anxious to meet her."

"Kris is with me."

"Oh." There was a sudden pause. "Well, then bring her along when you come." Abruptly, Mary Eulalie hung up, taking his acquiescence as a foregone conclusion.

Alex stared at the phone for a moment, and then lifted his gaze to Kris. She took the hand from her mouth and burst out laughing.

"If we're not there in fifteen minutes, she'll call again," Alex warned.

"Then I guess we'd better go."

"You don't mind?"

"Duty calls."

Alex hauled her to her feet. "Kiss me first," he growled.

She did just that.

"How do you feel about quickies?" he mumbled against her lips.

"The Minute Waltz is as much an art form as Beethoven's Fifth."

Alex was tempted, so tempted, but he set her firmly away from him. "Not for our first time together."

She ran a finger down his cheek. "Tomorrow, then? After the rehearsal dinner?"

"Tomorrow. We'll take all night."

It was an unshakable promise, a vow for the future.

Chapter Five

The rehearsal dinner was not the intimate little meal Kris had expected, for Devereaux and LeBlancs rarely missed an excuse to gather. Held at the Botanical Gardens in City Park, the affair was housed in a cavernous building that looked like a greenhouse, but had air-conditioning and was large enough to hold the wedding party, their guests, and a multitude of relatives.

"Go on in, Kris. I'll join you in a minute," Alex said, waylaid by a relative requesting free legal advice.

Nodding, Kris trailed in behind the other members of the wedding party, her palms sweating, a faint smile tacked onto her face. She itched to hold a pencil, to release the energy building inside her with a few quick strokes of lead.

The rehearsal had gone smoothly, with only a

few of the glitches and hitches that explained why a rehearsal was needed. The maid of honor had been miffed at having to walk back up the aisle with a woman, but they'd solved that problem by letting her go first with Kris following.

Her masquerade with Alex was a success, Kris decided as she responded to greetings from people she'd met over the week. Beyond the occasional arch look, there was a comfortable acceptance that she and Alex were paired. She should have been delighted with the results.

So, why this edginess? Anticipation warred with uncertainty, leaving her stomach in a nervous knot. Nothing Alex had said or done tonight stepped beyond the bounds of propriety, yet she was extraordinarily aware of him. He'd barely touched her, yet her skin felt warm and tight and sensitive to the least caress, like the casual touch of his fingers when he handed her a hymnal or his warm hand on the small of her back when he escorted her into the church. The spicy, masculine, citrus scent of him had become a longed-for part of each breath she took.

Why the edginess? Be honest, Kris, you know why. Because what she planned for later tonight had nothing to do with the charade and everything to do with her feelings toward Alex Devereaux.

Excitement. Desire. Friendship. Admiration. An incredible sense of rightness. And underlying it all, the stark reality of fear.

Fear of letting him get closer, fear of watching him walk away when he decided she lacked some essential trait, fear of the hurt if she allowed herself to care. Or love.

Kris rubbed her sweating palms together. She could no more refuse tonight than she could refuse to breathe. If she didn't take this one chance, she sensed she'd regret it for a long time to come, and she had never been one for caution.

She'd just have to be very careful to keep the last masks in place, to keep the barriers to her heart and soul intact.

Uncle Richard came up and hugged her. "How you doing, Kris? Going to save me a dance?"

His exuberance warmed her. "Sure thing."

Aunt Heloise—or was it Aunt Hilaire? the two were identical dumplings—bustled over. Her chocolate-drop eyes gleamed. "I heard you're an artist. Do you draw those sweet pretty pictures we see on greeting cards?"

"Something like that." Her cartoons had never been described as pretty or sweet, even the ones on cards.

"What do you think of my Elvis painting? It's going to be very valuable some day."

Elvis painting? Must be Aunt Hilaire. "I haven't had a chance to see it," Kris answered with more tact than truth.

She heard a rustle, caught a faint whiff of lime. Inside her, intimate spots began to tighten and tingle, sure signs that Alex was near.

"Good evening, Aunt Hilaire." Alex kissed his aunt's powdered cheek.

Would she ever get over this annoying tendency to get weak-kneed at the sound of his voice?

The maid of honor swept over, her silk gown

flowing elegantly about her ankles, and linked her arm with Alex's. "Would you join us at our table, Alex darling?" She arched a brow in Kris's direction. "Being best man, you must have some old friends you're dying to talk to." She patted Alex's arm with possessive red nails. "I'm sure you'll excuse us."

"Jennifer, I don't think—" Gently, Alex tried to extricate his arm, but Jennifer held on with the tenacity of a squid.

Kris tilted her head, studying Jennifer, and the beginnings of a cartoon image blossomed. Half female, half tentacle, a frantic fish . . .

"Kris." The annoyance in Alex's voice popped the image. *Our agreement,* he mouthed toward her, and then draped his free hand across her shoulder. A shiver coursed down her spine at the masculine strength beneath his suit jacket. If she were drawing herself right now, she'd surround herself with a halo of wavering, quivering lines.

Jennifer refused to take Alex's unsubtle hint. Her crimson suckers had found their prey, and Alex was too much the gentleman for rudeness, even to Jennifer.

Time for the act. Kris summoned her high-wattage smile and sagged against his side, relishing the hard support. Act? This part was as much an act as New York was a sleepy burb.

"He's mine," she said simply, staring at Jennifer, "but you can borrow him for a few minutes. I'm not selfish."

Jennifer gaped at Kris, then turned narrowed eyes to Alex. "Is she serious?"

Alex returned an innocent look. "Am I protesting?"

Her mouth snapped shut to a straw-thin line, before curving into a catty smile. "Well, well, Alex Devereaux tamed. And by a—" Her gaze swept across Kris, lingering at her dress's short hemline and spaghetti straps. "What did you say you did in New York?" Walk the streets was the clear implication.

Kris's chin jutted forward as she ignored the reminder that she just didn't fit in with this crowd. No way would she let this woman see the wound, however. "I tend bar."

Alex scowled at her. "How come every time someone asks, you've got a different career?"

"I'm a Renaissance woman; I've done them all." Kris gave him a grin. "Starving never appealed to me."

"Why not just say you're an artist?"

"An artist?" Coming from Jennifer, it sounded like sewer scourer.

"A damn good one," Alex retorted.

Warm pleasure stole through Kris. Her father had never said one kind word about her "doodling," yet Alex defended her when he hadn't even seen her best work. Or hadn't realized he had.

She kissed his earlobe. "You're being generous."

Despite the pirate exterior, Alex was caring and supportive. His protests aside, he would marry some day—his people always did—and his wife would be a very, very lucky woman.

His wife. The mere thought ripped a tear into her.

For tonight, though, she could pretend she had

a claim on his sexy sweetness and fierce loyalty.

She leaned forward and whispered in Jennifer's ear. Jennifer glared, dropped Alex's arm, pivoted on one spike, and then took off in a huff.

"I never saw Jennifer give up that easily. What did you say?" Alex asked.

"That if she didn't let go of your arm, tomorrow I'd escort her down the aisle and sing 'My Girl' at the top of my lungs while I did it."

Alex tilted his head back and laughed. His arm tightened around her shoulders. From the corner of her eye, Kris saw Jennifer send her a poisonous glare.

It was after dinner before Alex found a private moment with his sister. They stood together, alone in one quiet corner, watching the crowd of friends and relatives in general, Kris and Ross in particular.

"You like her, don't you?" Olivia said, as Kris and Ross executed the turns of an intricate waltz.

"Yeah," Alex agreed, although *like* seemed a wimpy word for what he felt. He cleared his throat. "Don't let Mama get upset if she finds out Kris is late coming home tonight." Rather than look at his sister, he followed the flame of Kris's hair across the dance floor. "In fact, don't let her check up on us at all."

"Oh, ho. So that's the way it is."

Alex shoved his hands in his pockets. "Don't read more into it, Olivia. I'm not looking for anything long-term. I can't split myself like that."

"You figure, like father like son? You're different, Alex."

"I was late to Ross's bachelor party."

"But you made it, and you took an afternoon off to shop for that wonderful camera."

Startled, Alex tore his eyes from Kris. "How did you know?"

"Kris let it slip. Apparently she didn't realize what a momentous occasion it was."

"She wouldn't. Her idea of a schedule is to say, 'Let's wander.' "

"But Kris isn't like Mama."

"I realize that."

"There's truth in the old saying that opposites attract."

"Attract doesn't begin to cover it." As he studied Kris's laughing visage, sudden longing pounced on him like an ambulance-chasing lawyer—persistent and unwanted, yet offering tantalizing promises.

"People combine marriage and careers all the time."

Could they? "What's their secret?"

"They love each other enough to make it work. Until now, you just haven't met anyone you wanted to make the effort for." Olivia smoothed a hand over her hair and tightened the back of her earring. "Now, I am going to steal my fiancé from his best man and claim a dance." She gave him an impudent grin over her shoulder. "I'll keep Mama off your back, but you'll owe me big time for this one, brother."

They love each other enough to make it work. Olivia's words haunted him. Was it that simple? And that complex?

Did he love Kris? Could it happen that fast? Was love this hot and sharp?

He feared the answer to all the questions was an undeniable yes. His claim of perpetual bachelorhood suddenly seemed hollow, the spoutings of a desperately wary man.

They love each other enough to make it work. It took both people to make it work. Kris knew her mind, said she needed nothing permanent. They'd agreed to the ground rules of this charade, but now Alex found himself wanting to forget those unwritten rules.

Across the room, Cousin love-em-and-leave-em Larry led Kris onto the dance square for a two-step. The twist in his gut told Alex he was in deep, deep trouble.

Kris. She wanted him; he knew that. A burning anticipation kept him alert and half-aroused so that he could barely wait for the niceties to be over. He needed to take her home with him and love her through the long, long hours of the night.

They wouldn't sleep much tonight.

What could possibly go wrong? He'd asked Kris that question when he'd first proposed this mad masquerade to her.

What could go wrong?

She wanted a few nights.

He now wanted forever.

Alex straightened his cuffs. He'd settle for sixty years.

Despite the air-conditioning, the room was warm. Kris reclipped a straggling strand of hair and then stifled a yawn. She expected the party would break up soon—after all, everyone had a wedding to attend tomorrow—but until it did, she needed a breath of air. Hoping the garden would be cooler than the interior, now that the sun had set, she stepped outside. Tiny white lights twinkled in shrubs and bonsai trees, creating a fairyland atmosphere. Kris followed one of the grassy paths toward a wrought-iron bench.

The metal was cool on her stockinged legs, and she spread her bare arms across the top, ignoring the hard curlicues, in favor of relief from the heat. The scent of tea roses, rich and sweet, perfumed her small corner. As she watched the people inside, her hands reached automatically into her purse for pencil and paper.

Swiftly she sketched. Simple strokes that carried only the essences. A face here. A hat there. The waiter's patient look as Mary Eulalie expounded. Claude tilting his head back in laughter. Table decorations. A pattern of lights. Shapes and patterns to be studied and manipulated and used later.

Voices drifted from the hedge behind her. "Olivia must be downright mortified. Imagine, having your fiancé choose a woman for the *best man*."

Kris stiffened. She recognized the speaker as one of the bridesmaids.

"Can you imagine how utterly ridiculous *I* feel?" Jennifer was there, too. "And that red hair."

How many more things about her were they going to trash? Kris's hands moved across the paper on her lap, her pencil expressing the agitation, the pain, with swift strokes.

"You know," Jennifer whispered confidentially,

"Olivia showed me the wedding present she gave them. Would you believe it's a *cartoon*? Hand-drawn. A real collector's item." Her voice quavered in a perfect imitation of Aunt Hilaire, and the two women snickered.

No mother likes to be told her baby is ugly. The pencil snapped beneath the sudden pressure of Kris's hand. She looked down at the picture she'd drawn. Then she smiled.

Jennifer didn't look nearly as attractive in squid form.

She tore the paper from her pad, not hiding the ripping sound, then stood and strode around the hedge, back toward the party. Jennifer didn't seem a bit surprised to see her, but the other woman flushed with embarrassment. With a flourish, Kris handed the paper to Jennifer. "I don't tend bar, I don't decorate cakes, and I don't walk the streets. I draw *cartoons* for a living. Humor reveals the sharpest truths."

It wasn't the best of exit lines, but it would do. Especially punctuated by Jennifer's outraged gasp as she looked at the paper.

Inside, Kris strolled over to Alex and linked her arm through his. "I'd like to leave now," she said in a husky whisper. "Are you ready?"

Desire flared across his face. "Very ready."

For once, Cinderella was leaving the ball with the prince, instead of a bunch of mice and an over-ripe pumpkin.

"Where's Sunny?" Kris looked around for the boisterous dog.

"The ten-year-old boy next door was thrilled to

have her over for the night. He adores Sunny." Alex picked up her hand.

Kris sucked in a breath as he kissed her fingers, one by one. "A baby-sitter for the kid while Dad's on a hot date?" she gasped.

His dark eyes widened, and he stared at her, as though her offhand comment made a surprise connection to another thought. "You're right. Sunny *is* like a kid, a family."

A grin curved across his lips, though he didn't relinquish his attention to her fingers. He drew her closer with the simple motion of an arm about her waist, then placed her hand around the back of his neck. He tightened his grip, pressing her flush against him.

"Do you know what I'd like?" His hips circled against her.

Kris moaned softly, the bud of anticipation within her belly blooming from the erotic caress. "I can guess. I want it too." One hand lay flat upon his buttocks and flexed against the play of muscle beneath her palm.

Alex clucked with tender amusement. "That's for later, Kris. We're taking this nice and slow."

"Nice? I object, counselor."

"Sustained. State your preference. Raunchy, raw, steamy, vigorous, sweaty? Stop me when you hear one you like."

"All of the above."

He brushed his lips against hers, once, twice, three times, a barely-there possession that set her heart spinning. His fingers speared through her hair. "Do you know how much I love your curls? I expect my hands to burn when I touch them."

Kris's insides tightened at the L word, until she decided Alex spoke it only in the heat of the moment. She buried her face against his neck. "So many compliments for the carrottop?"

He gave her head a tiny shake. "When are you going to just accept one of my compliments? You must have gotten tons of them."

"Not that many," she whispered.

Alex reared back and studied her face.

Kris looked away, unwilling to share the emotions that always hovered so near the surface with this way-too-perceptive master of body language. She was the strong one, the fun one, the funny one, not the one who ached inside and who wanted this night with a relentless hunger.

"Look at me, Kris."

Another command she couldn't resist. His dark eyes, outlined with lashes as long and pretty as the fringe on her favorite shawl, crinkled with hints of humor.

Her heart sped under the influx of pleasure.

"I'm going to help you with this deep-seated fear of compliments." Teasing lifted the corners of his mouth. "It's called immersion therapy."

"You're a lawyer, not a doctor."

"But I played one as a child."

"I'll just bet."

"I'm going to give you compliments, and you're not going to speak until I tell you. You will simply think, 'Alex never lies,' after each one."

"Never lies? You're a lawyer."

He gave her a disgusted look. "Alex never lies."

"Alex never lies," she parroted dutifully.

He nodded. "That's it. Now, no more talk, until

I say. Your hair is not carrot, it is burnished rose-gold, and the curls make it dance like flames. And you know how partial we New Orleanians are to hot." He lifted one brow.

Alex never lies.

"I love the way a smile lingers at the edge of your mouth. When you enter a room, you hesitate, then walk in with a jaunty little swing."

"I am not *jaunty.*"

He lifted that brow again. Kris subsided. *Alex never lies.*

This was getting to be kind of fun. As he talked, he caressed, his hands endlessly skimming in a teasing, tickling motion until her skin felt as if it glowed as bright as her hair. Prohibited from speaking, she leaned into him and gave his ear-lobe a nip and his neck a kiss.

"I love your sexy rear." He slid his hands beneath her slip of a dress and deftly removed her stockings and panties before massaging the part in question. "Almost as much as I love your breasts." He unsnapped the clasp on her strapless bra with one hand.

This man was entirely too adept at removing women's clothing by feel. Kris started to ask, then retreated at the sight of his raised brow.

Alex never lies.

He held up the lacy black bra. "I definitely love your taste in undies. One day, would you give me a fashion show? From the contents of just your lingerie drawer?"

What would he think of the yellow thong? Arousal, sharp and sweet, caught her in its velvety steel grip at the mere thought of modeling for him, the wisp of fabric, and nothing else. Her lungs dragged in necessary air.

Through the thin material of her dress, he palmed her, avoiding suddenly turgid nipples that ached for the rough stroke of his thumb. Or his tongue.

Kris groaned softly, threading her fingers through the warm softness of his hair.

He nuzzled her ear, even as his hands worked magic on her cloth-covered breasts. "I love the fact that I don't get a crick in my neck every time I want to kiss you." He demonstrated, thoroughly, how much he appreciated her height.

Kris returned the compliment, her breathy sighs and her roaming hands sharing the need and the pleasure he'd forbidden her to speak.

"I must admit," he said, "you're an ideal patient for this immersion therapy. Taking you on the hardwood floor, however, is not part of the treatment." The room tilted as Alex picked her up in his arms and headed down the hall to his bedroom. He looked down at her, his face in shadow, for they had turned on no lamps, relying only on exterior light—yellow streetlamps, silver moon, white stars—all bright and clear.

I'm too heavy, she started to protest, then bit down on her lip to stifle the impulse. Alex didn't seem to be having any trouble carrying her. After hearing the way he saw her, she did feel beautiful and wanted. Even the fact that his compliments began with, "I love," didn't bother her as it might have a quarter of an hour ago.

Instead, she wound her arms around his neck and laid her head on his shoulder. The wild thumping of his heart matched the pounding of hers, and the unsteadiness of his breathing wasn't from the exertion of carrying her.

Alex set her gently down on his wide bed, but did not follow her down. Instead, he toed off his shoes, and then, with an economy of motion, removed the rest of his clothes until he stood naked before her.

Kris drank in the magnificent sight of him. The dark theme of hair, eyes, and brows carried onto his chest, with a jet mat between brown nipples that tapered to a thin line bisecting his firm, flat stomach. His bold erection jutted from its dark nest.

Alex never lies. He did find her attractive. His need for her matched hers for him.

He hesitated at the side of the bed. "You can talk now, Kris. Do you want this?"

Kris opened her arms, but Alex stubbornly refused to move.

"I need to hear the words. We lawyers aren't much on assumptions and implied consent; we want it all spelled out in contracts."

"Will an oral contract do?" Her voice sounded dry and trembling.

"For the moment."

"I want this. I want you." She leaned forward and kissed him. His deep rumbling groan quaked through her, a definite six-pointer on the damage scale, as his fingers at her scalp held her close.

"You've got me so crazy, Kris, my brain is too jumbled to think of another compliment."

"Then let me give you one." She drew him in

deeper, and would have gone further, longer, except he stepped away.

His hot gaze swept across her. "If you'd like to keep that dress intact, then I suggest you take it off real fast. Because I'm not stopping once I put a knee on that bed."

With one easy motion, Kris grabbed the hem and pulled the stretchy fabric over her head. In less than thirty seconds, she was as naked as he.

Alex whistled. "Hot damn, I knew I liked that dress."

I found it at a consignment shop, she started and then stopped. Alex was right. She didn't need to apologize—for what she wore, for her hair, for who she was. Kris leaned back, bracing herself on her hands, letting him look his fill.

"I love what's underneath even better," he added, flicking on a dim bedside light.

His obvious admiration brought a flush to all her cheeks.

"You blush all over," he observed delightedly. He knelt beside her on the bed and touched the tip of her nipple with his tongue. Her tingling response made her breasts feel heavy and needy. She arched toward him, and he answered by taking her more fully with his mouth, sucking, running his tongue around her sensitive tip before lavishing attention on her other breast.

Kris slid her hands up and down Alex's skin, soft velvet encasing solid muscles. "I love the way you feel," she murmured.

He'd left off the air-conditioning, and a thin sheen of sweat smoothed her strokes. The lazy, spinning fan above circulated the air with languid ease, a slow-motion counterpoint to the increasing activity on the bed below.

She rained kisses across his shoulders, his chest, behind his ear, while Alex slowly bore her down the rest of the way. He spread her hair out on the crisp, white cotton sheets.

"I fantasized about your hair, you, in just this position, but the fantasy was a pale imitation of reality." He settled himself between her legs, and she opened to welcome him. "Ah, Kris," he groaned, rubbing against her with slow, tender strokes, "this feels so damn good. I love the feel, the scent"—he kissed behind her ear—"the taste of you." His hand joined his body in its tender torment of her.

Never wanting to let him go, Kris tightened her arms and legs around him, urging the closeness, the completion to come. She writhed beneath and against him, while her hands fluttered across each inch she could touch. "Now, Alex."

"Bossy little thing, aren't you?" He groaned as she reached and stroked him intimately. "I could get used to that." He stopped only long enough to rip open a foil packet he'd put at the bedside and sheath himself; then he entered her with one swift, sure stroke, his gaze never leaving hers.

Kris gasped at the invasion, the instant of pleasure—as he filled her, as she stretched to accommodate his size—so intense, she knew she could never find it again unless the man was Alex. She clutched him closer, suddenly scared.

As if sensing her hesitation, Alex buried her under an avalanche of pure pleasure from his strokes and his kisses. He murmured words and promises—some raw and raunchy, some tender and tasty, one or two in French—and drew her gasped answers into him with deep kisses.

Overwhelmed, Kris could only feel. The spiraling tension. The hot-pepper bite of desire. The exquisite sensations of skin on skin, tensing muscle, silky hair.

She reached for the elusive completion, the need in her a panting, keening urgency. Tension wound tight, and tighter, tightest, until it exploded, released with a long, exultant shout.

Alex, his scent, his sound, his strength, surrounded her, held her together, reassembled her. "I love watching you climax," he said in a raspy whisper. "I love being inside you when it happens, and I'm gonna love coming inside you."

His strokes grew steadily stronger, deeper, more urgent. Kris rose with him, drawn by his scorching desire into the maelstrom. The explosion shattered her as she surrounded his short, rapid pumping.

Beads of sweat highlighting his handsome features, Alex stiffened, gave a drawn-out, hoarse groan, and then collapsed atop her.

Kris drew in a long, shuddering breath. She lifted her hand to stroke his hair.

"That was great. I love you, Kris Lucas," Alex whispered. He withdrew, relaxed against her, and dozed.

I love you.
Alex never lies.
Kris's hand closed into a fist.

Chapter Six

Alex didn't doze long. Kris squirming beneath him soon roused him. Again? He murmured appreciatively into her neck. Despite the fabulous, mind-blowing, most . . . important sex he'd just experienced, he felt himself grow hard.

Never one to waste time, Alex thrust against her while he reached for another foil packet.

"No!" Kris hissed.

No?

Her sideways shimmy lifted the sensuous haze that fogged his brain. Much to his sorrow, she wasn't preparing for another pleasurable round.

She was trying to escape.

Remembering, Alex cursed very softly and stilled. He'd told her he loved her. He didn't regret the words, only the fact that Kris wasn't willing to hear them.

An astute lawyer knew when to make his points, and he'd always prided himself on his ability to organize for maximum impact. Unfortunately, his brain hadn't been the organ controlling his actions just then.

"What's your hurry? Didn't we say we had all night?" Alex clamped an arm around her waist and buried his nose in the silky mass of her hair.

"Hey, you know me, always late. No watch." She sounded breathless. "Can't be late to the wedding. After all, I'm in charge of the groom."

"Kris, it's not even midnight."

"Yeah, well, I really think I should go." She wiggled her shoulders, attempting to slip beneath his arm, but the action only served to brush her breasts against him, increasing the heat in his groin.

Alex rested his forehead on the pillow. It was a good thing he was a man who'd learned patience at his mother's first crisis. "Are you going to pretend you didn't hear me?"

He gave her credit for not pretending to misunderstand him.

"I heard you. Don't worry, I know you didn't mean it."

Didn't mean it? She'd soon know different, for no words he'd ever spoken had sounded so absolutely right. His predator instincts urged him to demand her acquiescence; his tender, protective ones insisted she be given time and choice.

"If you know I didn't mean it, then why are you trying to escape?" He turned to look at her.

"You changed the rules of our masquerade."

If she'd been standing, she'd have had her hands

194

on her hips. As it was, even buried beneath him, she managed to pack a pile of indignation into that scowl.

"Manipulated them. A redheaded bird once told me I was—um, inflexible. I'm trying to adjust."

A hint of a smile chased across her features before she could clamp down on it.

He rolled to his side and propped his head up with a bent arm. Idly he traced her ribs, pleased by the shudder that traversed her. She might be denying the words, but she couldn't deny the feelings. "I want something more."

"Well, I don't. I told you that."

"Would it be so bad?" he asked pensively.

She closed her eyes. "For a while it would be wonderful," she whispered, the vivacious shell cracking. "It's the after that's so hard. You'd come to loathe my odd schedules, my ingrained habits."

"How many more have you got? Ingrained habits, that is."

"I squeeze the toothpaste tube from the middle."

"Well that tears it then. No way I could marry someone who squeezes toothpaste tubes in the middle."

Her green eyes widened, and fear flared briefly amidst the wild flame of her hair. So, he hadn't managed to slip that "marry" in there without her noticing.

Moonlight dappled across the bed, giving her skin a luminescent glow that he wanted to capture. Alex shifted away slightly. Her lush, exotic scent distracted and aroused him, and his non-brain portions were clamoring to make the decisions again.

This moment was too delicate for him to trust to hormones.

He remembered something she'd said when he'd asked her why she didn't want to marry. *Who could put up with me?* Her answer had been flip, but Kris, he was realizing, was most flippant when her emotions were most involved and she was most vulnerable.

There was more here than simply her inability to accept compliments, but he wouldn't find out what by asking directly.

"Why *do* you keep odd schedules? Because of the various jobs you do?"

"Partly."

He waited in silence, feasting on her with all his senses, unable to deny himself a lover's delicate touches. Kris, he noticed, did not sidle away. Arousal flushed her pale skin and tightened the buds of her breasts.

"I've always done my best thinking at night," she said eventually. "It's when I get most of my ideas."

"Ideas for what?"

Kris looked away—to the wall, the ceiling, the foot of the bed—anywhere but at him. Finally she dragged her gaze back to his steady regard. "For my cartoons," she said, her finger tracing the sheets. "I'm KK George."

Alex's fingers clenched convulsively. And he'd told her he couldn't be comfortable around KK George. Never in his life had he regretted an offhand remark so much.

"Is it what I said about KK George?"

"That's a common attitude. People get uncomfortable when they find out I draw the strip. Afraid I'm analyzing them."

She was back to tracing pictures on the sheets with her finger. People get uncomfortable? It was more than that, Alex sensed deep in his soul. More like Kris got uncomfortable.

He tilted her chin, forcing her to look at him. "Right now, I could tear my tongue out for having said that. That was about a KK George I didn't know. I trust *you*, Kris."

Her gaze slid away again. "Why should you? I'm the undependable one, the wild one. I'm too . . . unconventional. Sooner or later, you'll leave."

"Why are you so sure I won't stick around?"

She shrugged. "That's just the way my life is."

A cube of fear hardened in his gut. He'd been thinking Kris just needed time to get used to the idea of being in love. Everything was happening so fast, he was wary, too, but he'd thought her emotions were as engaged as his.

Perhaps it wasn't enough.

Kris needed more than to love; she needed to trust and to believe. Trust that differences could be managed with compromise and tolerance from both of them. Trust that he accepted and celebrated the unique meld that constituted Kris Lucas. Believe that she deserved his love.

He could use every fluent word at his command and could show her how he felt with his body, but unless Kris trusted him, the words were useless. The decision was out of his hands. Until she was willing to take the enormous risk of loving, there wasn't a damn thing he could do.

The very real possibility that, after tomorrow,

she would walk out of his life hit him like a Mississippi surge, drowning him. No one else controlled his destiny. He believed that life could be bent to his will, categorized and prioritized. He'd fought chaos all his life. Yet, Kris, with her wild hair and slinky dresses and mix of vivacity and vulnerability, had flooded across his life, leaving tumbled emotions and hopes in her wake, scattering his previous plans into disarray.

"Coward," he accused, although which of them he was accusing he wasn't sure.

Her nostrils flared. "I have the right to remain silent about my work, counselor."

"Cut the lawyer crap. I wasn't talking about that. I was talking about you and me. Us."

"Look, Alex, I know men—when their brains are disengaged—say things they don't really mean. I'm not going to hold you to it. That's why we started this charade, isn't it? To avoid tricky, mushy scenes." She patted his arm.

Alex listened in disbelief, in alarm, in growing anger, but it was the patronizing pat on the arm that roused the beast. He rolled over, trapping her within the cage of his arms braced on either side of her. A vein throbbed in his temple. "Was that all this was to you? Part of the charade? I don't do casual sex, Kris. I love you—and yeah, I know it's too fast to be believed, but that doesn't change the feeling. I don't give a damn whether you're KK George or Vickie the bag lady; I'll still love you. And that's for keeps."

Her eyes widened, and she pulled in a gasp. Alex leaned over and kissed her, short but thorough. "That is not a charade."

Kris clutched at the sheets. "I don't believe in casual affairs either."

Her skin was pale in the darkness, the dusting of freckles standing out in stark relief. Her hair fanned out on either side of her head, a rose-gold cloak, and her eyes glittered with undefined emotions. Green eyes, red hair—he felt as if he was terrorizing a Christmas elf.

Alex groaned and dropped his head to his arm. "Oh, damn, I didn't mean you did."

He felt her hand flutter against his hair, then move to his wrist to trace his watch. "We're just too different, Alex."

"Not in the fundamentals. Not here." He touched her breast right above her heart; he couldn't resist following it with a butterfly kiss and was pleased to see a shudder of desire spread across her.

"We won't always agree," he said, "and I can't promise I'll never grit my teeth if you keep refusing to wear a watch, but I do know that without you, my life will be missing a wealth of laughter and caring. I'm willing to make the adjustments, Kris, but I can't, won't, do it alone. It takes two to make a marriage work."

"Marriage?" Her voice was barely audible.

"Not now, maybe not even soon." A ghost of a smile crossed his face. "But you know how we lawyers like contracts."

"I don't know . . ."

"I know, darling." He shifted to his back, drawing her atop him, giving the control over to her. He ran his hands up and down her arms. "Shall we have just tonight, then, *all night*, and let to-morrow fall as it may?"

It wouldn't be enough, but he would take what he could get.

Kris hesitated, then nodded and stroked his shoulders and chest, sending waves of pleasure throughout his body and bringing his semi-arousal to hard attention.

"I told you before, Kris, I need the words."

"Love me, Alex. For tonight, just love me." She moved her hips in invitation while she opened another foil packet.

Alex accepted and slipped into her slick, hot welcome.

For the rest of the long, and too short, night, he buried himself in sex and sensation, in loving Kris, but underneath it all was the hard, desperate knot of knowledge that this might be the only time they had.

For it had been good-bye he'd heard in her voice.

"What's bugging you, Luke?" Ross lifted his chin so she could straighten his bow tie.

"What makes you think I'm upset?" Kris gave the tie a final pat, then stepped back to eye her friend. "You look fabulous. You're going to knock the hat off every woman there."

Ross preened under her admiration, straightening the cuffs of his black tuxedo, but he wasn't going to be distracted. "I know you're upset when you talk nonstop."

Kris grimaced. "Spare me from the insight of childhood friends."

He touched her cheek. "It's Alex?"

She nodded.

"What did he do?" Ross's voice tightened.

"Said he loved me."

"Good for him." Ross handed her the ring box, and then headed toward the car out front. "Shall we go?"

Startled, Kris nearly dropped the box before tucking it in her tuxedo jacket pocket. "Is that all you're going to say?"

"What do you want me to say? That you should turn down what he's offering? Agree that you don't deserve happiness because you don't fit a mainstream norm?"

"I thought you might try to talk me into . . . seeing more of him," she said in a small voice.

Ross grinned at her. "You mean there's a part of him you haven't seen?"

Flushing, Kris punched him lightly in the arm. "You know what I mean."

"I can't talk you into that. Neither can Alex. That has to come from you, kid. Are you willing to take a chance?" He ran a knuckle across her chin. "Take as big a chance as the girl who befriended a lonely boy who called her Luke-ass?"

Tears welled in Kris's eyes. "I don't know. Let's just get you married."

As best man, Kris got Ross to the church on time—barely—and in pristine condition. She, however, had not fared as well.

"What the hell happened to you two?" Alex exclaimed as they raced, breathless, into the groom's waiting area. "You've only ten minutes until the service starts."

"My car had a flat," Ross explained.

"We had to change it," Kris added.

"You mean *you* changed it. I just worked the jack." Ross scowled and shook his head. "Luke, you are so blasted stubborn."

Changing the flat tire had left dirty smudges down the length of one trouser leg and grease on her palms. Her hair had escaped its pins and clips and dangled across her face.

Kris stuck out her chin. "I couldn't let you show up at your wedding covered in grease."

Alex enveloped her in a hug. "I was so afraid you'd had an accident."

"You didn't think it was my chronic lateness?" she mumbled against his chest.

He shook his head. "I knew you'd have him here on time. I trusted you." He stepped back. "Now let's get you cleaned up. We have a wedding to attend."

He brushed a smudge from her pants, while another groomsman handed her a paper towel for her hands. With the worst of the grease off, she fumbled with her hair.

"Leave it," Alex advised. "I like it with just those clip things holding it."

Kris smiled up at him, warmed by his solicitousness, his trust, and removed the remaining pins.

Alex leaned over and kissed her forehead. "You make a great best man," he whispered. "I'd ask you to be mine someday, but I'm planning on you as the bride."

She'd been nervous before, but his words made her stomach do a flip-flop.

Kris Lucas, the endless bridesmaid, a bride?

The thought didn't seem quite so foreign, so impossible now.

She *was* a good best man, even if she never had come up with a better term for it. Alex's words left a glow that sustained her throughout the service as she watched her best friend say his vows to the woman he loved. She saw the cherishing in the way Ross put the ring on Olivia's finger, saw the pride in the way he wore his own ring. Ross and Olivia had found something very special.

Had she found that same thing with Alex?

Did she have the courage to risk finding out?

The organ music vibrated within her soul as she knelt at the altar beside Ross while he received the priest's blessing. The full chords spoke of rejoicing and celebration. Of new beginnings and new chances.

As the priest proclaimed Ross and Olivia husband and wife, as Ross, a great joy on his face, lifted his bride's veil to kiss her, Kris looked over her shoulder at Alex standing beside her. He watched her instead of the bridal couple, naked love and hope in his expression.

She turned away without giving him the answer he needed, still unsure, still torn.

The organ announced the recessional. Arm and arm, Ross and Olivia began their life as husband and wife.

A tear of happiness welled in Kris's eye. *Goodbye, Ross. Take care of him, Olivia, as he will take care of you.*

Kris moved into her place to follow them down the aisle and met Jennifer in the middle. The maid of honor's gaze traveled from Kris's wild hair to the still visible dirt on the tuxedo, and she gave a sniff of annoyance.

I don't care what she thinks. The amazing thought stunned Kris. She didn't care if Jennifer or the others disapproved of her greasy palms and mussed tresses. *I know what happened, and why, and that's what matters.*

She gave a graceful bow, ushering Jennifer ahead of her, then glanced over her shoulder and gave Alex a big wink. He grinned in response.

Head held high, tuxedo wrinkled and dirt-stained, hair a wild halo about her head, the best man followed the maid of honor up the aisle.

At the reception, Kris decided she wanted to toast the bridal couple. It wasn't customary at a New Orleans wedding, but it was something she wanted to do. During the band break, she stepped up to the microphone and cleared her throat.

The feedback squeal demanded attention. All eyes were raised to her. Everyone waited in expectation, watching her.

Kris waited for her palms to start sweating and for the rush of insecurity.

Neither appeared. She didn't have to entertain the crowd. She had only to toast her friend and his new bride. A simple task and a profound one.

As simple as taking a step forward into the future.

As profound as opening your heart to another.

Kris lifted her champagne glass toward the

wedding couple. "New Orleanians love food, and we need no excuse for a party. Today, however, we gather to celebrate and share in the joy of Ross and Olivia, two people who have taken that risky step of marriage, joining not to diminish, but to strengthen and to grow together. Their love and devotion endures, a bright and shiny beacon to the future for us all. Or, as Henri Byrde might say, 'You humans have the strangest customs. What a gift!' To Ross and Olivia." To answering echoes, she lifted her glass and sipped her champagne.

She stepped away from the mike to find Alex at her side.

His dark eyes studied her, questioning, waiting. Kris felt her heart swell, the blood a steady beat of assurance. Doubts and fears dissipated under his steady regard, replaced by wonder and the soul-deep belief that this man was well worth the risk.

Effervescent delight bubbled through her, more potent than the champagne bubbles she sipped. She was tired of being ever the bridesmaid, or the best man. It was time to grab the bouquet with both hands.

She sat at a nearby table and tugged Alex down beside her. Quickly she pulled out a pen, then sketched on a napkin and slid the napkin in front of him.

Alex stared at it, his entire body tense and still as he understood. She'd drawn a picture of the two of them. He was looking at his watch. She was staring off at the clouds. But between them, their hands were clasped firmly together. And she'd surrounded them with a heart. Henri Byrde's chubby face peered over the edge of the heart, abeam with curiosity.

"You like pictures. I need words," he said, looking up.

Kris lifted her champagne glass to him. "Here's to taking risks. I love you, Alex Devereaux." She sipped, set the glass down, and then slowly, oh-so-slowly, a smile brightened her face.

He'd heard and said many words in his life, but he didn't think he'd ever again hear any so sweet. He leaned over and kissed her, his tongue tangling with hers even as his fingers tangled in her hair.

Alex reveled in the taste of her, her lips soft and yielding beneath his. When they parted, her cheeks were flushed, her mouth moist and open in wonder. "And I love you, whether you're Kristen Lucas or KK George or bashing one of my schedules to pieces. Think Olivia would consent to be my best man?"

"I want Ross as my matron of honor."

"We've got to find a different name for *that*," they chorused together, sharing a laugh.

Kris unfastened Alex's watch and slipped it on her wrist.

Alex took his pristine white handkerchief and wiped a spot of grease off her palm.

He threaded his fingers through her hair and brought her forward for a long kiss. She gripped the front of his shirt and held him in place.

Grandmother Desirée thumped over to them. "See," she called in her clarion voice. "I *told* you Alex was getting married."

"That's Olivia Elizabeth . . ." Mary Eulalie's

voice trailed away. "Oh my! You may be right, Mama."

Kris lifted slightly from the kiss, her green eyes gleaming. "I think I'm going to fit right in with this family."

"You've already found your place in my heart," Alex answered.

Then, the best man and the groomsman kissed again, pledging their hearts and lives.

Go for the Gold

Constance O'Banyon

This one is just for you, Jody.

Chapter One

Aspen, Colorado

Dr. Abigail Taylor Hunt watched the snow drift unremittingly past the window of her hotel room. She felt suspended in time, as if she were a lone figure imprisoned inside one of those small snow globes, and someone had just picked it up and shaken it, tilting her whole world.

Here she was in Aspen, the playground of the rich and famous, occupying the honeymoon suite of the best hotel, just as she and Donald had planned. The only trouble was, she was there alone. It was her wedding day, but there would be no marriage. Donald had broken their engagement because he said that he was in love with someone else.

Turning away from the window, Abbie stumbled to the bathroom, grabbed several tissues, and gave in to the anguish she'd tried to fight off since Donald had told her that he no longer loved her. She cried quietly at first, but then her sobs built to a crescendo, deep, ripping, heartrending. Had she been so blindly in love that she hadn't noticed the telltale signs that Donald didn't love her? In retrospect, she should have realized that something was wrong with their relationship. The signs had been there—the broken dates, the nights when he'd taken her home early, and the days that had passed without his calling her at all.

Straightening her shoulders, Abbie realized that she was giving in to self-pity. Maybe it hadn't been such a good idea to come to Aspen, even though it was the last place anyone would expect to find her. She just couldn't face her well-meaning friends and relatives, whose sympathy would only make her more miserable than she already was.

She'd made only one phone call since arriving, and that had been to her mother, so she wouldn't worry. Afterward, Abbie was sorry she had called because all her mother could talk about was Donald and how he'd shown up at their house the night before, humble and contrite, and wanting to go through with the wedding after all.

Abbie moved back to the window and leaned her forehead against the cold glass. What he had done was unforgivable, dishonorable, and she would never trust him again. For her, there could be no marriage without trust. Did a man with honor really exist? she wondered. Not that it mattered. She would never marry now. She smiled bitterly. She could almost picture herself living out her life like her father's oldest sister, Clara, alone and pitiable, living only on the edges of other people's lives. Of course, she'd return to her practice of treating other people's children, but she'd never have children of her own.

Dark shadows had encroached on the corners of the room, reminding Abbie that it was getting late. She found her flight bag, which she had hurriedly packed, and removed a bulky white sweater and pulled it over her head. She ran a brush quickly through her dark hair and applied a thin sheen of lip gloss to her mouth. She had to regain control of her life, and that meant getting out of this room and facing other people.

Abbie threaded her way through the crowded lobby, which was decorated in the plush, ornate style of the early gold-rush. Paintings depicting the glory days of Colorado graced the walls, and a magnificent tapestry hung above the large stone fireplace.

When she reached the dining room, the maître d' seated her near the window, where she watched people rush in and out of the picturesque shops that lined both sides of the street. After the waiter had taken her order, she turned her thoughts inward once more. She swallowed quickly, trying to control the sobs building in her throat. When her salad was placed in front of her, she pushed the lettuce around with her fork, fearing she'd choke if she took a bite.

Suddenly, the sound of laughter penetrated her self-imposed prison of pain, and she glanced in annoyance at the culprits who sat at the next table. Three Barbie look-alikes were being dazzled by the most fascinating man Abbie had ever seen. He spoke with a French accent, was deeply tanned and bone-meltingly handsome, with black hair and piercing amber eyes. His female audience appeared to cling to his every word.

With a newly acquired cynicism, Abbie assessed the Frenchman. He looked like a ski instructor. The dark winter tan was a dead giveaway. She noticed his expensive, hand-knit sweater. Definitely a ski instructor. And he looked like the type who drew women to him with his bold magnetism— wealthy women. Women who would no doubt pay generously for the pleasure of his company.

At that moment, her glance collided with the Frenchman's, and he smiled, nodding at her ever so slightly. His intense gaze held hers for a breathless moment, until the waiter appeared at her table and distracted her.

"Come on, Luc," one of the women pleaded. "Let's fly to Denver tonight. There's nothing to do here."

His French accent gave emphasis to his words. "I like it here. *Oui*," he repeated to the woman beside him, but his eyes were on Abbie. "I like it here very much indeed."

Abbie couldn't eat because the Frenchman kept staring at her. Once, when she glanced his way, he lowered his eyes as if he realized he was making her uncomfortable. She wondered why he was watching her so closely—she certainly wasn't his type. Her hair was dark, and judging by his companions, he seemed to prefer blondes.

Luc Anglade couldn't help but stare at the woman seated at the table next to his. She had the kind of rare beauty that owed nothing to cosmetic surgery or heavy makeup. She would only grow more lovely with age, and he found himself wondering if she was as beautiful on the inside as she was outwardly. The casual way she was dressed conveyed that she had little interest in fashion. So far he'd seen her only in profile, and he wanted to look into her eyes—he could tell a lot about a woman from her eyes.

As if he'd willed it, she turned toward him, and he was thunderstruck. Silken, coffee-colored hair fell loosely about a heart-shaped face. She had a bone structure that any model would envy. Her eyes were as blue as the Colorado sky, and there was such sadness reflected there that he felt as if her sorrow was his own.

Luc had never had such a strong reaction to a woman, and in that moment, he realized that he had to know her better. What a disappointment it would be if she turned out to be just another beautiful face, with nothing more to recommend her. But he knew instinctively that she was different from any woman he'd ever met.

Abbie was becoming increasingly uncomfortable because the man kept staring at her, and she felt as if she were on exhibition. Giving him a defiant look, she placed her napkin beside her plate and stood, deciding to forgo the main course and return to her room. When she left the table and walked to the door, she was aware that the Frenchman watched her all the way across the room. She told herself that he probably had an ego larger than his IQ.

*   *   *

Abbie was up early the next morning and ate a surprisingly hearty breakfast. Dressed in a powder-blue ski suit she'd hurriedly purchased in one of the local shops, she took a gondola to the top of Aspen Mountain. She was not an accomplished skier and had only taken up the sport to please Donald, who was a ski enthusiast. Usually she kept to Buttermilk, the beginner's slope. Today, however, she felt reckless. She hesitated for only a moment when it started snowing and she couldn't see twenty feet ahead of her.

With trembling hands, Abbie gripped her ski poles tightly—it was now or never. Something inside her urged her forward, and she had the feeling that if she conquered the mountain she would prove to herself that she didn't need Donald—she didn't need anyone.

She pushed forward, swallowing the fear tightening inside her like a fist. Almost immediately, a sharp curve came into view, and she panicked. Now was not the time to remember what some ski instructor had told her months ago about negotiating a turn. Somehow she managed to stay on her feet through the difficult turn. But no sooner had she passed the first curve than another appeared. She closed her eyes and prayed as she approached a high embankment. Before she could react, she was airborne. She managed to land upright, but hit the ground with a jarring thud.

Just when she was congratulating herself for not falling, her feet became entangled and she lost her balance, falling forward, then rolling and sliding for what seemed an eternity. At last she came to a painful stop, her face buried in the powdery snow.

"You have not the experience to try such a slope, mademoiselle."

She heard a familiar French accent and raised her head to stare at the Frenchman from the dining room the night before.

"No bloody kidding," she said angrily. "Thank you so much for pointing out the obvious."

"Are you hurt?" He knelt down beside her, his eyes full of concern. "Can you move?"

"Just leave me alone," she told him, wishing he would disappear.

"I will not go until I know that you are uninjured, mademoiselle," he insisted. "Can you move your arms and legs? Do you hurt anywhere?"

Abbie tried to sit up, but to her dismay, she couldn't untangle her skis until he helped her. With a strong tug, he drew her to her feet.

"See, no harm done except to my pride," she assured him. "You can just go on your way now."

"Mademoiselle . . . it is mademoiselle, is it not?"

His charm was obvious, especially when he gazed at her with those fathomless golden eyes. His face could have been sculpted by Michelangelo, it was so handsome. He was tall; she guessed a couple of inches over six feet. He wore a black ski suit and a matching cap with an Olympic symbol—just like one that Donald had.

"No," she answered him in irritation, just wanting to be rid of him. "It's not mademoiselle—it's 'miss.' "

"I must warn you that the most difficult course is still ahead. You have come only a quarter of the way down. I insist on escorting you safely to the bottom."

The snow had stopped and Abbie glanced downward, but she was unable to see the bottom of the mountain. She would never make it without help. "Thank you," she said grudgingly. "I would appreciate your assistance."

He smiled. "It is a pleasure." He adjusted her goggles, tightening the strap on the side of her head, and then positioned his own. "The one thing you must always remember is to protect your eyes. Snowblindness is very common among amateurs, and it's extremely painful."

"Yes, I know that," she said, feeling foolish. She was a doctor, after all, and should have known to protect her eyes. "I will remember next time."

"Hold on to me and I will steady you," he said, reaching out his hand.

Without hesitation, she placed her hand in his. His presence had made her feel secure, and therein lay the danger. He probably preyed upon wealthy American women, making them feel safe, then getting whatever he wanted from them. By being a damsel in distress, she had probably made herself his next target.

He clasped her gloved hands, and with a strength that took her by surprise, he expertly guided her downward, steadying her as they descended the slope.

Abbie suddenly experienced the thrill that must come to a really good skier. She had always concentrated more on remaining upright than enjoying the sport. Now it seemed as if there were no land and no sky, that she was one with the mountain itself, one with the man beside her. She wondered if he felt the same. The sensation was fleeting, gone the moment they reached the bottom of the slope. Abbie felt a rush of disappointment, although she could not have said why.

Luc glanced down at her. "With practice, and the right instructor, you would soon master the slopes."

She could guess what came next. "I suppose you are going to tell me that you are just the right instructor?"

She felt him tense as he released her arm. Before he spoke, he lifted his goggles and looked deeply into her eyes in a way that robbed her of her breath.

"I would be pleased to instruct you, mademoiselle, if that is your wish." He seated her on a bench and gallantly bent to unhook her skis, then removed his own before he spoke again. "Perhaps we could discuss the matter over a cup of hot chocolate," he suggested.

Abbie nodded in agreement. Her teeth were chattering, and she didn't know if it was from the cold or a delayed reaction to the danger she'd encountered on the mountain. She'd been a fool to attempt a slope meant only for expert skiers. And no matter his intentions, this man had probably saved her life.

Moments later they were seated in a booth at one of the rustic taverns, and Abbie was warming her hands against a mug of hot chocolate.

"Do you give private lessons?" she asked, thinking she would learn faster if he could devote his time exclusively to her.

He seemed to hesitate, and she thought he might refuse.

"I would do that for you," he said at last. "When would you like to begin, mademoiselle?"

"First of all, stop calling me mademoiselle— my name is Abigail Hunt. Most people call me Abbie." She offered him her hand. "And your name is . . . ?"

He contemplated his answer. Obviously she didn't know who he was if she'd mistaken him for a ski instructor. At last he took her hand. "I am Luc Anglade." He saw that his name meant nothing to her. "I am glad to meet you, Abbie."

She took a sip of hot chocolate and then set the cup aside. "I suppose you will have to schedule my lessons around your other classes."

Luc leaned back, watching her closely. His eyes moved over her rich coffee-colored hair, across her lovely face, resting on the arch of her slender neck and then gliding up to the blue of her eyes. Luc saw sadness, hurt, and confusion reflected in them, and he wondered if some man had caused her pain.

"At the moment," he said, "I am on holiday and will be at your disposal anytime."

"Good. Shall we begin in the morning?"

"Why not today?" He wasn't ready to let her go. "It's still early."

Abbie summoned their waiter and handed him the money to cover their check. She did not see Luc flinch because of her actions.

"Thank you very much, but I've had enough excitement for today. Besides, I left home in somewhat of a hurry, and I need to purchase some items that I neglected to pack."

"I will go shopping with you to carry the packages, *non?*"

She gave him an amused glance. "Look, Luc, we may as well come to an understanding right now. All I want from you is ski lessons."

His eyes probed hers, and he saw more than she could guess. She had been hurt, and she was afraid to trust him. "I will teach you, Abbie," he said simply.

"If you get bored this afternoon, you can always find one of your Barbie dolls to play with," she suggested, half in jest.

"Pardon?"

"Never mind—it isn't important. I'm an early riser. I trust that won't be a problem for you. I'll meet you in the lobby at seven—sharp."

Abbie stepped off the elevator, wearing her workout gear. When she entered the exercise room, she was glad that she had it to herself. If she kept busy, she wouldn't have time to think about Donald. She ran two miles on the treadmill, then pedaled another two miles on the exercise bike. She was exhausted by the time she had swum five laps in the pool, so she went to the steam room, where a peacefulness settled over her.

Had she really loved Donald? They had known each other all their lives—or she'd thought she had known him. She hadn't really.

She tested her bruised thigh, a reminder of the spill she'd taken that morning. Donald would have applauded her tenacity for taking on the big mountain.

Pulling her thoughts together, she belted her robe and stepped out of the steam room, only to be met by the sound of laughter. Luc Anglade was splashing in the pool, surrounded by his usual entourage of beautiful women. Abbie watched him for a moment, fascinated in spite of herself. He moved with the grace of a beautiful animal, sleek and muscled. She was surprised that he wore a simple black boxer-type swimsuit instead of a skimpy bikini.

When he saw Abbie, Luc climbed out of the pool and walked toward her. "I see you have been working out. This is good." He took her arm, running his hand up and down it in a clinical manner. "You are strong. This is in your favor. Concentrate on your leg, ankle, and stomach muscles. I will work up an exercise program for you."

"I don't need you to tell me how to get in shape," she said bluntly, her glance moving to the women who had begun to migrate toward them.

"Mademoiselle, if I am to instruct you, I insist that you follow my orders. Everything I ask of you will be done with a specific purpose in mind."

He was clearly annoyed, and she found satisfaction in breaking through his calm assurance. If he thought that she was like the women who idolized him, he was mistaken. Never again would she allow a man to dictate her life.

She dabbed her face with the towel draped about her neck. "Please excuse me. It's getting late."

Luc frowned as she left. He'd never had a problem conveying his feelings to a woman before Abbie. What could he say to her? "Abbie, what are you doing with the rest of your life, and can I do it with you?"

Chapter Two

Abbie had half expected Luc to be late, but as she emerged from the elevator the next morning, she saw him near the fireplace, surrounded by the usual bevy of leggy blondes. In her present state of mind, he represented the epitome of male egomania that could be fed only by a captive female audience. Why had she suggested taking lessons from him? She must have been out of her mind.

Luc watched her approach, and he could almost read her every thought. He was troubled that she viewed him in such an unfavorable light. Her disinterest in him as a man was something he'd never experienced before, and it fueled his own interest in her.

"Je vous demande pardon," he said to his companions. "Excuse me, *mesdemoiselles.*"

"No," a disappointed chorus chimed together. "Don't go, Luc."

"I fear I must. *Au revoir*, for now."

Abbie moved past Luc and stood at the door while she pulled on her gloves. When he approached, she gave him no more than a sideways glance. "It seems such a pity to take you away from your harem. Perhaps you would rather cancel our appointment?"

"*Non*," he replied offhandedly. "I always honor my commitments."

She jerked open the door and stepped out into the frosty air. "I just bet you do."

Luc appeared undaunted by Abbie's ill humor. A slight smile curving his lips and tiny laugh lines fanning out from the corner of his eyes were a sure indication that he laughed often.

Luc looked at Abbie and she could feel the pull of his passionate nature. A woman would have to be halfway in her grave not to be affected by his male magnetism. But she was in no mood to be just another of the adoring masses that worshipped at his feet—she was too vulnerable to open herself up to any man. Donald had almost destroyed her, and if she allowed it, Luc Anglade could easily finish her off.

A valet handed Luc a set of keys, and without ceremony, he ushered her into the plush, black-leather seat of a sleek, red Ferrari, then went around to the driver's side and got in himself. Evidently he had already been out early this morning, because their ski gear had been lashed to the rack on top of the car.

Abbie's eyes were on the strong hand that

gripped the gear shift. "I see you like your cars and your women flashy," she said scornfully. She was immediately sorry for her sarcasm. Her anger should be aimed at Donald, and not this ski instructor who had shown her nothing but courtesy.

Luc shifted the car into gear before answering her. "You might be surprised to know the kind of woman I prefer," he said. "And as for my Ferrari,"—he made a stab at humor—"you will have to forgive me if I don't feel obligated to 'buy American,' I believe the slogan goes. Actually, I didn't buy it at all. It was a gift."

With a sick feeling in the pit of her stomach, she could imagine some wealthy widow giving him the car as payment for services rendered. "And do you have a woman in France who has gone into decline waiting for your return?"

He turned to look at her now with a serious expression on his face. "*Non*, I left no one behind. I have no woman in my life at the moment."

"Not even one of the groupies who follow you around?"

He looked puzzled. "What is the meaning of this word 'groupies'? I am not conversant with American slang."

She smiled and then laughed, wondering why she drew such satisfaction in baiting him. "To put it simply, it means devotees, followers, adoring fans."

"I see what you are saying. You speak of my friends, the ones you call Barbie dolls?"

She was embarrassed. "Perhaps I should not have said that."

"I hope you will always speak your mind with

me. I find your candor refreshing, although you are in error in your impression of me."

"Jumping to conclusions is a failing of mine which I can't seem to control. But tell me honestly, have you often had a woman disagree with you?"

Again his mouth slid into a smile. "Hardly ever—until you came into my life. And now all the time."

"I'm not in your life," Abbie said hurriedly, nervousness making her voice tremble. "I hired you to teach me to ski, and that's all I want from you."

"Who is the man who hurt you?"

She jerked her head around to stare at Luc in astonishment. "What makes you ask that?"

"Like many of your countrymen, you choose to answer a question with a question." He turned a corner and pulled to the side of the road, shutting off the engine. "I see the sadness in your eyes," he said simply. "You are easy to read, Abigail Taylor Hunt."

He removed his glove, and she flinched when he softly touched her cheek, but she did not pull away from him. "Even on such short acquaintance, I believe I know you very well. I can tell you have been hurt because you strike out at life, and I also believe it is not in your nature to be so critical of others."

She closed her eyes, wishing she could lay her head on his shoulder and find comfort there. "You don't know me at all," she said without conviction.

He dropped his hand away. "I know you better than you think. For instance, you occupy the honeymoon suite . . . alone."

"How do you know that?"

He shrugged. "It's very simple—I asked the night clerk at the hotel about you."

She felt a rush of pain and was fighting against the bitter tears that stung her eyes. "I have not asked about you at the front desk, but I have a sketch of your character all the same."

His eyes narrowed. "I would like to hear it."

"Very well. You took up skiing in France as a boy. Your dream was to be in the Olympics, but you were either not that dedicated, or not good enough to make the team. So, instead, you came to America and became a ski instructor at a hotel that caters to the wealthy. Here you'll remain until you are too old to ski, or break a bone and have to return to France."

He stared at her, his jaw tightening. "I would prefer that you not sketch my character until you know me better." Reaching across her, he opened the door. "Shall we begin your first lesson?"

She got out of the car and looked about her in confusion. "Where are we?" This is not the beginner's hill."

He shrugged. "You said you wanted private lessons—nothing could be more private than here."

She was not amused. It was as if they were alone in the world. There were several gentle slopes, and beyond that a line of dense pines. "This is not what I had in mind."

"You must trust me to know what is best. If I am to teach you, Abbie, you must put yourself in my hands."

"Said the spider to the fly," she murmured beneath her breath.

His penetrating eyes, so amber and so intense,

stabbed into hers, and for a moment she felt that he was drawing all her secrets from her.

Wordlessly, he went to the rack on his car to remove their equipment.

In truth, he was a man like none she had ever known. He inspired her to trust him, to confide in him, yet she dared not. After all, he was a stranger, and a dangerous one at that because he seemed so sincere.

It would have shocked Abbie if she could have read Luc's mind at that moment.

As he watched her lock her ski boots into her skis, he was thinking that she looked almost ethereal, her white suit blending with the snowflakes that drifted around her. In that instant, Luc knew that she was the woman he'd been waiting for all his life, the one he wanted to give his name, to have his children. He wanted to make her laugh, to make her eyes burn with the same passion he felt for her, to make love to her, and to wipe the memory of the man who had hurt her completely from her mind.

With difficulty, he forced his expression into a noncommittal mask. Somehow he had to make her trust him; then perhaps love would come later.

"I'm ready," Abbie said, working her fingers snugly into her gloves.

Luc examined her to make sure her skis were locked in properly. "I want you to forget all you have learned before, Abbie, and listen to me. Let us begin," he said, pointing at her goggles and indicating that she should pull them into place.

Abbie was quick to comply as she waited for him to continue. She loved the sound of his voice and found herself so mesmerized by his French accent and deep tone that she missed what he was saying. "I'm sorry," she said, looking sheepish. "Would you mind repeating that last part?"

"I was explaining the importance of learning how to stand and walk on uneven terrain. After you have mastered this, I shall show you how to control your turns and how to stop."

He was so near that she could see that his amber eyes were flecked with brown. She had never noticed that he had a cleft in his chin—how had she missed that? There was just a stubble of beard, as if he'd shaved in a hurry. She wanted to touch his face and allow her fingers to move up to his midnight-colored hair.

Horrified, Abbie tore her mind away from her provocative thoughts. What was wrong with her? She had been jilted and was supposed to be too miserable to think of any man except Donald—wasn't she?

Luc took her to a small slope and continued with his instruction. "I want you to do a short swing-turn. When you do everything I teach you correctly, Abbie, you'll be able to turn smoothly."

She nodded, gripping her poles in her gloved hands. "I'm ready."

Abbie fell several times, but she always got up and tried again. Luc was a better instructor than she had expected, and she was learning more from him in this short time than in all the lessons she'd had before.

Once when she fell, he helped her to her feet and pulled her against his body to steady her.

"Relax, so you can learn to react quickly."

Relax! How could she relax when he was so near that she could feel his warm breath on her cheek?

"You have good balance," he complimented her, as he handed her poles to her and moved a few paces away. "Now concentrate on what I have told you."

The morning passed quickly, and Abbie was surprised when he suggested that they break for lunch. She had expected him to drive her back to the hotel, but instead, he ushered her into the car, then went to the trunk, removed a basket, and slipped into the seat beside her.

"I hope you brought your appetite. If I know Jean Paul, he has prepared a feast."

"Who is Jean Paul?" she inquired as he handed her a white linen napkin.

"The chef at the hotel. He's a countryman of mine."

"Of course," she said matter-of-factly. "And do you often call on his services to impress your . . . students?"

His glance rested on her face with a serious expression. "I see where you are going with this. You might be surprised to find I am not nearly the fun-loving bachelor you think I am."

I doubt it. To Luc, she shrugged. "I only know what I see."

Luc made no reply, but instead unpacked the picnic basket. "Try *le faisan*," he said, handing her a foil-wrapped package.

"What is it?" she asked. Nothing was going into her mouth before she knew what it was.

"I believe you call it pheasant."

"Oh."

He produced two crystal wineglasses and filled them with white wine.

Abbie took a sip of the sparkling liquid and smiled. "This is delicious! She read the label. *"Châteauneuf d'Anglade."* She raised her gaze to his. "This is my favorite wine!" she said in surprise.

"At last I find something we agree on."

She leaned back against the seat, taking a sip of the wine and letting its warmth spread through her body. "Luc, you have the same last name as the wine. Is that a coincidence?"

"I am but a humble ski instructor, remember?"

"Ski instructor, yes—humble, no."

She turned her head to find him watching her with such warmth that it took her breath away. "Don't do that," she said, handing him her glass. She dared not take another sip of wine.

"Do what?"

"Look at me like that."

His sensuous lips curved into a smile. "Was I looking at you in any particular way?"

She grasped the door handle and swung the door open. "Thanks for the pheasant and wine. I'm fortified now and ready to get back to the lesson."

Luc got out of the car and slammed the door. Getting to know Abbie Hunt was not going to be easy.

He led her to a steeper slope, and when she looked doubtful, he encouraged her. "You can do it, Abbie. You are going to learn how to sidestep up this hill." He showed her how to accomplish it, and then watched her.

"*Non*. Do not look at your feet," he said gently. "Now the wedge stop. That's right—knees and ankles forward. You are progressing quite well."

He had hardly gotten the compliment out of his mouth when she tottered and fell forward, one ski lapping over the other. He reached to help her, and when she was only halfway up, she lost her footing again. This time, she grabbed Luc with both hands and took him down with her. They both slid to the bottom of the slope, where she landed right on top of him.

Abbie was the first to recover. She slid off him and lay on her back, laughing in amusement. Luc sat up and attempted to untangle his skis from hers. Abbie was laughing so hard, she was almost hysterical. "What would your Barbie dolls say if they could see you now, Luc?"

He reached for her, pulling her forward so her face was only inches from his. "What do I care about them?" he asked, his voice almost a caress. "I have made you laugh, and to me that is the sweetest music."

She could not see Luc's eyes behind his goggles, but she could imagine their intensity. She was hypnotized by his nearness, and by the sound of his voice.

"Luc, don't."

Her words came out like a plea, so he released her immediately. For a moment, neither of them moved or spoke. Then he managed to stand and helped her up with him.

"You have had enough lessons for one day, Abbie. Tomorrow we shall continue."

She was almost disappointed. When she slid

onto the leather seat of the Ferrari, she groaned. "I am sore in places I didn't even know I had."

Luc started the engine and guided the car forward. The ride back to the hotel was silent, and Abbie realized that she had not thought of Donald at all.

Chapter Three

Abbie had taken a long, leisurely bath, hoping to soothe her aching muscles. She slipped into her cashmere robe and curled up in a chair. She flipped on the television, clicked through the channels, and then in boredom turned it off, staring at the blank screen. Again, she asked herself what she was doing in Aspen, Colorado, in the middle of winter, taking lessons from the Don Juan of the ski set.

The phone rang and she lifted the receiver, thinking it might be Luc. He probably found her dull company today and was calling to tell her to find another instructor.

"Hello."

There was silence on the other end of the line, but she could hear someone breathing. "Hello," she said impatiently.

"Abbie, thank God. I've called everywhere looking for you. Then I took the chance that you might have gone to Aspen."

Abbie thought she was going to be sick. "I'm not your concern anymore, Donald."

"Yes, you are, honey." There was uncertainty in his voice. "I don't blame you for being mad at me. I love you, and I made a terrible mistake. Can you ever forgive me?"

She paused for a long moment while she examined her feelings. Shouldn't she be overjoyed because Donald still loved her? She was numb, dead inside. She knew him so well, always needing everyone's approval, but his little-boy appeal no longer touched her. "I don't know what you want from me, Donald."

"I want things to be the way they were. I want you to be my wife, honey."

A tear of anger trailed down Abbie's cheek, and she quickly brushed it away. "You fall in and out of love so quickly, Donald. What happened to the woman you loved enough to break our engagement?"

"Everyone's entitled to one mistake, honey. I realized that same day that I didn't love Mary Ann, but you had disappeared and I couldn't find you."

Abbie closed her eyes, feeling nauseated. "Damn you, Donald. You didn't tell me the other woman was Mary Ann—she's my best friend! How could the two of you do this to me?"

There was a long pause on Donald's end of the line. When he spoke, it was with caution. "I thought you knew Mary Ann and I had been seeing each other—she told me you did. I'll make it up to you, honey—you'll see."

Her voice sounded mechanical. "What about poor Mary Ann?"

"She's nothing—forget about her. I have," he said almost flippantly. Then his voice took on a pleading tone. "Your mother's been wonderful. She says every man has doubts before he takes the big leap."

"And my father?"

"He . . . well . . . Mr. Hunt is not as understanding as your mom."

"Everyone says that I'm like my father, Donald, and apparently they're right because I don't understand either. I'm going to hang up now. Don't call me again."

"You know I love you!" There was amazement in his voice, as if he couldn't believe she was turning him away. "And you love me."

"No, and I don't think I ever did, Donald. I'm glad you have my mother's sympathy, but I'm more inclined to trust my father's judgment."

"Abbie, don't you dare hang up. We need to talk this out."

"Good-bye, Donald. Don't call me again."

"When are you coming home?" he persisted.

She hung up the receiver, allowing the dial tone to be her answer. She closed her eyes and leaned her head against the high-back chair, feeling suddenly lonely and bereft. Mary Ann and Donald had both betrayed her. How could she have misjudged them so?

Abbie's painful musing was interrupted by a knock on the door. She considered ignoring it, but whoever it was seemed persistent and only knocked louder. She tightened the belt of her robe and opened the door, surprised to see Luc standing there, a bottle of wine under one arm and a small black zipper bag under the other. He wore jeans and a green T-shirt that was open at the neck, revealing the curly black hair on his chest.

Gathering her thoughts, Abbie leaned against the doorjamb, giving him a knowing look. "I see you travel light. Planning on moving in?" she asked bitingly.

"That would be my first hope," he answered with humor. "But I'm here to make you feel better." He moved past her and into the room.

Donald's conversation still rang in her ears, and she was not feeling too charitable toward any male at the moment. "Do all your students get this personal attention?"

Before she could protest, he went to the bar and deftly uncorked the bottle. "Actually, I am very selective about who shares my wine," he said, smiling. He held out a wineglass to her. "Here, take this—you look like you could use it."

"Is it your intention to get me drunk, hoping that I'll invite you to share my bed?"

His amber gaze was suddenly serious. "If I wanted to be in your bed, I would not need to ply you with wine to get an invitation.

"*Non*," he said with assurance. "I'm here because you took several tumbles yesterday and again today. Thinking your muscles might be sore, I came to help you."

Abbie dropped her gaze, trying to decide if he was being earnest. Donald's actions had reminded her not to trust any man. Still, Luc had been a perfect gentleman today. In fact, he had been very patient with her. "I do feel sore," she admitted at last, deciding to trust him. "What miracle have you got for me in that little black bag?"

"First the wine," he urged. "It's part of the therapy."

Suddenly she welcomed his intrusion. Perhaps it would help her forget about Donald's phone call. She took the wine from Luc and raised it to her lips, taking a quick sip and welcoming the warmth that trailed down her throat.

"Now," Luc said in satisfaction, taking her arm and leading her toward the couch. "Take another sip and then lie down on your stomach."

She tossed her head back and looked at him suspiciously. "Maybe you think I'm a fool, but I can assure you I'm not. I know what you're trying to do."

"Abbie, you don't have the slightest idea what I want from you." Firmly, he took the wineglass from her and held it to her mouth. "Drink."

She was suddenly too weary to object. She took a large gulp of the wine and then another. When he would have drawn the glass away, she took it from him and drained it. "There. Now are you satisfied?" She moved to the counter, refilled her glass to the brim and drank it down.

Wordlessly he stared at her. He intended to find out who had hurt her and if she still loved the man. In her present state, she wasn't ready for a commitment, and she certainly wasn't ready to hear about his growing love for her.

"My problem is how to convince you that my

motives are honorable." He knew he'd scare the hell out of her if he admitted that he wanted her to be his wife and to have his children. "Abbie, I'm not here to take advantage of you, or to get you drunk. If we don't work your muscles, you will be too sore for lessons tomorrow."

"All right," she said, sitting on the couch, clutching her robe tightly about her because she had nothing on underneath. "If I don't like what you do, Luc, you'll stop?"

"But of course. Now, move to your stomach. That's right." Luc dropped to his knees and slowly moved the robe aside so her bare shoulder was exposed. He could tell she was tense. "Relax and put yourself in my hands."

Abbie wondered how many times he'd used that line; she was sure he'd always met with success. She heard him unzip the bag, and soon she smelled the pleasant scent of almonds.

"What is that?" she asked.

He chuckled. "Would you believe me if I told you it is my grand-mère's elixir? I never leave home without it."

She felt his hands touch her shoulders and the warmth of the liquid penetrate her skin. He had wonderful hands, and the recriminations she was about to spout died in her throat; a soft groan escaped instead. He worked magic on her skin, or perhaps it was his grandmother's elixir that lulled her into passiveness.

"Mmm," she murmured. "What's in that anyway?"

"I'm not certain. Grand-mère never shares her secret recipe with anyone. I know it has elixir of almonds, but I believe the prime ingredient is emu oil."

"You should bottle this stuff and sell it. That would assure you a better future than catering to wealthy women."

Abbie didn't see him stiffen, but she felt his hand clamp tightly against her shoulder. "Are *you* wealthy?" he asked.

She turned her head and looked at him. "Not wealthy enough to attract you, I fear."

She saw his golden eyes dance mischievously before he pushed her head back against the sofa. "You are assuming I would want you only for your money," he said, moving his hands lower and pushing the cashmere robe further down. His hands glided across her shoulder blade. "What is your profession?"

"I'm a doctor," she murmured, wishing he'd never stop massaging her body. "To be specific, I'm a pediatrician."

His hand paused at the small of her back. "A children's doctor?"

"Um-hmm. I love children. Donald didn't want any, though."

"But you do?"

"Of course—don't most women? Now that I think about it, Donald didn't want many of the things I wanted."

A muscle tightened in Luc's jaw while his hands moved lower, making a circular motion on the small of her back. He applied more lotion before he spoke. "Who is Donald?"

Abbie was feeling warm and lethargic and a little drunk, so she spoke openly about her private life to a man she hardly knew. "Donald is my fiancé—no, that is not right, he *was* my fiancé. You see, he jilted me, and I came on the honeymoon without him."

Now Luc understood why she was like a tigress when anyone came too near her. "This Donald is a fool, Abbie."

She groaned as he made circular movements from her shoulders to her waist. "Do you really think so? Well, my ex-best friend, Mary Ann, wouldn't agree with you. Or maybe she does now." Abbie took a deep breath. "Poor Donald can't make up his mind—first he wants me, then Mary Ann, then me again."

Luc could hear the raw pain in her voice, and he was beginning to get a clear picture of the betrayal she had suffered. Well, luck was with him, because he wanted Abbie, and if this Donald hadn't jilted her, she'd be a married woman now. "So," he continued, probing her mind while he soothed her body, "is Donald a doctor, too?"

Now that Abbie was talking, she couldn't seem to stop. "Donald Pennington IV is in public relations—advertising. My father always said that Donald wore his profession like a badge he'd won. You see, my father didn't like Donald very well. It turns out he was right about him." The wine had loosened her tongue and she spoke without hesitation. "On the other hand, my mother was happy to join our family to the Penningtons by marriage."

"I believe I like your father."

Abbie would have agreed with him, but his hands were moving sensuously from her shoulders to her waist, and it took her a moment to speak. "My mother is not going to be happy when she learns I told Donald to go away when he called tonight."

"He knows you are here?"

Abbie suddenly sounded like a lost little girl. "I had hoped that no one would find me here, but in his usual efficient manner, Donald did."

Now Luc was the one who was tense. "He wants you back?"

"Yes, but I don't want him—at least I don't think I do. What do you think, Luc?"

He weighed his words carefully. "If you have to think about it, you probably don't. What *do* you want in a husband, Abbie?"

She said without hesitation, "I want a man who allows me to practice my profession and won't feel threatened because I have a brain."

"Did Donald do that?"

Abbie's voice sounded far away, as if she were getting drowsy. "He asked me to give up my practice, and after agonizing over the decision for weeks, I finally agreed. The hardest thing I ever did was turn my patients over to my partner."

"What other qualities do you want in a husband?" Luc felt pangs of guilt because he was taking advantage of her vulnerable condition, but his guilt didn't stop him from trying to learn more about her.

"I should have put this one first because it's the most important," Abbie said with feeling. "I know it's old-fashioned, but I'll never love a man who can't place honor above all else. I would never lie to him, and I would want him to always be honest with me. My father is fond of the saying, 'All that glitters is not gold.' Donald isn't gold—but I thought he was. How easy it is to be mistaken about someone's true nature."

"Donald is a fool if he doesn't realize that you are a rare diamond, Abbie. The man who wins your respect will be fortunate indeed." This was spoken with passion, but Abbie didn't notice.

"Not my heart, Luc?"

"That, too, of course."

She hiccupped and then giggled. "I think I'll just give my body to every man who comes along and keep my heart locked up in a safe place forever."

With a movement that took her by surprise, Luc turned her over so fast that her robe fell to the floor. Suddenly he had lifted her to her feet and was holding her so tightly that she could hardly breathe, but she was too astonished to react.

Luc's voice was sharp, his accent more pronounced because he was disturbed. His eyes darkened with anger. "Do not say that, Abbie—never say it again! You know you don't mean it."

"No, I don't mean it," she replied in confusion. "I don't know why I said it." What she didn't understand was why it seemed to matter so much to him.

Luc's face was swimming before her. She thought she saw tenderness in his expression—but surely she was mistaken. She should never have drunk all that wine.

"Let go of me," she said, trying to wedge her arm between them.

"Not just yet." He fitted her body to his, and his

241

amber eyes flamed as if someone had lit a fire behind them.

Abbie realized that Luc was going to kiss her, and unwittingly, her lips moved toward his. It flashed through her muddled senses that she must have lost her mind completely. She was naked in the arms of a Frenchman she'd known for only two days. Everything flew out of her mind when his mouth touched hers, sending shock waves through her body. She clung to him, pressing tighter to his warmth and becoming pliable in his arms.

Luc felt her melt into him, and he deepened the kiss. He felt her arms slide around his neck, and she pressed even closer. His hands moved down her back, and then he stopped and pushed her away abruptly.

Abbie was startled back to reality when he retrieved her robe and draped it around her naked body.

"I don't want it to happen like this between us," he said in answer to the unspoken hurt in her eyes. "When I make love to you, Abbie, I won't ply you with wine to do it."

Her pride came to her defense. "I will never allow you to make love to me, Luc. I am not so drunk that I don't know what you are."

"Do you?"

"Yes. A Barbie doll collector."

He clasped her chin and turned her face up to his. "I could have had you tonight. When I'm gone, ask yourself why I stopped."

"Go away," she said, pushing her tumbled hair out of her face. "Just leave me alone."

He moved to the door and paused, his hand on the knob. "I'll meet you in the lobby at the same time as today."

She refused to look in his direction. "I won't be there."

"You might want to rub the emu oil on your legs and thighs, since I never got that far."

She turned to him, more hurt than angry. "I never want to see you again, Luc Anglade."

"Tomorrow we move to a steeper hill," he said, going out the door and closing it quietly behind him.

Abbie stood there for a long time, trying to make sense out of what had happened. Luc had been right. She had all but begged him to make love to her. Why had he pushed her away? Didn't he find her desirable?

She saw his black bag on the floor and kicked it, wishing it was Luc himself. She didn't need men in her life. They only complicated everything.

But that night, as she tossed and turned in bed, she did not dream of Donald. She dreamed of golden eyes that danced with mischief and a deep French voice whispering in her ear, "I could have had you tonight, Abbie."

Chapter Four

The next morning, Abbie was determined not to meet Luc. She walked to the door, then stopped. "No," she said aloud. "I won't go." She dropped onto the edge of the sofa and rested her chin on her hands. Luc could have taken advantage of her last night and he hadn't. She had never met a man like him. He was an enigma, mysterious and totally desirable. She was sure her blood reached a boiling point every time he looked at her with his golden gaze.

She was indecisive. Again she went to the door. Why shouldn't she be with Luc? They were both free, assuming he didn't have a wife or two hidden away somewhere in France. She paused with her hand on the doorknob. She never wanted to see him again!

Luc was relieved when he saw Abbie exit the elevator. If she had kept him waiting much longer, he'd have gone to her room and dragged her out himself. No woman had ever gotten under his skin the way she did. He was thirty-two years old and had thought he was in control of his life. But that was before he met Abbie.

Trying to act as if nothing had happened between them the night before, Abbie worked her fingers into her gloves as she approached Luc. She watched his expression to see if he would give her that I-knew-you-would-come look. He didn't. He merely held the door open so she could precede him.

"I hope you haven't gone to the trouble of providing lunch," she said, stepping into the frosty air, her breath coming out like puffs of smoke.

"*Non.* I thought that after the lessons we would rent a snowmobile and ride to a restaurant at the top of the mountain. Do you like Italian food?" he asked courteously.

Abbie had given him an easy out, but she was glad that he wanted to be with her. "I love *good* Italian food," she said with a smile.

"As you Americans say, it's settled then."

The morning passed quickly, and Abbie listened intently while Luc patiently instructed her on controlling her moves.

He stood at the bottom of a steep incline and called up to her. "Concentrate and allow your mind to respond to the slope, Abbie, so you can react ahead of time, and the mountain will be yours."

She nodded and began her descent, gliding confidently down the slope, and expertly stopped in front of him, beaming because of her progress. "I'm actually beginning to enjoy skiing." Her cheeks were rosy from the cold and her eyes were shining with excitement. "It's all because of you, Luc."

"You're the one who did it, Abbie," he said with warm encouragement. "You have good balance and the potential to be, if not expert, at least above average."

She sat on a tree stump and gazed at the beauty surrounding her. The sky was unsullied by smog, and the snow made everything seem pristine and clean. "I never thought I would like it here, but I do. I owe much of how I feel to you, Luc."

His golden eyes seemed to glisten. "In what respect?"

"Don't misunderstand me. I'm just trying to say thank you, and to offer you my friendship."

He bent down to unhook her skis, keeping his head down, as if it took all his concentration. "Friendship," he muttered. "That's better than nothing, I suppose."

"I beg your pardon?" she asked, leaning closer to him since she hadn't heard his remark.

Luc stood and offered her his hand. "Are you hungry?"

"Starved."

"Then I prescribe lunch at the summit, Doctor."

Abbie had expected to have her own snowmobile, but Luc had rented only one. Without hesitation, she climbed on behind him and slipped her arms about his waist. She was having fun, something that had been missing from her relationship with Donald.

With a loud whirr of the motor, they were off, leaving a spray of snow in their wake. Cold air stung her cheeks and she laid her face against Luc's back. Unexpectedly, and with the power of an avalanche, Abbie felt a warmth deep inside her. She was falling in love with Luc. She hadn't wanted to—it had just happened. There was no future for them, but she could content herself with the present.

Luc expertly guided the snowmobile steeply upward, and Abbie's arms tightened about his waist. She wasn't frightened, not with him. It was exhilarating just being near him. She found herself smiling, and then laughing out loud as he wove in and out through a line of tall pine trees. When a shower of snow fell off the branches and hit Luc in the face, Abbie bubbled with laughter.

The rustic atmosphere of the restaurant made it seem a part of the surroundings. They sat on wooden benches, drinking hot apple cider to warm them, and wine with their meal. Mood music reminiscent of Italy played softly in the background.

Abbie glanced up to find Luc watching her with a soft expression on his face. Oh, he knew so well how to reach a woman's heart, she thought, dropping her gaze.

"Have you ever been to France, Abbie?" he asked quietly.

"Unfortunately, I haven't." She swirled the wine around in her glass and watched the candlelight play on the shimmering liquid. "I'd like to go there someday."

"I would be pleased to show my country to you, and to show you to my country, Abbie."

She could think of nothing she'd like better at the moment than to be in Paris with Luc. "Tell me about yourself," she said, neatly folding her napkin and placing it on the table. "Your English is excellent. Have you been in the United States long?"

"Not so long as you might think." He placed his wineglass down and studied her face. "Do you speak French?"

"Strictly high school and college French, I'm afraid."

She wrinkled her nose and shook her head, looking very little-girl-like. It was one of the many endearing qualities she had that could twist a man's heart. It made Luc want to hold her close to him and never let her go.

"College French is good, is it not?" he asked, tearing his gaze away from her soft lips.

"I doubt I would be able to carry on a conversation with you in French without reverting to English."

"But you could learn."

She looked puzzled. "I suppose. I hadn't really thought about it."

"I want to know more about you, Abbie. Your accent is softer and more pronounced than most Americans I have met. Where do you live?"

"I was born and raised outside Arlington, Virginia. Near Washington, D.C." She closed her eyes, picturing the stately white colonial where she'd lived most of her life. It sat atop a hill with a sweeping view of the Potomac River. She suddenly felt terribly homesick for her parents, especially her father.

"My father's a doctor, and I grew up wanting to follow in his footsteps. I even went to Johns Hopkins because that's where he graduated and did his internship. The difference between us is that my father is an obstetrician and delivers babies, while I'm a pediatrician and treat the children after they're born. I have an older brother, Robert, who is a heart specialist in Philadelphia." She suddenly realized that he'd cleverly turned the conversation away from himself, and she smiled, shaking her head. "Enough about me, Luc. I insist that you tell me something about yourself."

He studied the delicate hand that rested against the white tablecloth. Her fingers were long and graceful—she had healing hands to comfort a child, he thought. "I suppose you could say my family are farmers," he answered, bringing his thoughts back to her question. "Our vineyards have been in my family for nine generations. It is my hope that they will be in our family for many more."

"I'd like to hear about your family."

Luc shifted his weight, and Abbie's heart skipped a beat when his leg brushed against hers. She kept remembering him holding her in his arms last night, and she ached to be close to him again. She had to stop thinking about him that way. She raised her gaze to his and found him watching her.

"Abbie, in my home, there is my father and my

younger sister, Dominique. My mother died when I was twelve, and Grand-mère has taken care of us ever since." He smiled as if remembering something pleasant. "Grand-mère is eighty-three, and in excellent health. I believe she would like you a lot, Abbie."

She heard the pride in his voice when he spoke of his home and family, and she wondered why he had chosen to come to the United States. Probably a small vineyard did not hold enough excitement for him. "How long have you been in Colorado? Don't you miss your family?"

He felt guilty for not telling her the truth about himself, especially since she placed so much importance on honor. "*Oui*, I miss them."

She loved the sound of his voice and could listen to him all day. "Yet you left the family vineyard and came to America to teach wealthy women how to ski?"

He was saved from answering when their waiter opened another bottle of wine and handed the cork to Luc. He passed it beneath his nose and nodded. But when the waiter attempted to pour wine in Luc's glass, he covered it with his hand and shook his head, smiling at Abbie. "No more for me—I'm driving."

When the waiter left, Abbie was determined to learn more about Luc. "What do you want to do with your life?" She paused, wondering why his answer was so important to her. I mean what do you *really* want?"

He took her hand and held it in a warm clasp, and she did not pull away. "What do I want? I will answer you in this way, Abbie. Grand-mère says that eyes are the mirrors to the soul. If that is so, then look deeply into my eyes, Abbie, and see what's mirrored there. Then you will have your answer."

Abbie extracted her hand, somehow reluctant to look into his eyes, but she could not resist the temptation. Slowly, she raised her gaze to his, unprepared for what she saw. The brilliant amber eyes were gentle and sparkled with the softness of . . . love. She gasped and lowered her eyes, feeling as if a sudden storm had just swept through her body, leaving her breathless. She pushed her wineglass away, thinking she'd had too much to drink again.

Luc was watching her closely, and he could read much of what she was thinking. "What did you see in my eyes, Abbie?" he asked, the tone of his voice laced with meaning. "And why did you look away so quickly?"

"I saw nothing," she answered, refusing to look at him because she was still shaken to the core of her being. She stood up abruptly. She had to get away from him. "I should be getting back to the hotel so I can call my mother. She worries about me," she said, her excuse sounding contrived even to her ears.

Luc stood, tossing money on the table. "We shall leave, if that is your wish, Abbie. Bundle up well; it is very cold because the sun is setting."

She blinked her eyes. "I had no idea it was so late," she said in astonishment. They had talked for hours. Time always passed quickly when she was with Luc.

As they stepped out into the twilight, Abbie's

thoughts were troubled. If she wasn't careful, she was going to be terribly hurt by this man. She had always considered herself a sensible woman, but she wasn't so sure about that now. She didn't love Donald, and never had. What disturbed her was the fact that she was falling deeply in love with a Frenchman who probably took what he wanted from a woman and then tossed her aside like last year's model.

Silently, Luc helped her onto the snowmobile behind him and started down the mountain.

Abbie's cheeks were wet with tears, and when she placed her head against his back, her hands locking about his waist, she felt the pressure of his hand on hers. The tears flowed unchecked down her face. She dared not see him alone again because she couldn't trust herself.

Tonight she would make arrangements to return home.

Chapter Five

When they reached the hotel, Abbie slid off the snowmobile before Luc had time to help her. She saw one of the women who always hung around Luc hurrying in their direction.

Abbie spoke quickly, needing to say what was on her mind before the blonde joined them. "I won't be needing any more lessons, Luc, but I'll leave a check for you at the front desk."

Before she knew what was happening, Luc was standing before her, gripping both her arms. "What do you mean?"

It almost hurt to say the words that would end their relationship. "I'm going home tomorrow, Luc."

By now, the blonde was beside them, and she placed a hand on Luc's arm possessively. "Where were you today, Luc? I missed you on the slopes."

His gaze never left Abbie's face. It was as if the other woman didn't exist.

Abbie felt momentary pity for the young woman because of Luc's indifference to her. His actions only cemented Abbie's resolve. She didn't want to be treated with such disinterest at some point in the future.

"You can't leave," Luc said. "Why would you consider it?"

Abbie shook her head sadly. "I'm going home." She nodded at the other woman. "I believe your friend wants you."

She rushed away before Luc had time to answer. When she reached the hotel entrance, she went inside without a backward glance.

Wearing her cashmere robe, Abbie was curled up on the sofa, listening to the wind whistle outside her window and trying to fit the pieces of her life together again. In two days, the old year would end and a new one would take its place. What would the new year mean for her?

She leaned her head back and closed her eyes. She could remain in Aspen for the New Year celebration. It would certainly be spectacular, with Gold Medalists from all over the world skiing down Aspen Mountain, carrying torches. Donald was such a fan of the Winter Olympics that he knew all the winners' statistics—their names, ages, and every published aspect of their lives. The thought of seeing them, even at a distance, was the reason he'd wanted to honeymoon there.

Abbie thought of Luc and her growing feelings for him. She dared not stay one more day because she was too vulnerable where he was concerned. She was reaching for the phone to call the front desk so she could make her reservations for the early morning flight, when someone knocked on her door. This time she was not surprised to see Luc standing there. He wore black dress pants and a white, hand-knitted sweater. His golden gaze rested on her, and as always it was electrifying.

"What's the matter?" Abbie asked flippantly. "Were you afraid I'd skip town without paying you?"

His jaw tightened in anger. Wordlessly, he entered the room and closed the door behind him. Then he grabbed Abbie and held her firm.

"Damn you," he murmured as he jerked her forward, slamming her body against his. "I didn't know anything was missing from my life until I saw you." His lips were very near hers. "You have complicated my life, Dr. Abigail Taylor Hunt. And now you want to leave me. I won't allow that to happen until you understand how I feel about you."

Abbie couldn't speak past the tightening in her throat. He rested his chin on the top of her head and just held her for a long moment, while she closed her eyes, allowing his essence to fill her mind and body.

"You feel something for me. I know you do, Abbie—don't deny it."

"Lust," she managed to say flippantly, trying to relieve the tension between them. "Pure, unadulterated lust."

He lifted her chin and brought her face upward so she had to meet his gaze. "I think not." He managed a smile. "Although lust is not a bad beginning between a man and a woman. Shall we build on that, Abbie?"

She was aware that her lips were moving, but it was as if someone else spoke the words. "Please don't do this to me, Luc."

"Do what? Love you until the day I die?"

"I'm sure your definition of love and mine are entirely different. You think of it as a contact sport, while I think of it as something spiritual."

He laid his face against hers. "Don't confuse me with any other man you've known. Let me love you with my body, as well as my soul. Trust me, Abbie."

Before she could utter a word of protest, his lips descended, covering hers, crushing, devouring, relentlessly draining her of any resistance.

Her body seemed to float toward his warmth. She fit snugly against him, molded to him, clinging to him as if he were the sun and she a sunflower that needed his brightness to survive. She threw her head back when his hot mouth moved down her neck, teasing her, taunting her, driving her out of her mind. Her arms moved about his muscled shoulders, and she was drunk with the feel of him—only this time she couldn't blame it on wine.

"I knew there was fire in you, Abbie," he whispered against her ear. "You have depths that have not yet been tapped."

"I don't understand."

His hands moved up and down her back possessively. "You know that I want you and you want me."

She didn't bother to deny it. "Yes."

His hands moved to her waist. "What you don't know is that I want more then just your body. I want all of you."

She pulled away from him as if he'd dashed cold water in her face. "Those are pretty words, Luc, but I doubt that you are interested in any woman's heart."

His golden eyes flamed, his nostrils flared, and Abbie knew she'd gone too far this time.

"I have borne your insults with good grace, Abbie, because I knew you'd been hurt. But you're tearing me apart. All I need is a chance to prove that you're wrong about me."

Suddenly his motives didn't matter. Tomorrow she would go back to Virginia and an empty life. Would it be so bad if she took what Luc offered tonight?

Abbie raised her head and parted her lips in a bold invitation. "Kiss me, Luc."

He gave a sharp intake of breath and lifted her in his arms. "I'll kiss you, Abbie, but it won't stop at that. If you don't want more, say so now."

For her answer, she buried her face against his chest, listening to the drumming of his heart, the rhythm matching her own erratic heartbeat. She was amazed by the deep, painful longing that raged through her like an inferno. She was almost mindless when he laid her on the bed and eased his weight down beside her.

Luc's hands moved downward as he untied her robe, sending shivers of delight dancing all through her. Since she wore nothing underneath, her naked body was exposed to his appreciative gaze.

"You are perfect," he said, lightly moving his hand around her breasts, across her flat stomach, to her rounded hips. He dropped his dark head, his sensuous mouth following the trail blazed by his hands, draining her of the last bit of protest she might have made.

Abbie moaned, turning her head from side to side, biting her lip to keep from crying out from the desire coursing through her body.

Luc's lips found hers, and he kissed her tenderly, lovingly. He held her close to his body, his hands gliding across her hips to press her tighter against him. "I knew when I first saw you that we would share this moment."

"You couldn't have," she said, groaning when his hand moved lower and then lower, stirring up even more longings. All at once, she was frightened by the intensity of her desire, and she pulled away.

But Luc drew her back to him. "Don't be afraid, Abbie. I will give you only joy."

He fought to curb his impatience so they could savor each moment. He would make it pleasurable for her, and show her that she had been created to love and be loved by him. He poised so he could enter her, slowly, sensuously, filling her aching recesses.

Luc trembled as her velvet softness closed about him. He had been right; theirs was a perfect uniting.

Chapter Six

Abbie awoke smiling and untangled herself from the sheets. She reached for Luc, but the impression he'd left on the pillow beside her was the only evidence that he'd been there at all. Joy filled her heart as she remembered all they had shared. Luc had asked her to trust him, and she would.

She curled up, resting her head against his pillow. "I love you," she whispered. "I always will."

Hearing footsteps, she sat up and watched Luc advance into the room, carrying a tray. His gaze was tender as he placed the tray on her lap.

He dipped his head and placed a kiss on her lips. "Breakfast for my mademoiselle?"

"I'm famished," she said, reaching for a glass of orange juice.

He arched a dark brow. "I don't doubt it."

She saw that the tray contained breakfast for

only one. "Aren't you going to eat with me?"

"I already ate. Will you forgive me if I leave you now? I have arrangements to make. We'll talk about them later."

She nodded, hiding her disappointment. "Of course."

After Luc left, she poured herself a cup of coffee and lost herself in thought. She was trying to re-call what Luc had said to her last night. She couldn't remember either of them mentioning love.

Absently, she reached for the remote control and switched on the TV. The morning news was on, and she only half watched it while she de-voured a bowl of bananas and cream.

Suddenly her attention was riveted on the TV screen. Had she heard correctly? She thought the announcer had said he was going live to Aspen, Colorado, to interview French Gold Medalist Luc Anglade.

Abbie sat transfixed when Luc's image flashed across the screen.

"Mr. Anglade, it's a pleasure and an honor to speak to you. Unless I lost count, you have won five gold medals and three silvers. That's an ex-traordinary record. Can you tell any of our younger skiers your secret?"

Luc flashed his familiar smile, and it seemed to Abbie that he looked right at her. "I have been fortunate to be able to do what I enjoy. I would say that if anyone is serious about competing, hard work and dedication are the keys to success."

"For those of you who don't know it, Mr. An-glade is the heir to the prestigious Anglade wine empire. His family has been producing wine since just before Columbus discovered the New World." The camera cut to France, sweeping across an immense vineyard, and then to the Château Anglade, which was larger than most hotels while the reporter explained how Luc's home was also famous for the large collection of medieval tapestries housed within it.

Abbie covered her mouth with her hand, trying to smother the building sob. Luc had asked her to trust him, but he'd lied to her all along. She felt her heart shatter into a million pieces. Never had anything hurt so deeply, and this time, the pain would never heal.

Luc was standing beside his Ferrari, his dark hair blowing in the wind. It was hard to believe that this world-famous man was the same one who had made love to her last night.

"Mr. Anglade, I understand the people of France gave you this car as thanks from a grateful nation for your feats in the last Winter Olympics." The interviewer looked into the camera. "Folks, if you haven't bought your tickets for the drawing, you can buy them at most of the shops in town. Mr. Anglade has graciously donated this beautiful Ferrari to the Handicapped Children's Foundation of America. Even if you don't win the car, you'll have the satisfaction of knowing that your money went to a worthy cause."

He glanced back at Luc. "What does your family think of your fame, Mr. Anglade?"

Luc appeared impatient for the interview to end. "They want to know when I will come home to stay."

"We all hope that won't be for a very long time. It has been a pleasure to watch you over the years. I believe you have as many fans in the rest of the world as you have in your native France."

"I am going to honor my family's wishes," he said simply. "I am going home to stay this time."

"Does this mean we won't see you compete on the slopes again?"

Luc seemed subdued and evasive. "If everything goes as I plan, I shall be leaving for France right after the New Year's celebration."

Abbie hit the off button on the remote and the television went blank. At first she was too stunned to react. Then she picked up Luc's pillow and lobbed it at the offending screen. Tears lingered behind her eyelids, and she huddled in the bed as vivid memories of the night before enveloped her mind. She was besieged by emotions that she was incapable of dealing with at the moment. In a daze, she reached for the phone to make her flight reservations.

"You are probably one of the most eligible bachelors in France, if not in the world," the interviewer continued. "Do you plan to marry soon?"

Luc smiled. "*Oui*. I have plans."

The interviewer perked up, feeling he had just stumbled onto an exclusive. "Can you tell us who she is?"

"I will say only that she is an American."

The more the interviewer pressed for answers, the more Luc dodged his questions.

"Will you be married here, or in France?" The

interviewer struck with a directness that usually worked, but Luc shook his head.

"I will speak only of the upcoming New Year's event and the raffle for handicapped children. I'm sure you will understand my desire for privacy."

Abbie spoke hurriedly to the desk clerk. "But the flights can't all be full. Can you put me on standby? There's no chance for me to leave today?" She gripped the phone so tightly that her knuckles whitened. "Then reserve a car for me. Oh, none available. How soon can I leave?"

She hung up the phone, feeling dejected. All the flights had been booked, and there were no rental cars available. She quickly dressed and rushed out of the hotel without her coat and cap. She couldn't blame Luc for what had happened last night because she had been a willing participant. But he had lied to her, and she could never forgive that— never!

Abbie slipped out of the hotel through a side door, then walked hurriedly down the street. She walked until she was tired, then found a deserted spot and sat huddled on a bench, her mind whirling. It had started snowing heavily, but she hadn't noticed because she was numb.

Abbie heard someone call her name and glanced up to see Luc striding toward her. She wanted to run from him, but it was too late. She clasped her hands tightly, praying she wouldn't cry in front of him.

"Abbie, I have been searching everywhere for you. I called your room several times, but you were not there. When I couldn't find you at the hotel, I began walking the streets, looking for you. What are you doing out here? Don't you know you could catch cold?"

He removed his down jacket and placed it about her shoulders, but she jerked it off and handed it back to him.

"I don't want anything from you."

He sat down beside her. "You saw the interview on television?"

"Only enough of it to know you've lied to me." Her voice sounded devoid of feeling.

"I never told you that I was a ski instructor, Abbie. That was a conclusion you came to on your own."

"But you didn't deny it."

"*Non*, I did not, and I ask your forgiveness for that. I wanted to tell you about myself, but the time never seemed right. And as long as you thought I was merely a ski instructor, I could be with you."

She slowly rose to her feet, afraid her knees might buckle. "How convenient that I helped you weave your lie, Luc. You must have laughed at my gullibility."

He was beside her, reaching for her, but she moved away and he dropped his hands to his sides. Then he leveled his golden gaze on her. "It wasn't like that, Abbie." He realized that if he lost her, he would miss her for the rest of his life. "Had you listened to the entire interview, you would understand. Come with me to the coffee shop and let's talk. It's too cold for you out here."

She moved farther away from him. "Leave me

alone, Luc. There is nothing you can say that I will believe."

"I won't allow it to end like this, Abbie."

Anger and hurt battled for supremacy within her. "Do you leave, Luc, or do I?"

"I'll leave if you will promise to return to the hotel. But this isn't over between us, Abbie. You know it isn't."

She watched him walk heavily away, wishing she dared call him back. He was soon lost from sight by a dense curtain of snow. One thing she knew for certain—she must avoid seeing Luc again because it would only prolong her agony.

The numbing cold made her shiver, so she walked quickly back to the hotel. She went directly to her room and dialed the front desk, directing them to hold all calls. The desk clerk told her that a Donald Pennington had been trying to reach her.

"I don't want to be disturbed by anyone," she said emphatically, glancing down at the flashing message light.

Like a sleepwalker, she moved to the window, thinking how much she'd changed in a few short days. She had come here to grieve about losing Donald, and now she could hardly remember what she'd ever seen in him. She could imagine him calling every five minutes, demanding that the desk clerk put him through to her room. Donald always insisted on having his way; she could see that now. There had been a time when she thought his little-boy traits charming. Now she realized he had just never matured.

Her thoughts went to Luc. There was nothing

little-boyish about him—he was a man who knew who he was and what he wanted out of life. She was puzzled by his attentions to her. Probably it was only the chase that interested him, and not the capture.

She took a long, leisurely bath and then dressed in jeans and a pink cashmere sweater. Feeling restless, she curled up on the sofa and picked up the newspaper. There, on the front page, was Luc's face staring back at her. The bold headlines ripped at her heart.

French Gold Medalist and wealthy heir to Anglade wine fortune, Luc Anglade, to wed American Beauty.

Abbie set the paper down without reading it and went to her room. She didn't want to know about the beauty who was to be Luc's wife. Most of all, she didn't want to think of him being faithless to the woman he was to marry—it was too close to what Donald had done to her. He'd made her an unwitting partner to his treachery and had betrayed her as well.

Dropping onto the bed, she closed her eyes. Sleep came to her at last in the small hours of the night, but she awoke often and slumbered restlessly.

Chapter Seven

At first the sound came to Abbie like something out of a dream, but it became louder and more persistent. Someone was knocking on the door and wouldn't go away. She buried her head under her pillow, but the annoying sound continued.

At last she slid out of bed, pulling on her cashmere robe as she marched to the door. Yanking it open, she was ready to vent her anger on her faithless lover.

"Luc, I told you not to—"

But it wasn't Luc—it was Donald. She stared at him in amazement, noting the anger on his face.

"Abbie, what in the hell do you think you are doing, rushing off like this and barricading yourself in your room like a little girl who wasn't invited to a party?"

She continued to stare at him as if he were a

stranger. "I was sleeping, Donald, and if you'll leave, I'll go back to sleep. What time is it, anyway?"

He was disconcerted because she was so calm. He had never seen her looking more beautiful than she did at that moment, with her dark hair tumbling over her shoulders.

"It's six, I suppose," he said striding past her into the room.

She followed him, but left the door ajar. "What are you doing here, Donald?"

"I've come to take you home, so pack your things. You needn't worry. As far as everyone knows, we had to postpone the wedding because you were ill. I have already rescheduled it for next Saturday."

Abbie found the situation humorous. She could almost see him and her mother with their heads together, attempting to contrive a believable story to tell everyone. "I'm not going to marry you next week, next year, or ever, Donald."

He merely smiled indulgently. "I know you've been hurt, Abbie, but I'll make it up to you."

"I don't want you. I never loved you, Donald, I only thought I did."

"What? You can't mean that!"

"Oh, but she does," a cold voice said in accented English.

Abbie and Donald turned in astonishment.

"I assume this is the Donald you told me about?" Luc said, pulling Abbie into his arms.

Abbie nodded, realizing that Luc was merely trying to help her out of a difficult situation. She felt laughter bubble inside her—it was all so ridiculous! After she had dealt with Donald, she would still have to deal with Luc. Maybe she ought to sell tickets.

"Donald," she said, leaning into Luc, "meet Luc Anglade. Luc, you will remember I told you that Donald and I were supposed to be married a few days ago?"

Donald was speechless for a moment. "You are *the* Luc Anglade! I watched you take the gold in the last Olympics. I was rooting for you all the way—I'm one of your biggest fans, Mr. Anglade."

"You will excuse me if I don't return the compliment," Luc said, planting a kiss on the top of Abbie's head and pulling her even closer to him. "I don't like you at all. But I suppose I do owe you my gratitude for not marrying Abbie. She belongs to me now, and if you don't mind, we'd like you to leave so we can be alone."

Abbie almost found it within her to feel sorry for Donald. His throat was working convulsively, and he was obviously having a hard time breathing.

"Abbie, what's going on here?" he asked at last, his voice shaking with emotion. "Have you thought how your behavior will affect your parents? And what about me? What will I tell everyone?"

"Perhaps you should tell them that Abbie jilted you," Luc said, glancing down at her lovingly. In a show of affection, he brushed a tumbled curl from her cheek. "As for her parents, once they see how happy I make their daughter, they'll give me their blessings."

Donald looked suddenly suspicious, as though

he'd been the injured party. "Abbie, how long has this been going on between you and Mr. Anglade?"

Her eyes sparkled with tears as she looked from Donald to Luc, and then back to Donald again. "Love knows no time limits. What I thought was love was merely a fondness for someone I'd known all my life." She suddenly felt terribly sorry for him. "I don't want to hurt you, Donald, but go home. There is nothing for you here."

Donald held out his hand to her. "I really do love you. Come with me."

She shook her head.

Luc made a gesture toward the door. "Let me show you the way out, Donald."

In stunned silence, Donald moved through the door and out of Abbie's life forever.

She was surprisingly calm. "Thank you, Luc, for helping me out of a difficult situation. Now I think it's time for us to say good-bye, too."

He caught her hand and pulled her to him. "Don't think you can dismiss me as easily as you did poor Donald."

"I don't feel like talking now."

"But we have a wedding to plan, and there's not much time. I thought it would be nice to be married on the stroke of midnight New Year's Eve. That way, we can tell our children we'd known each other for two years before we got married."

Abby smiled feebly. "Donald's gone now, Luc. You can drop the pretense."

For the first time since she'd known Luc, she saw doubt reflected in his eyes.

"You had better love me, Abbie, because I am

hopelessly in love with you. Besides, you can't disappoint my family. I have already called them and told them that I have found the girl of my dreams."

She looked into his eyes, searching for the truth. "You love me?"

He enfolded her against him, wishing his body would stop trembling. He was still afraid she would walk away from him. "Love you—I can't take a breath without thinking of you. If you don't marry me, you will condemn me to a life of loneliness." He raised her face and looked into her eyes. "Will you marry me, Dr. Abigail Taylor Hunt? Will you come with me and be my love?"

She threw her arms around his neck and tears ran down her cheeks, sweeping away all her doubts. "Oh, yes, Luc. I will definitely marry you."

He still held back, as if there was something unsettled between them. "If you have any questions about me, ask them now, Abbie."

"I have many questions, Luc, but I already know the answer to the important ones."

"How would you rate my character, Abbie?"

"You're 24-carat, Luc." She saw by the brightness in his eyes that she had pleased him. Suddenly she thought about his family—this would surely be a shock to them. "What will your grandmother and your father say about your marrying an American?"

He rested his face against the top of her head. "My father said that this is one of the most sensible decisions I've made in my whole life."

"And your grandmother?"

"She said to hurry up and make babies. She

wants to hold her great-grandchildren before she dies."

"Oh, Luc, I know it isn't reasonable and I can't explain it, but I do love you with my whole heart."

His lips settled on hers, just as if they belonged there. It frightened her when she thought about how close she'd come to marrying Donald. If she had never met Luc, she would have missed her soul mate. She clung tighter to Luc, as if he would disappear if she let him go.

After a while, with her head cradled on his arm, she asked. "When did you first love me?"

He became serious. "The moment our eyes met, I felt as if I were falling off a mountain, and I haven't hit bottom yet."

"Will we live in France?"

"*Oui*. Do you mind?"

"Wherever you are will be my home, Luc." A playful light came into her eyes. "But what will you do about your Barbie dolls?"

He shook with laughter and hugged her tightly. "I'm going to be too busy playing house with you to think of anyone else. I will make wine, and you will make babies. I have a feeling that I'll never know a dull day with you at my side."

Something was still troubling Abbie. "I'm a doctor, Luc." She looked into his eyes. "I will not want to give that up. I did for Donald, but I was terribly unhappy about it."

Luc knew how important her profession was to her. "We'll find out what you must do to practice in France and take the proper steps." He touched her cheek softly. "I don't want to change you, Abbie. I fell in love with the woman you are, and I want you to have whatever makes your life complete."

Abbie dropped her gaze, fearing she would cry. Less than a week ago, she'd thought her life was over; now she knew it was just beginning.

It hadn't taken long for the contingent of reporters that descended on Aspen for the New Year's show to discover that Luc Anglade's intended bride was Dr. Abigail Hunt of Arlington, Virginia.

Most of the time, Luc managed to protect Abbie from the eager press that followed them everywhere they went. But they did find her when she was shopping for a wedding dress. She graciously gave them a short interview, and they agreed to leave her in peace, at least for a while.

It was Abbie's wedding day, and she was bursting with happiness. Through Luc's influence, the French ambassador had obtained a special marriage license for them and a passport for Abbie.

Most of the people in Aspen had emptied into the streets to watch the spectacle that was ushering in the new year. The skies exploded with fireworks, and laser beams searched and stretched heavenward, brightening every dark corner.

In a small chapel tucked away in a secluded valley, Abbie stood beside Luc as they repeated the vows that would bind them together until death. Only a few of Luc's closest friends were in attendance, mostly fellow Olympians and their spouses.

Abbie's heart was so full, she could hardly respond to the minister's prompting. When he pronounced them man and wife, Abbie raised her lips to Luc and he kissed her tenderly.

Clasping her hand, Luc hurried them out of the chapel and into the night, while his friends showered them with rice. With a hasty good-bye to everyone, he helped her into a white limousine and slid in beside her. Their destination had been a well-kept secret so the press wouldn't intrude. The driver was taking them to the Denver airport, where they would catch a flight to Paris.

The car sped away from the town and wound its way around the mountain. "You are mine now," Luc said, pulling her into his arms. His heart was so full that it took him a moment to speak again. "I knew it from the beginning—my trouble was in convincing you that we belong together, Abbie."

"I love you," she said, looking into his golden eyes, while fireworks burst around them.

"You say that now," he said mischievously. "But wait until you've lived with me for forty or fifty years."

"A lifetime wouldn't be long enough," she said, hiding her face against the front of his tuxedo.

"Do you realize that we'll spend our wedding night traveling?" Luc asked, lacing his fingers through hers. "All I can do tonight, Abbie, is hold you, when I want to rush you to the first hotel I find and make love to you all night."

That was what she wanted, too, but she managed to smile. "There will be other nights."

"I'm sorry to tell you that we will only have a week alone before I take you to meet my family. I thought it would be nice if we surprised grand-mère on her birthday. Will you mind?"

"Not at all. I want very much to meet your family."

Luc glanced down at the diamond ring he had placed on her finger only moments before, and a great possessiveness came over him. "My family will love you, Abbie."

Through the rear window, the skies still exploded with fireworks, but Abbie didn't notice. She was nestled in her husband's arms, and his hands were moving over her body as if he were memorizing every curve. She heard him groan in frustration because he could only touch her, and they both wanted much, much more.

She glanced up to find him smiling at her, and her heart caught in her throat. Her husband was truly a man of honor—a man of the purest gold.

Lottery of
Love

Bobbi Smith

For Dennis Lennaman and Larry Lennaman of Community Auto Body for all their help with research. I even appreciate their input on choosing a title for the story, but somehow "Zach's Racks" just didn't sound romantic enough. Thanks, guys!

Chapter One

Strains of the Beach Boys' "Little Deuce Coupe" played in the background as Zach Thomas made an adjustment to the engine of the '65 Mustang he was restoring.

"That should do it. . . ." he said to himself, satisfied that he'd finally found the problem and fixed it.

This red, 2+2 Fastback was the car of his dreams. He'd been working on it in his spare time for over a year now and had been enjoying every minute of the challenge.

Ducking out from under the hood, Zach wiped the grease from his hands on a rag and slid behind the wheel of the car. He turned the key, and, as the engine roared to life, a smile of pure masculine satisfaction lit up his face. His hard work had paid off. Life was good.

"Hey, Zach! You working late again?"

Zach looked up to see Rod Matthews coming through the garage's side door. He turned off the engine and climbed out to talk to the nineteen-year-old college student who worked for him part-time. "What are you doing here this time of night?"

"I was driving by and saw the lights on. I thought you might be working on your baby." Rod gazed at the classic car with admiration. "Sounds like you finally got it right."

Zach threw the greasy rag at him in good humor, and Rod agilely dodged it. Zach turned back to the engine to make one more final adjustment.

"There. Now, turn it on for me. I want to listen and see if—"

Rod didn't need to be asked twice. He loved the old Mustang and hurried to climb in. He gloried in the fantasy of sitting at the wheel. This '65 was one cherry machine. The engine roared to life like a finely-tuned instrument.

Zach frowned in concentration as he listened. Finally, he nodded to himself and waved to Rod to shut it down.

"All it takes is a gentle touch, the right tools, and perseverance," he said with satisfaction, slamming the hood and wiping any imaginary fingerprints off the paint job.

"Wouldn't those rules work for women, too?" Rod asked with a laugh as he came to stand beside his boss. He'd known Zach for years; Zach had been part of the group of friends his older sister, Elise, had hung out with during high school. Rod had always admired him and was glad to be working for him. Zach's Collision Plus, his garage and auto body shop, was the best in town. Zach had worked hard to build and maintain a sterling reputation, and Rod knew it was well-earned. No one was more honest or did better work than Zach.

"Who has time for women?" Zach quipped in return. "This little beauty takes up all my spare time."

"What are you going to do with it, now that it's finished?"

"I haven't decided yet," he said evasively, but in his heart he knew exactly what he wanted to do with it. He wasn't about to share that with Rod, or with anyone for that matter.

"Well, it's worth a pretty penny. You ought to sell it and start on another one. What was it worth in '65?"

"Retail ran about thirty-two hundred dollars."

Rod laughed. "You could get twenty grand for this one, easy, if you ever decide to sell."

"We'll see." He turned away from the car and started back toward his office at the rear of the garage with Rod following. "So, you were out just driving around bored?"

"No, I was studying at the library."

"What's your sister up to tonight?" Zach asked casually.

Rod glanced at his watch. "Right about now, she's making a sales pitch to Aaron Benedict."

"Aaron Benedict—the new owner of the Tigers?"

"The same. She's trying to land a contract with him to handle all of his catered affairs for the football team."

"That's exciting."

"I'll say. She sent him the proposal a week or so ago, and his office contacted her earlier this week to set up the appointment. This morning she was really nervous about making the presentation."

"She'll do great. She's a class act. This catering business of hers is sure to succeed."

"I hope so. It would really mean a lot to her. The contacts she'd make through the pro football team alone would be fantastic."

"If anyone deserves a break, it's Elise." Zach's words were heartfelt.

Elise had taken over raising Rod all by herself after their parents had died three years before. Her catering business had been brand new then and struggling, yet she'd assumed full responsibility for her younger brother. She was putting him through college now, even though their money was tight and they were scrimping on just about everything.

"It would be wonderful if she got this contract. Just think, I might get to meet all the pro football players."

"Let's hope she does."

"You like Elise, don't you?" he asked.

"Of course. I've known her since we were in high school."

"How come you two never hit it off? I think you'd probably get along great."

Zach shrugged. "I don't know. We've both been busy and just never got around to it."

"She was pretty heavy with that guy, Brad, for a while."

"And I was going with Diana."

"Your timing's just off, I guess."

"I guess." Zach refused to be drawn into any speculation with Rod. Any feelings he had for Elise were private. He'd always thought she was beautiful and he had been attracted to her, but somehow, things had never worked out. That's why they'd remained just friends through the years.

"You ought to ask her out sometime."

"You playing Cupid? It's not even Valentine's Day."

Rod grinned and trailed after him into his small office.

Elise could barely contain her excitement as she held out her hand in a very professional manner to Aaron Benedict. "Thank you, Mr. Benedict. You won't be sorry you hired me."

"I'm sure I won't. Your company has a wonderful reputation for innovation and excellence. I'm looking forward to our association and hope it will be a long and prosperous one." The tall, fair-haired, sophisticated millionaire took her hand in a warm, firm handshake.

Elise smiled up at him. "Me, too. I'll get started on the plans for your kick-off media party right away. I'll have the details to you within a week. That way you'll have plenty of time to decide exactly what you want."

"I'm counting on having your undivided attention during these projects. That will be possible, won't it?" He met her regard squarely as he held on to her hand just a moment longer to emphasize his words.

"Of course. I always work very closely with my clients."

"Good. Then we understand each other." He smiled and moved away from her. He'd first seen Elise Matthews, owner of Catering Elegance, the year before at a social event he'd attended. He'd found her to be a very bright, attractive young woman, and he'd been impressed with her work. Now that he'd bought the football team, he had the perfect opportunity to get to know her better on both a business and personal level. It would not present a hardship to him to have to work side-by-side with her on future projects. "I'll look forward to hearing from you."

"Yes, sir."

"My name's Aaron, Elise. We're going to be working together over the coming months, so there's no need to stand on formality."

"Fine, Aaron," she said his name softly, testing it, liking the sound.

"I look forward to hearing from you next week."

His phone was ringing, and he turned away to answer it. Elise knew she'd been dismissed and gathered up her briefcase and portfolio. She all but floated from his office. She managed to maintain her outward, controlled, businesswoman demeanor until she'd climbed into her car and shut the door. Only then did she let out the scream of excitement she'd been biting back since Aaron had told her he'd decided to go with Catering Elegance.

"Yes!" she shouted, victorious. At last, her life was changing . . . and this time for the better.

She headed home, eager to find her little

brother Rod and celebrate. They could make it now! She'd just signed a six-figure contract with the millionaire owner of the Tigers. Catering Elegance was going places!

Elise was feeling on top of the world as she drove home. Up ahead, she spied a gas station, and, feeling very lucky right then, she pulled in to buy some lottery tickets. It had been a long-standing family joke started by her father years before that one day someone in their family was going to be rich. He'd bought his lotto tickets twice a week, and after his death, Elise had continued his tradition. The last she'd heard, the pot was up to around ten million. She could be happy on ten million, and if she didn't play, she couldn't win. In a fit of extravagance, she bought five tickets and hurried off again in search of Rod.

It was by pure coincidence that Elise found herself driving past Zach's garage and caught sight of Rod's car parked out front. She pulled in near the side door.

"Rod? Zach? Are you in here?" she called out as she found the door unlocked and let herself in.

"We're back here!"

At the sound of their answering call, Elise rushed to tell them the good news.

"This is so exciting!!" she exclaimed when she reached them.

"You got it?" Rod asked, trying to contain his excitement.

"I got it!"

Shouts of happiness erupted from all three of them. Rod and Elise embraced. Zach, caught up in the celebration, gave Elise a big hug too.

"Congratulations!"

Elise was laughing as he set her away from him. "Thanks, Zach. I guess Rod told you all about it?"

"He was just filling me in. It's about time something went right for you."

"You've always been my biggest cheerleader." Her dark eyes were sparkling with delight as she looked up at him. She couldn't remember a time when Zach hadn't been there for her. He was one of her best friends. "I think this calls for a celebration. What about you two?" Elise said.

"Absolutely," Rod agreed. "Where can we go?"

"I'm not exactly dressed for a night on the town." Zach looked down at his grease-stained work clothes. They were hardly suited to dining at a good restaurant, and, as late as it was, it would take him too long to get cleaned up.

"We could order a pizza and eat here," Rod suggested.

"That sounds fine."

"Are you sure?" Zach asked Elise, who looked slim and elegant in her business suit and heels. "I don't want to ruin your big moment. You deserve to have a night out."

"A night out would be great, but pizza's all my budget can afford. I may have gotten the contract, but I haven't seen any money from Aaron yet."

"Aaron?" Rod said, surprised and awed. "You're calling him Aaron?"

"That's his name." Elise's color heightened a little. "He asked me to call him that since we'll be working so closely together."

"Cool." Rod grinned. His sister was calling the owner of the Tigers by his first name. With any luck, he could end up sitting on the sidelines with the football players during a game.

"Are you two game for pizza, or do I have to find myself two new dates?" Elise's question jerked Rod back to reality from his teenage fantasy.

"I'll eat pizza anywhere," he quickly answered her. "Wow! My sister and Aaron Benedict!"

"Don't get too excited there, big boy," she cautioned. "This is business."

"Yeah, yeah."

"What about you, Zach?

"Sure," Zach agreed, glad to be celebrating her good fortune with her. He knew how much it meant to her to be successful. Several times in the past few years, when he'd known they'd been strapped for cash, he'd found ways to give Rod a bonus to help out. He'd known better than to offer the money directly to her. As proud as she was, she would have refused it and struggled on her own. "But I'm buying."

"It's my celebration," she argued. "Let me."

"No, not this time. You can buy next time."

"Are you sure?"

"Positive."

The pizza was ordered and quickly delivered. As they settled in to enjoy the fare, Rod lifted his soda in toast to Elise.

"You done good, Sis."

"Here, here," Zach seconded, taking a deep drink of his own soft drink.

"Thank you, sirs. Now, all I have to do is the best work I've ever done." The thought was a bit unnerving, but she knew this was her big break.

She couldn't let any doubts or fears affect her performance.

"You will," Zach told her.

"I'm glad you have faith in me."

"There's never any doubt about that. What do you have to plan first?"

"A big kick-off party for the media at the end of the month."

"So, we're going to be hobnobbing with the rich and famous that soon?" Rod asked.

"You got it."

A silly grin spread across his face as he drifted off into his fantasy world again. "And to think, I used to resent dressing up and helping you with the catering."

"How times do change," she said with a shake of her head. "Well, I guess I'd better call it a night. I've got to get started bright and early in the morning. You ready to head out?" She looked at her brother.

"I'm all set." He rose and grabbed a piece of pizza to take with him. "Race you home."

"No way. The last thing you need is a speeding ticket."

"Aw, Elise . . . You're no fun."

"Good night, Zach." She dug in her purse for her keys and accidentally dropped her lottery tickets.

"You're still buying lottery tickets?" Zach asked.

"You'd better believe it, especially tonight. I was feeling really lucky after I left Aaron."

"Didn't your dad always buy them?"

"You remember that?"

"Oh, yeah. He always swore he was going to be a big winner one day."

"Well, I'm carrying on his tradition." She picked up her tickets and safely stowed them away again. "The pot's up to over ten million dollars. If I win . . . no, *when* I win, it'll be only the Ritz, limousines, and Dom Perignon for me—no more pizza in a garage at midnight."

"You ready, Elise?" Rod opened the door for her.

"Yes. Good night, Zach, and thanks for the party."

With that, she and Rod were gone.

Zach stood in the doorway of the garage staring after them until their tail lights had disappeared from view. He turned then and looked around him. The heavily shadowed workshop looked abandoned. It was certainly a far cry from the Ritz. The cars parked inside for repairs looked dead and abandoned. To the untrained eye, the walls where the myriad of tools of his trade hung looked like a scene from a nightmare. It wasn't pretty, artistic, or sophisticated. It was just his life. And he loved it.

"The Ritz, limousines, and Dom Perignon . . ." he muttered to himself as he returned to his office to finish off his daily paperwork.

Zach sat at the desk and picked up the last piece of pizza, intending to finish it off. As he stared at the cold pizza in his work-scarred hand, he realized he was not Ritz or Dom Perignon material. He was just Zach Thomas, who loved to work on cars.

In irritation, Zach tossed the slice aside. Scowling, he went back to work.

Chapter Two

Elise stood proudly in the banquet hall as all around her the entire press corps, along with reporters from all the major TV and radio stations, and the elite of the city's society celebrated the beginning of the professional football season. Players and coaches mixed with socialites, newsmen, and bankers. All were partaking of her fancy canapes and commenting on the wonderful decorations and theme for the evening's event.

"Magnificent, my dear," Aaron breathed in her ear as he came to stand next to her.

Elise glanced up at him and her breath caught in her throat. In a tux, she found him to be even more handsome and sophisticated than usual, and that was hard to believe. "You like the party?"

"I love it. The jungle theme . . . the waterfall . . . tropical flowers . . . How did you manage all this?"

"Secrets of the trade," she answered easily, with a smile. She wanted him to think that all had gone smoothly, but the truth be told, she'd had one heck of a time convincing the zoo officials to allow her to use some of their tropical birds in the setting.

"It was a stroke of genius. I especially love the tiger sounds in the background. It adds just the right touch of danger and excitement."

"This is football."

"Do you like sports?"

"I love sports, and I've been a big fan of the Tigers ever since I was a little girl. I used to watch the games with my father. I know this is only your first season as owner, but I think you're going places."

"I hope so. I want to win the Super Bowl, and with a few strategic trades and the right breaks, I think we'll have a run at it this year."

"I'll be rooting for you."

He grinned down at her as he slipped an arm about her waist and gave her a slight hug. "I'm counting on it."

"Mr. Benedict!" a reporter from the Daily News called him. "Do you have time for a short interview?"

"I have to go," Aaron told Elise. "We'll talk later?"

"I'll be here."

"Good." He flashed her one last, quick smile and moved off to join the eager reporter.

Elise watched him go and wanted to pinch herself, to see if all this was really happening. The comments she'd heard from the guests as she'd made the rounds of the room earlier had made her heart swell. Everyone was enjoying the jungle theme. The waterfall seemed the favorite of many, for cameras were flashing almost constantly as the team's Tiger mascot posed there with fans for pictures.

Taking a glass of champagne from a passing waiter's tray, she took a deep drink. It felt wonderful to be mixing with the rich and famous, and to be accepted by them. She glanced down at the sleek gown she wore. It was the one big splurge she'd allowed herself, for she'd known she had nothing suitable in her wardrobe for an occasion like tonight. Most of her clothes were practical business suits or jeans for relaxing. She'd never done any work of this magnitude before, but she was ready now. Today, she'd proven she was good enough, and she was glad everything had gone so well, for she'd wanted to impress Aaron.

"Well done, Sis," Rod said as he joined her for a minute. He was wearing a tux and had been overseeing the circulating waiters. "There are TV cameras everywhere."

"When Aaron does something, he does it right."

"I'll say. Wow! I even got to meet 'Concrete' McAllister!"

"You did?"

His eyes glowed as he recounted his conversation with his favorite player for the Tigers. "Zach is going to be so jealous!"

"Zach? He likes Concrete, too?"

"Oh, yeah. Zach's his biggest fan. He thinks Concrete is the reason the Tigers will be a contender this year. It's a shame Zach couldn't come with us tonight."

"Do you think he would have had a good time?" She glanced around at all the people dressed to the nines.

"He would have suffered through it for the chance to meet the players. You ought to see if you can get him invited to some of this stuff. He'd love it."

"We'll see." Elise pictured Zach in his tight T-shirts and jeans, and she smiled. She'd never seen him in a tux and wondered how he would have fit in with the rich and famous. Zach was a down-to-earth guy. He cut right to the heart of any situation and dealt with it straight on. It was one of the qualities she liked best about him—his complete honesty.

"I'd better get back to work," Rod told her. "I've got a real mean boss."

"I know . . . a slave driver."

"She brings out the best in me, though."

"You sure?"

"Positive." He winked at her as he moved off.

Elise smiled as she watched him go. Rod was turning into a fine young man, and he was pretty good-looking, too, with his dark coloring and quick smile. She knew their parents would have been proud of him.

The rest of the evening went smoothly. It was nearly two in the morning when she found herself supervising the last of the clean-up.

"Superb," Aaron said when he found her near the back of the ballroom.

"I'm glad everything went so well for you."

"For us. We're a great team, you and I."

"We are?"

He'd been holding a bottle of champagne and two crystal glasses behind his back and he lifted them up now for her to see.

"Here." Aaron handed her a glass and filled it for her, then filled his own. "Congratulations, my dear, on a job well done."

"Thank you," she murmured, enchanted by his thoughtfulness.

She lifted her glass to his and then took a sip just as her eyes met his. For that moment, she was caught up in the power of his blue-eyed gaze. She could easily understand how women fell under the spell of powerful men. Aaron was handsome, wealthy, and sophisticated. What was not to like? She found herself smiling at him, and she barely tasted the champagne.

"To us," he said softly, taking a deep drink from his own glass. He was about to say more when Rod called out.

"Elise! I've brought the van around. Are you ready to start loading?"

His call shattered the intimacy of the moment and jarred her back to reality. "I'd better finish getting things cleaned up." She set her empty glass aside.

"We'll talk next week?"

She nodded. "I'll have the first tentative plans for the big fund-raiser ready for you to go over by mid-week."

"I'll be looking forward to it."

She flashed him a smile and started to turn away.

"Elise?"

She looked back, and Aaron was still there, his gaze warm upon her.

"Good night," he said gently.

"Good night," she responded, and then hurried off to work with Rod.

Aaron had enjoyed the evening, but he'd enjoyed even more watching Elise pull the entire celebration together. Elise Mathews was a very talented woman.

Rod immediately collapsed into bed when they finally got back home in the early-morning hours. It was Sunday night, and he had classes the next morning.

Elise, however, was too excited to even think about sleeping. She'd done it! The media party had gone off without a hitch! She changed into comfortable casual clothes, then went to work on the fund-raiser. It had to be even bigger and better than the media party had been.

"Haven't you been to bed yet?" Rod's sleep-heavy voice jarred her from her work hours later.

"Oh, hi! No, I had a couple of ideas for the next party, and I wanted to get them down on paper." She suddenly realized that sunlight was shining through the windows.

"You must be exhausted."

"I am, but it's worth it. It went great, didn't it?" She turned to look at him.

"It was wonderful."

She beamed at his praise. "I've got to be even better with this next one. That's why I went straight to work on it last night."

"Well, get some sleep today. I'm gonna shower

and get out of here. I've got a nine o'clock class,"
he groaned.

"Do you work tonight?"

"No. It's my night off, but I've got a hot date with
Susie Johnson."

"Not too hot, I hope."

"Aw, Sis, you worry too much."

"It's my job," she said with a grin as he stumbled
into the bathroom to shower and shave.

Elise watched him go, proud of the man he was
becoming.

It was almost noon when she finally decided to
rest. She was so tired, she didn't even bother to
undress before she fell across her bed. She was
asleep almost as soon as her head hit the pillow.

The sound of the doorbell hours later finally
awakened her. She buried her head even deeper
in her pillow, but whoever was at the door was
not going away. Cursing under her breath, she
dragged herself from bed and went to see who was
so insistent on waking her. She smoothed her hair
back and opened the door, not caring that her
clothes were rumpled.

"What is it?" she asked, then discovered it was
Zach. "Oh . . . Zach. Hi."

A slow, lazy grin spread across his face as his
gaze swept over her. "You were sleeping?"

"Um . . ." she said, stifling a yawn as she held
the door wide for him. "You want to come in?"

"Sure." He moved past her into the small, two-
story house. "How did the party go?"

"Just great. I think Aaron was pleased."

"Good, I'm glad to hear that. Is Rod here? I

needed to tell him something about work tomorrow."

"No, he had a date tonight. I haven't talked to him since this morning."

"Well, just tell him that I need him to come in as early as possible."

"I'll tell him," she said wearily.

"How late did you stay up last night? You look completely worn out."

"Actually, I didn't get to bed until almost noon."

"Why?"

"I had a great idea for the next event. It's a charity ball, and I promised Aaron I'd have the first plans to him by Wednesday."

"You're not going to get anything to him if you kill yourself in the process. When was the last time you ate?"

She frowned. "I don't know. Some time early yesterday, I guess. I didn't eat last night at the party because I was too excited."

"How about I fix you something before I go?" He glanced toward her kitchen, knowing she probably had a well-stocked pantry.

It had been so long since anyone had worried about her that she was startled by the kindness of his offer. "What?"

"Something to eat. You're a caterer. Surely, you've got something in the kitchen I can turn into a meal for you."

"But—"

"You're tired, right?"

"Very."

"You need to eat, right?"

"Yes," she agreed with a small smile.

"Well?" Zach grinned at her.

He looked so earnest that Elise didn't know what else to say, so she simply said, "Thanks."

"Go rest. I'll call you when it's ready."

He disappeared into the kitchen, leaving her standing alone in the living room. She wasn't used to the luxury of someone waiting on her. She almost felt a little useless, but she was too tired to worry about it. Taking Zach's advice, she decided to take a shower and freshen up. She knew she must look a mess, and she would certainly feel brighter once she'd cleaned up her act.

While Elise showered, Zach checked out her pantry. He found the pasta he'd sought and then dug through her cabinets for the pots he needed. As he'd suspected, she had homemade sauce in the refrigerator. He tested it, searched for her spices and added his own twist to her concoction. A head of lettuce provided the base for a salad, and he added butter and garlic salt to rolls before popping them into the oven. Satisfied that she'd have enough to eat, he sat down at the kitchen table to wait for her return.

As he glanced toward the pantry again, he spied the stub of a candle on the top shelf. If he was fixing her an Italian dinner, the least he could do was provide the right atmosphere, too. . . .

Chapter Three

Elise emerged from the shower to find the mouth-watering aroma of Italian cooking filling the house. She threw on jeans and a sweater, then quickly dried her hair. Not bothering with makeup, she headed for the kitchen, more than ready for whatever her personal chef had prepared. To her surprise, the kitchen was dark.

"Zach? What happened? Did you blow a fuse?" she asked as she started into the room. She stopped short when she saw the one and only pitiful candle she kept in case of power outages burning brightly in the top of a two-liter soda bottle in the middle of her kitchen table.

"Welcome to Tomaso's Ristorante," he said in a terrible mock-Italian accent.

"Thank you, sir," she responded, playing along.

"We live to please our customers." He bowed

and held a chair out for her. "Have a seat."

Elise found herself giggling at his antics as she slipped into the chair. She'd been working so hard for so long that she'd almost forgotten what it was like just to relax and have fun. "It's a good thing you have a day job."

"I am sorely wounded." He put a hand to his heart and tried to sound aggrieved.

"Oh, I'm sorry. It does smell delicious, and I'm sure you must have worked hard to achieve this wonderful atmosphere—"

"I would have used a Chianti bottle and been really authentic, but I couldn't find one," Zach joked, dropping his accent. "How hungry are you?"

"Very."

He quickly placed a delicious-looking salad before her. "Do you mind if the hired help eats with you?"

"You mean I'm paying you?" she teased.

"You better believe it."

"How much? Union scale?"

"Better. One smile, and all the pasta I can eat. Deal?"

"Deal."

"I didn't know you liked to cook," she remarked, digging into the salad.

He shrugged. "If there's time, it can be fun, but usually I'm too busy or too tired when I get off work. Fast food can become a way of life if you let it."

"I understand completely."

"So tell me all about your media party. I read the gossip column in the paper this morning, and the columnist was sure singing your praises. I'll bet your phone at the office is ringing off the hook with job offers."

"Good. Job security and a guaranteed income are wonderful things, especially with college tuition and Rod's car insurance." She paused to take a bite. "Ummm—what did you do to the salad dressing? It's really different."

"An old family secret. My mother was Italian, so I picked up a few cooking hints here and there."

Zach dug into his own salad as Elise told him everything that had happened at the party.

"Aaron even said we made a great team," she finished, remembering clearly his words to her. A thrill shot through her, and her eyes gleamed with excitement.

Zach had been watching Elise as she talked. Her loose dark hair curled softly around her shoulders. It looked silken, and he wondered if it would be that sleek to the touch. Her complexion was flawless, and her eyes were dark and expressive. She was his idea of gorgeous. He wondered idly if she had any idea how he felt about her, and realized she didn't. She considered him a good friend, and he'd never done anything to disabuse her of that belief. Anytime either one of them had been available, the other had been involved with someone else.

Tonight, however, in the candlelight, celebrating her success with her, his feelings stirred and came fully to life. He wanted her.

"You know, I do have a bottle of Merlot in the basement if you want some," she said, thinking a glass of wine would go well with the meal.

"I should have thought to check your wine cellar earlier."

"I keep my aged stock downstairs."

They both laughed. Her throaty chuckle stirred him even more. "I think I would like some."

"I'll get it," she offered. "If you'll get the glasses. I have some fine plastic ones there in the cabinet over the sink."

"I've always been partial to better plastic," he responded, going to claim the poor man's substitute for crystal while she went to retrieve the bottle from the basement.

He opened it for her when she returned, then poured them each a glass.

"Ah . . . Candlelight, fine wine, a beautiful woman . . ." He settled back in his chair as he took a drink. "Not bad."

"You're right. Candlelight, fine wine, and a good-looking man make for a great evening," she agreed.

He chuckled. "How did your lottery tickets do last week? The jackpot's really up there."

"You know, I've been so busy, I didn't even check the numbers the other morning!" She jumped up and got the tickets off the front of the refrigerator where she'd left them under a magnet. She grabbed the morning paper and searched for the right page. "Let's see. Maybe I'm a winner!"

Zach watched in amusement as she scanned the numbers in the paper and on her tickets. Her expression went from hopeful to pained.

"Nothing," she complained. "Not even one number matched, and I bought all these tickets! I'm just a loser, with a capital L."

"Aren't we all when it comes to the lottery? I just figure we're donating to someone else's millions."

"That's the truth. But my dad always said I'd be rich one day, and I'm holding him to that."

"Was he psychic?"

"No, but my dad never lied to me."

"It's a happy thought, but in the meantime, I think we both have to keep working."

"There is a connection, isn't there?" She finished off her glass of wine and held it out to him for more.

Zach obliged just as the buzzer went off on the stove. "Are you ready for your next course?"

"It smells wonderful."

He dished up full plates of pasta and sauce for both of them, and put the platter of hot garlic bread dripping with melted butter on the table. They began to eat in earnest then, and her expression reflected her delight in his culinary talents. The look on her face was so rapt that Zach finished off his wine, poured another full glass, and downed most of it.

"Thank you." She sighed blissfully as she sat back after eating almost every bite on her plate. "I don't usually eat this much, but that was delicious."

"If my shop goes out of business, you can back me in a little Italian restaurant."

"You're on, but we'd have to think of a good name for it."

"You don't like Tomaso's Ristorante?"

"If I'm backing you, I want equal billing."

"Spoken like a true nineties woman. Let's just hope I don't end up cooking for a living. I'm much better with engines than I am with stoves."

"Rod says you do have a way with cars."

"I love them. They're sleek and powerful. There's nothing like the feeling I get when I've been rebuilding an engine, and I finally get it right. When it roars to life." A smile curved his lips at the thought.

Elise found herself staring at his mouth, wondering why she'd never noticed how handsomely chiseled his features were. The shadow of a day's growth of beard darkened his lean jaw. As she lifted her gaze to his, she found his dark-eyed regard upon her, his expression unreadable. Her pulse quickened in instinctive response, and that puzzled her. This was Zach.

"You like the feeling of power?" Her voice was almost breathless as she took another sip of wine.

"I like knowing these hands had the power to bring it back to life," he said quietly.

Elise let her gaze drop to his hands. They were strong hands, powerful, yet capable of the most delicate of touches, she was sure. Otherwise he wouldn't be able to do what he did so well. She looked up at him again, and, in that instant, their gazes locked.

Time stood still. Awareness of their surroundings faded, until it was just the two of them, alone in the soft, flickering candlelight.

The instinct was older than time, and Zach responded to it. He rose and went to her, taking her hand in his and drawing her up to him. He didn't speak, not daring to risk ruining the moment. There were just the two of them, alone in the semi-darkness.

Zach bent to her, slowly, gently, fearful of breaking the spell that had woven itself around them. Elise was caught up in the moment, aware only of the sensual scent of his aftershave and the warmth of his hand holding hers. When his lips sought hers, she gasped slightly, but did not draw away. Encouraged, he brought her into the circle of his arms.

The wine had cast a warm glow over the moment, and Elise gave herself over to the sweetness of it. Held close to his heart, she lifted her arms to link them around his neck. It felt right to be in his embrace.

Her move was an invitation that sent a jolt of awareness through Zach. He shuddered as he deepened the kiss, his mouth moving hungrily over hers. He had wanted—no needed—her for a long time.

Elise responded to his kiss with equal fervor, enjoying the feel of his hard, muscular body. She moved against him, tangling her fingers in the hair at the nape of his neck as she gave herself over to the unexpected thrill of his nearness.

"What smells so good?" Rod called out as he came through the front door.

At the sound of his voice, they moved quickly apart.

"Zach cooked dinner for me," Elise called back. She went to stand at the sink just as her younger brother strode into the kitchen with Susie on his arm.

"You cook?" Rod glanced at Zach where he was sitting in a chair at the table, looking quite relaxed, downing a glass of wine.

"You can't eat pizza every day," he returned easily, revealing none of the turmoil that was churning inside him as he finished off his wine and poured what was left in the bottle into his glass.

"I didn't know you were coming over tonight. If I had, Susie and I would have hurried home."

"I didn't know I was coming by either, but just as I was getting ready to close, three rush jobs came in. I stopped off hoping I'd catch you to tell you to come in as early as possible tomorrow."

"I'll be over right after class."

"Good." Zach drained the glass and stood up to go. "Elise, thanks for dinner."

"My pleasure," she answered with forced ease. "You did all the cooking."

Her smile was tight, but only Zach noticed.

"Good night. I'll show myself out, and I'll see you tomorrow," he said to Rod.

Zach got in his car, but he didn't immediately drive off. Instead, he sat there, staring sightlessly at the steering wheel. One minute he'd been in heaven and the next . . . In frustration, he started the car and pulled away from the curb. It was going to be one long, lonely night.

Elise visited with Rod and Susie for a few minutes longer as she finished cleaning up the kitchen, then excused herself and went to her room. She was still tired and would have slept, except the memory of Zach's unexpected embrace was burned into her consciousness. Restless and confused, she sat down at her desk and went back to work. Aaron expected these plans to be on time, and she wanted them to be perfect.

As the hours passed, though, Elise realized she

wasn't getting a lot done. Mostly, she'd been sitting there, thinking about Zach. She'd known him for years and had never realized just what a strong, handsome man he was. She wondered what had ever possessed him to kiss her that way and realized it had probably been the wine and the candlelight. It didn't get much more romantic than Tomaso's Ristorante.

Elise smiled, and tried to go back to work.

Chapter Four

"You have reached Catering Elegance. We're out of the office, but will be glad to return your call. Please leave your name and number, and we'll get back to you as quickly as possible. Thanks."

Zach glared at the phone, blaming it for his misfortune in missing Elise again. This was his fourth attempt that day. He hadn't left messages the other times and decided not to leave one now. Sooner or later, he was bound to catch her at her desk. He hung up and went back into the shop.

He started working on a car with a vengeance, wanting to banish the memory of Elise's kiss. It kept haunting him. It had even kept him up most of Monday night, and that was why he wanted to see her again. He needed to find out if she had reacted the same way as he had to their embrace.

He had spoken to her Tuesday morning, but the

conversation had been short and stilted. She'd been at the office, surrounded by her staff, poring over the plans for the Tigers' charity event that she had to present to Benedict that week. She'd ended their two-minute conversation by telling him to call her the following week.

Here it was a week later, and he still hadn't managed to get in touch with her. He'd been wanting to ask her out. The fund-raising event was that following weekend, and he was hoping she'd have some time to relax. Things just weren't working out, though.

Earlier in the day, he'd wondered if he was missing a subtle message, but when Rod had come in to work, he'd told him how hard she'd been working on the event all week, putting in fifteen-hour days, and how excited she was about her meetings with Benedict. It seemed they were meeting every day to go over the plans. Zach knew she was just doing her job, but he was finding it difficult to be patient when he remembered the sweetness of her kiss. . . .

"We are switching to our remote at Tigers Headquarters," the radio personality announced, interrupting their scheduled programming. *"Tigers owner Aaron Benedict has called a news conference to begin in three minutes. Reporter Dan Tyler is on site. Tell us, Dan, what's the word on the street?"*

"Rumors have been flying all morning about possible trades, but no one seems to know anything for sure. We'll just have to wait and see what Aaron Benedict has to say."

Both Zach and Rod looked up at the radio in surprise at this news.

"I wonder what's going on," Rod said.

"Hard telling with this new guy in charge," Zach replied.

"Good afternoon, ladies and gentlemen," Aaron Benedict said after coming to the lectern to make his announcement. *"I'm here today to announce some exciting changes we've just made in player personnel. As of today, Ace Knowlen and Concrete McAllister have been traded to the Washington Redskins for Derek Jones and a future first-round draft choice."*

"What?" Zach and Rod both yelled, sharing the same furious expression as they stared at the radio.

"That no-good—" Zach swore.

"I can't believe he'd do something like this!" Rod blurted out. "Trading McAllister! Doesn't he realize how important he is to the team? Doesn't he realize how many fans he's going to alienate?"

"I guess he just doesn't care." Zach was disgusted.

"This is terrible. The season might as well be over."

The announcer came back on as Benedict ended his announcements and left the podium. *"Fan reaction here in town is going to be interesting. Concrete is a favorite. His following is phenomenal."*

The station cut to an interview with a furious fan who wanted McAllister to stay and Benedict to go, and Zach walked over and turned off the radio.

"And Elise likes him? Unbelievable," he said. "The man's obviously an idiot. Trade Concrete McAllister? He's our best player!"

"*Was* our best player," Rod corrected.

Zach shot him an angry look. "How could Benedict get rid of Concrete? And why would he want to?"

"There has to be something going on. Maybe Elise will know when she gets home tonight. I'll ask her."

"It won't make any difference to me. I'll never root for the Tigers again. Not without Concrete."

"You're not going to start rooting for the Redskins, are you?" Rod was aghast.

"You just never know," he answered, still scowling. "I had some hope a couple of months ago when Benedict first bought the team, but now I think he's the worst owner ever. We should get all of Concrete's fans together and run Benedict out of town."

"It wouldn't bring Concrete back," Rod mourned.

"I know, but I'd feel better." And Zach knew he would feel better if Benedict was gone. Elise might have a free minute. Of course, she might be out of a job then, too. He scowled, wanting the best for her, but resenting the rich owner.

The sound of the phone ringing distracted him from his dark thoughts, and he wiped off his hands and went to answer it.

"Collision Plus," he answered in a gruff tone.

"Zach? Thank heaven you're still there!" Elise sounded upset.

"Elise? What's the matter? Is something wrong?" He immediately tensed at the sound of her voice. "Are you all right?"

"Oh, I'm fine, but my car's not. I was just leaving

Aaron's office, and it won't start. I tried to get Rod, but he wasn't home. Could you come down and tow me in? I don't know what's the matter with it, other than it's just worn out." Her worry was obvious.

"Where are you?"

"In the high-rise garage right across from Aaron's office building. It's at Sixth and Broadway."

"I'll be there in less than half an hour." He asked her a few more detailed questions about what was wrong with the vehicle and hung up.

As much as Zach was sorry she was having car trouble, at least this presented him with the perfect opportunity to be alone with her. He would have preferred to be cleaned up when he went to see her again and not wearing his dirty work clothes, but if she was having car trouble, she'd be glad enough to see him no matter what he looked like.

"Rod, that was Elise on the phone. Her car's quit on her, so I'm going down now to tow her in."

"I'll go with you." Rod stopped what he was doing, ready to help.

"No, you stay here and keep working. We gotta get that car back to the owner tomorrow." He gestured toward the vehicle Rod had been working on. "I'll be back as soon as I can. If anything else comes up, just call me on the radio."

"You got it. Geez, I hope it's nothing too bad with Elise's car. Of the two we've got, hers is the best."

"If anybody can fix it, we can," Zach said confidently. "I'll be back."

He made the trek downtown in record time, considering the near rush-hour traffic, and located the garage she was parked in with no trouble. He found Elise standing next to her dead car on the third level. She looked so downhearted that he found himself smiling as he climbed out.

"It's not that bad. It's not like your best friend died or something."

"It feels like it," she countered, managing a weak smile as she looked at her older, very overworked car. It had more than a hundred and fifty thousand miles on it, but it was all she had. "The day was going so well, and now—"

"Relax. It could be something really simple. Let me take a quick look."

He opened the hood of her car. After getting into her vehicle and trying to start it up several times with no luck, he took one last look at the engine and slammed the hood shut.

"Well?" she asked expectantly.

He approached her solemnly, like a doctor reporting on life-or-death surgery, but there was a twinkle in his eyes. "It's going to require work—but it'll live."

"Oh, you!" She was laughing now. It always amazed her how Zach could lighten her mood. No matter how bad things seemed to be, he always found a way to make her feel better. A distant memory of how he'd been there for her when her parents were killed returned. He'd been her rock, always there, always supporting her in a quiet sort of way.

"I'm going to have to take it in to figure out exactly what's wrong, but I can drop you by your house on the way, if you want."

"That'd be great. Thanks."

Zach climbed back into his truck and positioned it to hook up to her car. After taking care of all the cables and making sure it was secure, he opened the passenger-side door and spread a reasonably clean towel on the seat. She looked so elegant that he didn't want to risk getting her dirty.

"Want me to help you climb in? We're about ready to go."

"Thanks."

Even though she was wearing her best business suit and heels, Elise didn't hesitate. She grabbed her briefcase and purse and went to Zach. He took her things from her, stowed them safely behind the seat, and then offered her a hand up. She took it and allowed him to help her up into the cab. As she settled in, Zach shut the door and circled the truck to climb in himself.

"I really appreciate all your help with this," Elise said as he put the truck in gear.

"That's what friends are for."

"What a mess." She sounded exhausted. "I've got so much work to do with the charity event on Saturday, and now I'm going to be car-impaired."

"So that's the socially correct term for it?"

"Car-less, wheel-less and car-deprived work, too," she quipped.

Zach was laughing as he started to pull away with her vehicle in tow. He was about to swing clear when a limo blocked his way. He slammed on the breaks to avoid a collision.

"What the hell . . . ?" he snarled, angry that the

other driver could have caused a wreck right there in the garage.

As he was swearing, the window rolled down in the back of the limo and Aaron Benedict looked out at him.

"Elise! My secretary just told me about your misfortune. There's no need for you to ride home in a tow truck. I'm leaving the office now, and I can drop you by your house."

She was completely caught off guard by Aaron's offer. She'd made the call from his secretary's desk because he'd been in a business meeting, and she hadn't even known that he'd been aware of her problem.

"Well, Zach was going to—"

"I'm sure Zach wouldn't mind delivering your car to you once it's repaired," Aaron said with challenging arrogance as he looked straight past Zach at her.

Zach's grip tightened on the steering wheel. He wanted Elise with him. He'd been looking forward to having a few minutes alone with her for days, and now Benedict—

"We can go over those last few details you were talking about earlier," Aaron called out, appealing to the businesswoman in her.

"Zach?" Elise looked to him, to see what he thought. "Do you mind?"

"Do whatever you want to do," he replied nonchalantly. His own acting ability was amazing him. "You know where I'll be."

"Thanks," she told him, thrilled that Aaron thought enough of her to offer her a ride.

Gathering her things, she slipped quickly from

the cab and hurried to get into the limo.

As she entered the luxury vehicle and settled back on the leather seat, Zach was treated to a quick glimpse of slender thigh before the door slammed shut. He stared after the limo as it pulled away and then looked around himself at the well-used interior of his tow truck. He gave a shake of his head as he pulled out with her car in tow.

Zach knew he couldn't be angry over Elise's decision to ride with Benedict. Who would want to ride with him when they could ride in a limo? He'd known all along how Elise felt about being rich; no doubt riding with Benedict would feel like a dream come true, and he wouldn't want to deny her that chance. She'd have been crazy to pass it up.

He sighed and maneuvered his way out of the parking garage and into traffic. He wanted to get back to the garage as quickly as possible so he could start working on her car tonight. As he headed for Collision Plus, the only thing that was really bothering him was that she was riding with Benedict.

"I'm sorry about your bad luck with your car," Aaron was saying as he sat back next to Elise in the plush interior.

"Me, too. Car trouble was the last thing I needed with the event coming up Saturday."

"Do you think he'll be able to fix it in time?"

"If it can be fixed, Zach can do it. He's the most talented mechanic I've ever met. He has a way with cars that's just amazing."

"Interesting," Aaron replied, not really caring.

He just wanted to make sure she was taken care of. "Well, if things don't work out right, just let me know and I'll send a car for you."

"That's very kind of you, but I should be all right."

"Do you have plans for the evening?" he asked, changing the entire mood of the moment.

"Only work, why?"

"What do you say we have dinner?"

"Now?" Her eyes widened at the prospect. Aaron Benedict had just asked her out.

"Now," he replied. "I've got a nine o'clock meeting, but I'm free until then. I'd been wanting to spend some time with you away from work—to get to know you better."

His statement surprised and pleased her. "I'd love to have dinner with you."

He smiled at her and gave orders to the driver to take them to one of the best restaurants in town.

"At last, we can relax for a while."

"I don't think I remember how," she said with a rueful laugh.

"I'll teach you," he said in a low voice.

His words sent a shiver of awareness up her spine.

Their conversation turned to other topics as they settled into an easy companionship.

"I'm sure my brother Rod and Zach aren't happy with you right now."

"The trade?"

"Exactly. Concrete has been their favorite player for years. Trading him is not going to sit well with them or the other fans. Why did you do it?"

"It was strictly a business decision," he answered, having anticipated the reaction that he knew would be forthcoming from the disgruntled fans. "I'm sure they'll get over it in time."

"Maybe, maybe not," she countered. "Concrete was involved in a lot of charity work around the city, and people really relate to him and like him."

Aaron gave her a benign smile. "Once they see what a great team we're building, they'll get over it."

"I hope you're right for the team's sake. It doesn't pay to alienate the fans."

"If we're winning, they'll be with us. Everyone likes a winner," he answered confidently as the limo stopped at the door of the restaurant.

Their dinner was magnificent. Elise had dined there before when she'd been trying to come up with new and more exciting ways to promote her business. She'd been impressed then and was even more impressed with the standard of service and the delicious food tonight.

"Aaron, this was wonderful. Thank you so much for this evening," she said as she finished dessert.

"It was my pleasure, believe me. What's your calendar look like for the rest of the week?"

"Work, work, and work. Being self-employed is rough. The boss knows exactly what you can get done in any given length of time and expects you to deliver."

"It's not much easier being in the corporate world. At least as your own boss, you have some semblance of control."

"You have control," she countered. "You own the team."

"And that's precisely why I bought them without taking on any investment partners. I want to be the one who makes the decisions—good or bad. It will fall on my shoulders, and I'll take the praise or the flak, whichever comes."

Elise found herself admiring him even more as she teased, "You're going to get a lot of flak about Concrete."

"I just want them to give me a chance. Like I said before, once we're winning, they'll understand why I made the moves."

She lifted her glass of wine to him. "To a winning season for the Tigers."

"Here, here," he seconded, and touched glasses with her.

Aaron had met a lot of beautiful women, but there was something about Elise that set her apart from the others. Maybe it was her willingness to speak her mind with him or just the openness of her personality, but whatever it was, he was drawn to it.

"Elise, I was wondering—"

She looked at him expectantly and realized again just how good-looking he was. His blond hair was razor cut, and the short style was perfect on him. Fierce, competitive intelligence burned in his blue eyes, and she knew he was a force to be reckoned with.

"Would you be my official date for the charity event?"

She blinked, surprised and thrilled by his offer. "I'd love to, but . . ."

"No buts." He stopped her. "I know you have to supervise everything. I'll be busy with the media and players, too. We'll both be taking care of business all night, but I would love to have you on my arm whenever you can get away from your responsibilities for a few minutes. What do you say?"

"Thank you, Aaron. I'd love to be your date Saturday night."

A short time later they were in the limo on the way to Elise's home.

"I'll see you tomorrow?" Aaron asked.

"I don't know. I'm going to be running all over town taking care of last-minute details."

"Well, if you get the time, stop by the office for a few minutes. I'd love to see you."

At his words, she looked up at him as he sat beside her, and in that moment, Aaron boldly took her in his arms and kissed her.

It was Elise's Cinderella dream come true. She was in a luxury car being kissed by a rich, handsome man. She turned to him, kissing him back, enjoying the moment as the car came to a halt in front of her house. When he released her, she smiled at him.

"Good night, Aaron."

"Good night, Elise. I'm looking forward to Saturday night."

His words followed her as she left the car, and she stood there on the walk up to her house watching as his driver pulled away. Only when she turned around did she realize that Zach and Rod were standing on the front porch waiting for her.

Chapter Five

A heated flush stained Elise's cheeks as her gaze met Zach's, and she was glad for the concealing darkness.

"Not too shabby coming home in a limo, Sis," Rod quipped, completely missing the tension between them.

"Aaron decided to take me out for dinner," she returned as she moved to join them. "Hi, Zach. Did you manage to get my car fixed already? I was just telling Aaron how good you were."

"I'd love to tell you that it was that simple and already repaired, but it's not. That's why I came over. I know you've got the big fund-raiser Saturday and you'll need wheels, so I brought you something to drive until I get the part in I have to order for you."

"How long is it going to take?"

"If the distributor has it in stock, I can have it Monday and have your car ready by Monday night. Until then . . . Well, here are the keys to the car I'll give you as a loaner." He held the key chain out to her.

"Are you giving me the tow truck to drive?" she asked with a laugh. Their hands touched as she took it from him, and she realized how kind it was of him to have taken care of her this way.

"No way, Elise," Rod spoke up. "Zach knows how much that charity event means to you. Take a look at what he parked around back for you to drive for the rest of the week."

She glanced quizzically at the two men, then left the porch to circle the house, leaving them to follow. She was amazed to find Zach's restored '65 Mustang Fastback waiting for her. She couldn't believe he was being so generous. She knew how much the car meant to him, how long he'd been working on it.

"Your carriage awaits you, ma'am," Zach said gallantly.

"I can't drive this," she protested.

"Why not?" He was startled by her refusal, and thought for a moment that, since she'd been riding around in limos all night, she didn't want to be seen in such an old car.

"Because this is your pride and joy." She looked at him with amazement. "You've worked hard to restore it. What if something happened to it? I'd never forgive myself."

"It's heavily insured. Besides, if something does happen, I know this guy who does great auto body work—"

She laughed at his good humor. "But Zach . . ."

"Don't worry about a thing. I want you to drive it. You'll look great in it."

Elise was grinning at the thought of being behind the wheel of the shiny red Fastback 2+2. "I will, won't I?"

"It may not be as classy as the limousines you're getting used to, but—" he began.

"It's classier," she said in all seriousness. "Thanks, Zach. This is so sweet of you." On impulse, she leaned toward him and kissed him on the cheek.

"Ah, Sis," Rod said lightening the moment. "Zach isn't being sweet. He's being a good businessman. This is just good customer service."

"So you loan your Mustang out to all your customers?" she asked them both.

"Hardly," Zach said with a grin.

"That's what I thought, but you know, it's an idea. They have Rent-A-Wreck. How about opening Rent-A-Hot Mustang? You'd do a booming business on Prom Night."

"And think of the cost of insurance. Great idea, Elise, but I think I'll pass for now." Zach shook his head at the thought of a teenager on Prom night behind the wheel of his favorite car.

"You know, you ought to come to the fundraiser Saturday night. It should be fun."

"How dressy is it?"

"Formal."

"I'd hate to pull up in the tow truck wearing a tux. Since you're going to have my best set of wheels, would you want to pick me up?" he suggested, thinking that at last they'd be having a real date and get to spend some time together.

"I would love to, but I can't."

"You're going to be working too much?"

"That, and Aaron asked me to be with him for the evening. I can get you tickets and Rod could pick you up, though—if you'd like to go," she offered, trying to help solve his dilemma.

"I'll have to check and see. It'll depend on work," he replied evasively. "I'll let you know."

"Great." She looked back at his perfectly restored car and was thrilled at the thought that she was actually going to get to drive it. There was a twinkle in her eyes as she asked Zach, "You need a ride home, don't you?"

"I could walk, but a ride would be nice."

"Let's go, but there's one condition."

"What's that?" he asked, wondering what she was up to.

"I'm driving."

"You're on."

"Good. Rod, I'll be back in a few minutes." Keys in hand, she climbed into the sports car.

"The lady's driving." Zach shrugged and smiled, managing to sound carefree as he, too, got in.

Elise started the car and grinned at the roar of the powerful engine. She glanced over at Zach and gave him a daredevilish look. "You're really going to trust me with this?"

"Am I making a mistake?" he countered, meeting her regard with a challenging look of his own.

"Let's find out." She gave it gas and they raced from the driveway, turned sharply, and with a squeal of tires disappeared down the street. She glanced only once in the rearview mirror to see her brother running out into the street to watch them drive off.

Neither Elise nor Zach spoke as she drove around town. She was enjoying controlling the muscle car. Occasionally, she glanced over at Zach to see whether she was making him nervous, but he seemed relaxed and happy. They'd been driving for about twenty minutes when he spoke up.

"Turn in at White's." He pointed toward the old, circular drive-in restaurant where everyone went to hang out their senior year in high school.

"Think we'll impress the kids?" she asked as she pulled into a parking place.

"No, but I always promised myself that one day I'd show 'em. I'd come here in my hot car and look really cool."

"You did?" She stared at him in amazement.

"Yeah," he said, grinning at her and looking boyish. "But that was over ten years ago. The people I was trying to impress are long gone."

"I never knew you cared about impressing anyone."

"There's only one person I want to impress now . . ." Zach's gaze caught and held hers. He started to lean toward her, instinct guiding him. He wanted—no needed—to kiss her again.

"Nice car, lady!"

The intimacy of the special moment vanished as a teenage carhop came running up to take their order.

"Had it long?" he asked eagerly.

"Less than an hour," she replied. "It's really his."

"Excellent," the boy said, nodding approvingly

to Zach as he checked out the rest of the Mustang.

"Thanks. A lot of work went into restoring it," Zach told him.

"I can tell. Someday, I'm going to have a car like this."

Across the width of the car, Zach and Elise shared a knowing smile.

"What'll ya have?" the teen asked, forcing himself to get back to work and quit dreaming about fast cars.

They gave him their orders, surprising each other as they both ordered the same thing—a chocolate shake. When the boy had dashed off to place their order, Elise turned off the headlights, and they settled in to wait. They watched the comings and goings of the drive-in with easy companionship and discovered that it was still the popular place it had been years ago. Their shakes were delivered, and Zach insisted on paying. They devoured them quickly, and Elise groaned as she finished off the last of hers.

"That was delicious," she sighed, closing her eyes in ecstasy. "Thanks, Zach."

"You're welcome."

His gaze was warm upon her as he thought of how beautiful she looked tonight. He was about to tell her that when she sat up straight and started the engine and turned on the lights.

"Are you ready?"

"If you are," he answered, sorry that they couldn't stay longer, sorry that their earlier moment had been interrupted and he'd been unable to recapture it.

"Whether I want to be or not, I have to be back

at work first thing in the morning. The closer Saturday gets, the more harried I get."

"It'll be fine. You did a great job on the media party. You'll be great again Saturday."

"I'm glad you think so."

"I know so."

She felt buoyed by his confidence in her and smiled at him just as the carhop came for their tray. She pulled out of White's onto the main street.

"One more stop and then I'd better get you home. It's getting late," she told him.

"You don't have to worry about me. I don't have a curfew."

"So I wouldn't get into any trouble if I kept you out past midnight?"

"None whatsoever."

She pulled into a convenience mart and parked. "I'll be right back."

"What are you doing?"

"I haven't gotten my lottery ticket yet. The drawing's tomorrow night. Every Friday and Monday, you know."

"Well, wait a minute. I'll go with you and get one of my own."

They were back in the car a few minutes later, tickets in hand. Elise had bought ten, Zach only one.

"I can't believe the pot's over forty million, and you only bought one ticket."

"It only takes one ticket to win."

They drove off for Zach's house. Elise pulled into the driveway of the small, brick ranch house.

"I got you here all safe and sound."

"I appreciate it. You want to come in?"

Elise was tempted. They'd been having such fun together, but she knew her job had to come first. Later, when she had money, she would have fun. There was no time now. She had to get back to work first thing in the morning. "No. I've got to get home. I've got too much work to do to take time out for any more fun, darn it."

"Whenever you're ready, just let me know."

"I will, believe me."

Emboldened by the thought that she really would have liked to spend more time with him, he made his move.

"Elise?"

She turned and found herself in Zach's arms, his lips seeking hers in a passionate exchange. He deepened the kiss, drawing her as close as he could. As heady as her embrace was, Zach was silently cursing himself for not having restored a full-sized '60 sedan. He wanted to get closer to her, to hold her fully against him, and it was proving next to impossible in the cramped quarters of the Fastback.

The power of Zach's embrace left Elise's senses reeling. His gentle touch stirred her, and when his hand sought her breast, she didn't draw away. Logic told her to stop, but her desire overruled the logic of the situation. She'd wanted this ever since that night at her house when he'd first kissed her.

"Oh, Zach . . ." She whispered his name as his lips left hers to trace a pattern of fire down her throat.

She shifted positions then, trying to get closer to him. But the steering wheel and gear shift pro-

325

vided serious obstacles, and she suddenly realized just what she was doing. And she couldn't help herself. She started to giggle.

"Elise?" Zach frowned as he drew back, wondering why she was pulling away from him and why she was laughing.

"I'm sorry," she told him regretfully. "It just struck me as so funny that we're sitting in a driveway, necking like a couple of teenagers. I'm twenty-five and you're how old? Twenty-eight?"

Zach found himself smiling, too, as he gazed at her across the car in the semidarkness. He thought she'd never looked more beautiful. Her eyes were aglow, and there was a slight flush to her cheeks.

"You're beautiful, Elise Matthews." He reached out and touched her cheek.

She savored his caress and then leaned forward to press her lips to his once more. "I've got to go, Zach."

"I know."

He kissed her once more, softly, gently, then opened the door to get out.

"Let me know about Saturday?"

"I'll tell Rod tomorrow."

"Good night."

Zach watched until she'd driven away, then went inside to his solitary bed.

Chapter Six

"Yeah, right," Elise grumbled to herself as she sat at the breakfast table on Saturday morning reading the newspaper. Quoting from the paper, she read her horoscope out loud, " 'You will be irresistible to the opposite sex.' Hah! That'll be the day."

She thought of Zach and might have believed a little of the prediction if he hadn't asked Rod for two tickets for Saturday night—one for him and one for the date he was bringing.

Still in annoyance, Elise continued to read, " 'Money will come your way in a surprising manner.' Yeah, like a regular paycheck . . . 'cause I sure as heck didn't win the lottery again this week. I can't win if I only keep matching two numbers on a ticket! The good news is, they say it'll be worth fifty-two million for Monday night's drawing. 'The future holds unlimited potential for happiness for you as long as you are honest with yourself and follow your dreams.' "

"Who are you talking to?" Rod asked as he walked into the kitchen, yawning.

"Myself. I'm real good company."

"I know. I like you, too."

She smiled at him and tossed him the sports page.

"How soon are you leaving?" He glanced at the clock and saw that it was just seven.

"I need to be down at the hotel by eight to start setting up. I'm taking my change of clothes with me this morning. Aaron has taken a suite at the hotel, and he said I could use it to change and freshen up for tonight."

"So I won't see you again until tonight?"

"Right. You need to be there ready to work at five-thirty. Have you made arrangements with Zach to pick him up?"

"I don't need to. He found another way to get there."

"What's he going to do?"

"I have no idea. He didn't offer, so I didn't ask."

"And he never told you who his date is for the evening?"

"Nope." Rod eyed his sister, wondering why she cared. She and Zach had been friends forever. It seemed odd that she suddenly wanted to know whom he was seeing.

Elise was curious about what arrangements Zach had made for that evening, but she put her curiosity aside. She hadn't had time to talk to him since she'd dropped him off the other night, and he hadn't bothered to call her, either.

"I have to get ready. I want to stop by the gas station and pick up more lottery tickets. Wish me luck."

"On the lottery or tonight?"

"Both."

"I do. It's going to be great. You've done everything right. Tonight is going to be the best night of your life." He tried to sound encouraging.

"You sound like my horoscope." She laughed.

"I hope I'm right."

"So do I." Elise disappeared upstairs to get ready for the long day ahead.

Elise couldn't believe how perfectly everything was going. The Tigers' charity event for cancer had been a complete sell-out. The rich and famous were there in droves. Most of the other professional sports franchises were well represented by their players, and the movers and shakers of the metropolitan area were there in numbers. At last count, the charity event had raised over one hundred and fifty thousand dollars for the Cancer Society. The Tigers had adopted the Cancer Society as their main charity because their legendary head coach, Jim Cutter, had died of it when he'd been in the prime of his life a few years before.

"My dear, you never cease to amaze me with your talent," Aaron said as he handed her a glass of champagne. "The food is magnificent. The decorations are stunning. People are raving about what a success the night has been."

"I'm just glad you're happy with everything."

"If we raise money, I'm happy, and we've already surpassed our goal."

"That's fantastic. Everything has gone smoothly. There were no last-minute emergencies at all."

"That's because you're so organized. You covered every possibility and were ready for any scenario."

As he finished speaking, a photographer from the society page of the newspaper appeared. Aaron slipped an arm around Elise's waist and drew her close to his side just as the man snapped their photo.

"It'll run in Monday's paper," the photographer told them as he moved off in search of other noteworthy subjects.

"I hope I look reasonably intelligent in that. I take a notoriously bad picture."

"I don't know how that's possible," Aaron said in amazement. "You're beautiful."

Suddenly, the opening line of her horoscope slipped into her thoughts—*You will be irresistible to the opposite sex.*—and she found herself grinning. "Thank you, Aaron. That's very sweet of you to say."

"And very true," he responded.

"You haven't seen some of my past photos."

"Maybe someday you'll show me."

She looked up at him and saw that he was serious. It surprised her. "You're serious?"

"Very." He gave her a light squeeze, then released her as a business associate summoned him from across the ballroom. "I'll see you later."

To her shock, Aaron pressed a soft kiss on her

cheek before he moved off. She was watching him make his way across the room, greeting other guests, when she caught sight of Zach for the first time that night. He was wearing a tux and had his back to her, but there was no mistaking him. Elise wondered why she could never imagine what Zach would look like in a tux before. She knew he did justice to tight jeans and T-shirts, but he was even more gorgeous dressed in formal wear, and he looked as if he were completely at ease, confident and debonair.

As if he sensed her gaze upon him, Zach looked up in her direction and their gazes collided across the room. Zach smiled at her, lifting his champagne glass in silent salute. The petite, seductively gowned blonde on his arm said something. Zach turned away from Elise and concentrated on what his date was saying. When she'd finished talking, he threw back his head and laughed in seeming delight. The woman in turn laughed at his return quip.

Elise watched them move off together, looking to all the world like the perfect couple, and a troubling emotion began to gnaw at her—an emotion she didn't want to name. Her gaze sought out Aaron again, and she spied him working the crowd a short distance beyond Zach. She studied them both as she kept them in the same line of vision. Both men were tall, and each was good-looking in his own way—Aaron blond, wealthy, and sophisticated in manners and dealings; Zach darkly handsome and ever straightforward in his associations. They were both men she admired, but she wondered why, when she saw Aaron kissing another woman and laughing at her witticisms, it didn't bother her at all.

Taking another glass of champagne from one of the waiters, Elise went to check on how things were going. The evening would be a late one, and she wanted to make sure all her employees were doing all right and had everything they needed.

As the charity event came to a close, Aaron asked Elise to stand at his side as he thanked everyone for coming. They stood by the door shaking hands and making small talk with all those in attendance.

"You look familiar to me. I know we spoke briefly earlier in the evening, but I don't remember your name," Aaron said honestly as he came face-to-face with Zach.

"I'm Zach Thomas. We met the other day in the garage. I was driving the tow truck."

"Zach. Of course. It's good to see you again. Thanks for coming tonight. Who's your lovely companion?"

"This is Michelle Seton. Michelle, this is Elise Matthews and Aaron Benedict."

"It's a pleasure to meet you both," she said politely. Then, directing her next comment to Aaron, she added, "But Mr. Benedict, you made a big mistake trading Concrete McAllister."

Aaron grinned. "The trade seems to have been the main topic of conversation here tonight, and most of the crowd wanted to string me up."

"I'm one of them," Zach put in drolly.

"Give me a chance to show you what this team can do."

"We wanted to support you, but why trade a fan

favorite?" Michelle pressed. "A lot of folks care about Concrete and really like him. He's going to be missed in the community."

"Let's hope a big winning season wins back their loyalty," Aaron said, never conceding that he might have made a mistake in the trade.

"Good night," Zach said, knowing it was a pointless discussion. The deal was done and the man was obviously pleased with it. Then, looking directly at Elise, he repeated, "Good night."

"Good night, Zach. Michelle, it was nice to meet you," she told them, but all the while she was wondering where Zach had met her and how they knew each other.

It was nearly an hour later when the last of the guests had departed, and Aaron and Elise were finally alone in the midst of the hotel personnel doing the clean-up work.

"Let's go upstairs to the suite and have a drink to celebrate our success tonight, shall we?" he suggested.

"I'd love to," she accepted, not wanting to think about where Zach and his petite blonde had gone and what they were doing.

Aaron escorted her into the elevator of the plush hotel. She was weary, but exhilarated, for everything had turned out wonderfully. She stepped into the elevator car, and the moment the doors closed and they were alone, Aaron took her into his arms.

"I've been wanting to do this all night," he said in a low voice as he kissed her.

For Elise, it was her dream come true. She was in an elegant hotel, being kissed by a millionaire.

His kiss, along with the speedy rush of the elevator going up, thrilled her. When they reached their floor and he reluctantly let her go, she was breathless.

Neither of them spoke as he took her hand and led her from the car. They walked down the hall to the luxurious suite where she'd changed clothes earlier in the day. He unlocked it, held the door for her, and went straight to the bar, where an iced bottle of Dom Perignon awaited them. Fluted crystal champagne glasses were on a silver tray next to the ice bucket, and Aaron effortlessly opened the bottle and poured them both a glass.

One entire wall of the suite was a window, and Elise went to stand there and stare out at the skyline of the city. It was perfect . . . the luxury hotel, the fine champagne, the handsome man . . .

"To us," Aaron said as he held out one glass for her to take.

She dreamily took it and lifted it to his. "To us."

"Do you realize how great we are together?" he asked as he went to sit on the overstuffed sofa and patted the place next to him for her to join him.

"We do work well together," she agreed as she sat down. "It was a wonderful evening."

"And it's not over yet." He took her glass and set both their glasses aside, then took her in his arms again. "You are one beautiful woman, Elise Matthews, and I want you for my own."

Before she had time to say a word, his mouth covered hers in a passionate kiss. His declaration had left her in shock. *His own? He wanted her for his own?* The thought gave her pause. They barely knew each other. Not that there was anything about him she didn't like. What was to hate? His good looks? His kindness? His money? No, she would be hard put to find anything about him she didn't like—except his trade of Concrete McAllister—but *his own?*

Jolted out of the romantic haze the champagne and his kisses had created, she realized that he wanted more from her than a few kisses. Much more.

"You want me for your own?" she finally said when the kiss ended and she managed to put a little distance between them on the sofa. "Aaron, we've worked together for a number of weeks now, but we really don't know each other that well."

"I know all I need to know about you, Elise, and, in case you haven't figured it out yet, I'm a man of action. I know what I want when I see it, and I know I want you."

"But—"

He took her in his embrace again and held her close. "I love you, Elise. Will you marry me?"

She gasped out loud at his proposal, and he saved her from having to answer by kissing her again. She gave herself over to his ardor, enjoying his kiss, enjoying the comfort of being in his arms, but always, hovering just on the edge of her pleasure with Aaron, was the haunting memory of Zach's kiss and touch.

Aaron's kiss became even more heated as he lay back on the sofa and pulled her down upon him. They were stretched out body to body, full length, as he began to caress her and make love to her. She was the woman he'd waited all these years for, and at last he'd found her. He didn't ever want to let her go again, but when he felt her resistance to his advances, he stopped, puzzled, and drew away from her.

"Elise? What's wrong?" he asked as he sat back up and faced her.

"Nothing's wrong, Aaron. It's just that this is happening so fast. I never dreamed you felt this way about me. I need time . . . time alone to think. I'd better go." She rose and grabbed her purse. "I'll get my other clothes later."

With that, she was gone from the suite.

Aaron stared at the closed door. He hoped she'd change her mind before she reached the elevator. He hoped she would never leave him again. He wanted her with him. He found her intelligence and beauty to be a rare and devastating combination, and he didn't ever want to lose her. He waited quietly, hoping she would return.

But when the elevator came to the floor, Elise got on it.

A short time later, Aaron emerged from the suite in hopes of finding her there. All that greeted him was the empty hall. He turned back into the suite and put away the champagne. Tonight, he would drink the hard stuff.

Elise was trembling as she rushed across the nearly deserted garage, and she didn't feel safe again until she was sitting in Zach's Mustang. The drive home was a blur, and she was still feeling nervous as she let herself into the house.

"It's about time you got home," Rod called out

from the kitchen when he heard her come in the front door.

"Have you been here long?"

"No, not too long. Just long enough to get comfortable. How did it go? What do you think?" He went to stand in the kitchen door so he could see her.

"Oh, Rod . . . I don't know."

"You don't know how it went? Everything I heard was that it was terrific. You're making quite a name for yourself."

She didn't answer, but sat down heavily on the sofa.

"Elise?" He could tell something was wrong. "What's the matter?"

"Nothing. Everything . . ."

"I don't understand."

She looked up at her little brother, who'd come to stand before her sensing that something was troubling her. "It's Aaron."

"What about him?" Rod was instantly ready to go and defend her honor if the man had done something to hurt her. "What did he do?"

"Well, he—"

Rod was expecting the worst. "He what?"

"He proposed to me tonight," she blurted out miserably.

Rod stared at her in complete confusion, trying to figure out why a millionaire proposing to her would be so distressing. It seemed to him to be a wonderful thing. "You just got proposed to by a really rich guy, and you're unhappy? I don't get it."

"Oooh! You men!" She threw a pillow at him.

"What's the problem?"

"I don't know. . . . It's just all so sudden. I've only known him for a matter of weeks."

"Months, now."

"Whatever. It's just that I didn't know he felt this way. I didn't know he really cared about me."

"And this is bad?"

"No, not really. It's just—"

"Do you love him?" Rod knew just the right question to ask.

She looked up at him, her expression serious. "I don't know."

"I guess you'd better find out."

Elise didn't say any more, for she knew he was right. She liked Aaron, liked him a lot. But love him? Want to spend the rest of her life with him? She didn't know.

"I better go to bed and sleep on it. Good night, Rod." She got up to leave the room.

"If you want to talk any more, let me know. I'm here."

"You're a sweetheart. Thanks." She went to hug him. As she was leaving the room, she glanced back his way to ask, "Did you ever find out anything about Zach's date? Her name was Michelle Seton, but I'd never heard of her before tonight."

"Me either, but she sure was pretty."

Elise nodded and went on to bed.

As she lay there in the dark staring up at the ceiling, she realized her dilemma was real. The man she'd always thought was her dream man— a rich, handsome, successful businessman, who drove around in a limo and served her Dom Perignon—had just proposed.

Why, then, was she so miserable?

Chapter Seven

"Got the part in, did you?" Rod said as he showed up for work at the garage Monday afternoon and found Zach working on Elise's car.

"It got here about an hour ago. With any luck, I'll have it ready for her by closing time."

"Great, although I think you might have a fight getting that Mustang back. Elise likes driving it a lot. She took it out for a spin yesterday and didn't come back for hours. But don't worry—there are no big dents in it or anything."

Zach glanced up at him and found that Rod was grinning at him.

"Get to work," he growled good-naturedly.

"Yes, Boss. What have you got for me today?"

Zach pointed to a clipboard with the work orders on them. "Work on the Davenports' car. I promised them delivery first thing in the morning."

Rod checked what needed to be done and went to get the parts it required. As he walked past Zach on the way back, he knew he had to tell him what had happened with Elise. Even though she hadn't made up her mind yet about marrying the guy, which Rod could not understand at all, he thought it was pretty exciting.

"Guess what happened to Elise Saturday night after the charity event?"

"What?" Zach asked, not looking up from where he worked under the hood.

"Aaron Benedict proposed to her!"

Zach went cold inside at his words, and he almost hit his head on the raised hood as he jerked up to look at Rod. "He what?"

"He proposed to her. Said they made a great team and wanted her to marry him," Rod repeated simply as he started to work on the Davenports' car.

"When's the wedding?" The question was ground out of him as he stood there staring at Rod's back. Memories of Saturday night played in his mind—Elise looking as gorgeous as ever on Aaron Benedict's arm. Benedict kissing her there in the midst of the celebration. A society photographer from the paper taking their photo. He realized he should have known what was going on. She had looked happy that night, and marrying Benedict would make all her dreams come true— she'd have the Ritz and her limos and champagne.

"I don't know."

"They haven't set the date yet?"

"No. As of this morning, Elise still hadn't made up her mind."

A surge of hope jolted through Zach at Rod's response, but he fought to remain outwardly calm. "Why the hold up?"

"That's what I said to her. This Benedict guy's good-looking, wealthy, and owns a pro football team. As far as I'm concerned, a brother-in-law doesn't come any better than that, but then, I'm not the one marrying him."

With an effort, Zach brought his raging emotions under control and went back to work on Elise's car. Benedict had proposed . . . but Elise hadn't accepted yet. There was still time . . . there was still hope.

Zach paused in his efforts and wondered, hope for what? He frowned, staring down at the wrench in his hand. He couldn't kid himself any longer. He loved Elise. He hadn't said anything before because of her talk about marrying a rich man, and he knew he'd never be rich. He was an honest working man, born of working-class parents. He'd had to work for everything he'd ever gotten in life, and he didn't expect that to change. There was one other thing he knew would never change, too, and that was the way he felt about Elise. He had loved her for a long time now, and he knew he always would.

With a vengeance, Zach kept working on the car. She hadn't accepted Benedict's proposal yet. He would hand-deliver her car to her tonight and tell her exactly how he felt about her.

* * *

It was after eight when the doorbell rang, and Elise got up from her desk to answer it.

"Zach . . . Hi," she said, surprised to find it was him and glad that it was. He'd been haunting her thoughts. Every time she'd thought she'd made up her mind about Aaron, memories of Zach intruded . . . his kiss . . . his touch . . . his good humor and kindness.

"Your friendly auto mechanic delivering your car on time as promised," he told her.

"Thanks. Come on in."

He walked in and noticed a huge bouquet of roses on the mantel. "Nice flowers."

"Oh, thanks. Aaron sent them to me."

"He has good taste." Zach felt the jealousy rising within him, but kept it under control.

"You want something to drink? A soda?"

"Sure. Thanks."

While Elise disappeared into the kitchen to get their drinks, Zach wandered over to the roses and read the card.

" 'Call me—Aaron.' " He read it under his breath and knew what he'd call Aaron if given the chance. Not only had he traded Concrete, now he was trying to marry Elise.

"Zach, I was thinking—" Elise came back into the room carrying their drinks to find him sitting on the sofa waiting for her.

"About what?"

"About our cars. You wouldn't consider a trade, would you? My car for the Mustang?" she asked teasingly, then went on quickly. "Now that mine's running again, it's a real prize. In a few more years, it'll be a collector's item just like the Mustang, and since you like old cars so much . . ." She left the question hanging, knowing full well what his answer would be.

"That's a tough one. I'll have to think about it for a while."

"How long's 'a while'?"

"About thirty seconds."

"And?"

"I don't think so. Not that I don't think yours is a wonderful vehicle. It's just that I'm fond of the Mustang after working on it for so long."

"Darn. I was afraid you were going to say that."

"If you're serious, I could look around and try to find one to restore for you, but it isn't cheap to do all that work."

"I know. I guess I'll just have to wait until I win the lottery."

Or marry Benedict. The thought crept into his mind as he took a deep drink of his soda, but he didn't say anything.

"So how did everything go Saturday? It looked like everyone had a good time, and I read in the paper that you'd raised the most money ever at one of their charity events."

"It went great. Aaron was most pleased. Did you and your date have a good time? What was her name again? Michelle?" She was bound and determined to find out more about his date.

"Yes, her name's Michelle, and we did have a fine time. She was quite impressed."

"I'm so glad. Where did you two meet?"

"Why do you want to know?" He thought he heard more-than-just-casual interest in her tone, and it bolstered his hopes. Surely, she did feel

343

something for him. She couldn't have responded to his kiss that way unless she did.

"Oh, I was just wondering." Elise tried to sound nonchalant.

"I've known Michelle for years. What about you and Benedict?"

"What about us?"

"Are you going to marry him?" A muscle worked in his jaw as he asked the question, and he found he was holding his breath as he awaited her answer.

"So Rod told you about Aaron's proposal?"

"Yes. What do you plan to do?" Zach shifted so he was nearer to her.

Elise felt the heat of him as he moved closer. "I haven't made up my mind yet."

"Why not?" he asked, lowering his voice as he slipped an arm around her shoulders and pulled her to him. "He could give you Dom Perignon every night."

He kissed her then, his mouth moving over hers in a devastating, possessive exchange, meant to tell her without words the depth of his feelings for her.

Thoughts of Aaron troubled Elise, but as Zach deepened the kiss and drew her even closer to the hard wall of his chest, all thoughts of the other man were vanquished. She gave herself over to the glory of Zach's embrace. Somehow, they were soon lying on the sofa, their bodies pressed intimately together.

"Is champagne every night what you really want?" Zach asked as his lips left hers to explore the sweetness of her throat.

Elise arched toward him as he continued his sensual assault. When his mouth sought hers again, she gave a soft whimper. His kiss and touch were heavenly, and she felt so safe in his arms. Was this what she really wanted? The haven of Zach's embrace?

"Tell me, Elise," he demanded, drawing away from her a bit, a slightly harsh edge to his voice. "Do you want the champagne?"

"No . . . I . . . I don't know what I want."

"Look at me," Zach commanded. He wanted to look into her eyes and see the truth of her emotions. He had to know what she was feeling. "Tell me what you want."

She gazed up at him, her expression confused, the look in her eyes troubled.

Zach wanted to hold her to his heart and never let her go, but she had to come to him of her own free will. She had to come to him because she loved him. He would accept nothing less from her.

"I know what I want," he went on. "I want you, Elise. I love you."

He kissed her again, deeply, thoroughly, putting his whole heart and soul into the exchange.

"But you have to tell me what you want."

He waited, but she didn't speak. She closed her eyes, bewildered by all that was happening. She'd known she and Zach shared something special, but she'd never known he loved her until now.

Her silence was like a knife in his heart, and he moved away from her. Standing over her, he could think only of how beautiful she was and how much he wanted to make her his own.

345

"Elise," he said her name quietly, though his own passion was hot within him.

She opened her eyes to look up at him.

"When you decide what you want, you let me know. You know where I'll be."

With that, he turned and left her. He let himself out of the house and started up the Mustang using his extra set of keys.

Elise went to the door after him, wanting to stop him, but unsure of just what to say. She wasn't sure of anything right then. A lone tear traced a path down her cheek as she watched him drive away, and she turned back into the living room and sat down on the sofa to try to sort out what she was feeling.

Zach loved her.

She smiled as she thought of his fierce declaration.

But did she love Zach? Was he the man she should spend the rest of her life with?

Elise shook her head, as if that would clear her thoughts. She'd known Zach forever. They'd been friends for years. He was her buddy. She had always known how cute and smart he was. Why hadn't they ever felt this way about each other before? Why was it happening now?

She thought back over the years of their friendship. They'd never dated because she'd gone away to college. When she returned, he'd been involved with other women. There had even been one girl a few years back who, she'd heard, Zach had almost married.

Elise found herself smiling at the thought that it hadn't worked out for him with the other woman. Then she frowned, as the possibility that it might not work out for *them* reared its ugly head. The thought of a life without Zach scared her, and it was then that she faced the truth.

She loved him.

As attractive as Aaron was, and there was no denying that he was, money wasn't everything. She wanted the riches loving Zach could bring, even if it meant doing without material things in life. Those things didn't matter—she would have Zach.

The recognition of her true feelings freed her, and Elise laughed out loud.

She loved Zach, money or no money, champagne or no champagne, limousine or no limousine. He might not be rich, but he loved her and he owned one heckuva '65 Mustang. It didn't get any better than that.

Her laughter faded and she frowned. She had to think of a way to tell him. She just couldn't drive over to his house and blurt it out. She had to make this good.

Chapter Eight

It was six A.M. and barely light outside.

Zach had been up all night, waiting and hoping that Elise would call or come over. Neither had happened. Resignedly, half an hour before, he'd turned on the television and retrieved his newspaper from the front lawn. He was sitting at his kitchen table now, the newspaper open wide before him, a cup of hot, strong coffee in hand. He smiled to himself and took a deep drink of the potent, steaming brew. It was going to be a long day, and he might as well get ready for it.

His beeper went off, surprising him, and he was tempted to throw it across the room. He didn't want any more business. He didn't need any more business. He was tempted to get in the Mustang and take off. He didn't care where, as long as it was anywhere but here. The cold, logical electronic beeper, unaware of his dangerous mood, beeped again.

Swearing under his breath, Zach thought about ignoring it, but knew it might be someone in trouble. He pushed back from the table and got up to go to his phone. He dialed his answering service and waited for an operator.

"This is Zach with Collision Plus."

"There's been an accident westbound on Lambert Drive. The nearest cross street is Roosevelt. One car involved, no injuries. The driver will remain with the car until you show up with the tow truck."

"Thanks. Did you get the driver's name?"

"No, but the car is a '65 Mustang."

The thought of a '65 in a wreck sickened him. In less than five minutes, he'd closed up the house and was heading for the garage. Within twenty minutes, he was on the road in the tow truck making his way straight to Lambert and Roosevelt. It took him less than forty-five minutes to reach the site of the accident as reported by the answering service, but when he arrived at the scene there was no sign of a wrecked vehicle anywhere.

"This is Zach with Collision Plus calling back. I've just reached westbound Lambert near Roosevelt, and there's no sign of any accident or broken-down cars. Can you recheck the message please?"

"One minute, sir." The operator's voice was cool and disinterested. After at least two minutes on hold, the woman came back on. "It was a woman who called in the accident. She didn't leave her name, but westbound Lambert near Roosevelt was the location she gave."

"There's no one here. She hasn't called back?"

"No, sir. That was our only contact with her."

He gave a snarl of disgust and hung up. A wasted effort and here he thought he was going to help somebody out of trouble this morning—so much for all his good intentions. His mood grew blacker as he returned to the garage. When he got there, it was after seven, and neither of his other two employees had shown up yet. He was really angry. Any other day, he might have laughed it all off, but today he just wasn't in the mood.

Feeling positively surly, Zach parked the tow truck, unlocked the garage, and stalked inside. The only light that was on was coming from his office. Cursing his own stupidity in forgetting to turn it off when he'd gone out on the emergency call, he strode toward the light, ready to phone his errant employees and ask them why they hadn't shown up for work.

Or at least he was until he reached his office door and looked inside.

Elise was sitting at his desk, dressed as if she was going in to work. She looked up. "Hi, Zach."

"Elise? What are you doing here?" Zach's heart lurched at the sight of her, but he was too afraid to let himself hope about her reasons for coming here.

"There wasn't any Mustang at Lambert and Roosevelt?" she asked, giving him a very seductive smile.

"You called that in?"

She nodded as she stood up and crossed the room to stand before him. "I had to think of a way to get you out of here. I didn't want to take any chances—"

"Any chances with what?"

"With the surprise I have planned for you."

"Surprise?" Zach knew he sounded less than brilliant, but he had no idea what she was up to.

"I even sent Charley and George out for coffee and doughnuts, just so I'd have time to set everything up. You see, I made you something." She moved away to show him what looked to be a pizza box on his desk. "Open it."

He was frowning and smiling at the same time as he lifted the lid. Inside was a heart-shaped pizza made with all his favorite toppings.

"Zach?"

He looked up at her, all the love he had for her shining in his eyes.

"I love you, Zach, and I love pizza in the garage at midnight or at seven in the morning—as long as I'm sharing it with you."

"Elise—"

He opened his arms to her and she went into them. They stood that way, neither speaking, just enjoying the beauty of the moment. Then carefully, gently, he bent to kiss her. It was a kiss of delight and promise, a kiss that told of the loving wonders yet to come.

"Will you marry me, Elise?"

"Yes, Zach. I can't think of anything more wonderful," she sighed, nestling against his chest and listening to the heavy, steady beat of his heart. This was Zach. She loved him. He was hers.

He kissed her again, more deeply this time, as if not really believing what was happening. The last twelve hours had taken an emotional toll on him, but that didn't matter now. The only important thing was that Elise loved him and had come to him of her own free will.

"You're sure?"

"I'm positive."

"I know what Aaron Benedict can give you. That's your dream, isn't it? The Ritz, limousines, and Dom Perignon?"

"For a long time I thought it was, but now I know different. My dream is loving someone as wonderful as you."

"When are you going to talk to him?"

"I already have."

She drew him down to her for a flaming kiss that told him all he needed to know about the truth of her feelings for him.

"I love you, Zach Thomas, and if you want to open a restaurant instead of running a garage, I'll help you with it. I'll even wait tables for you if you want me to."

"We could sell heart-shaped pizza," he suggested.

"It would probably only be big on Valentine's Day," she said, laughing in delight as she hugged him close.

They both sighed as they stood in the middle of the room, wrapped in each other's arms.

"How soon do you want to get married?" Zach asked.

"As far as I'm concerned, we could go to a justice of the peace today, but I know you have a pretty big family. There's only me and Rod and a few distant cousins on my side."

"We can talk to my parents today and see how they feel about a small, quick wedding and reception."

"Quick. I like the sound of that." She kissed him again. "But I won't be cheated out of a honeymoon. You've got to promise me that we'll have at least a week together. Okay?"

"I don't know if I can afford to take that much time off."

"Oh." She looked momentarily downcast, then brightened. "We'll figure something out. I want you all to myself with no danger of interruptions."

"That sounds great to me," he agreed, remembering how Rod had walked in on them that night at her house. "Uninterrupted, hmmm?"

He kissed her again, then drew away.

"I have something I want to give you."

"What?"

"Just a little something I picked up the other night."

She was smiling brightly, wondering if it was a ring, but instead he pulled out his wallet. She couldn't imagine what he had.

"Here." Zach held a lottery ticket out to her. "This is for us to begin our life together."

"That's so sweet of you. You know how I feel about lottery tickets."

On his desk was a copy of the morning paper. He opened it and handed her the pages with the lottery number listings.

"Check them out."

"Now?"

"There's no better time than the present."

She sat down at his desk to go over the numbers as he took a piece of her pizza to eat. He stood back, watching her expression as she went over the numbers listed. He noticed when her hands began to tremble.

"Zach . . ." Her voice was hoarse as she looked up at him, her eyes wide with excitement. "You won!"

"I know," he said simply.

"Oh, my God! That's fifty-six million dollars!"

"I know."

And she was in his arms, jumping up and down, kissing him. She was unmindful of the pizza he held, unmindful of anything but the joy of loving Zach. He took her in his arms and twirled her around the office.

"I think we're going to live happily ever after," he said, claiming her lips in a passionate kiss.

"I know we are."

She started to kiss him again when she noticed that Charley and George were standing outside the office door holding a bag of doughnuts and cups of coffee, watching them

"Good morning, Boss," they said, giving Zach and Elise a curious look.

"It's a very good morning," Zach agreed.

"You're celebrating?"

"Elise just accepted my proposal. We're getting married." He decided to save their other good news until later. This was more important.

"That's great! Congratulations!"

"Come on in. Enjoy the pizza and the doughnuts. I'm taking the day off."

"You?" They were shocked. Zach never took unscheduled time off.

"That's right, gentlemen. You are your own bosses today. I'll see you later."

Grabbing Elise's hand, he hurried off through the garage and out into the parking lot.

They kissed once more right there in broad daylight and then climbed into the Mustang.

"Are you ready to have some fun now?" he asked, remembering how she'd feared taking time away from her work schedule to play.

"Yes. I'm more than ready."

"Let's go."

Epilogue

"I now pronounce you man and wife," the minister intoned. "You may kiss your bride."

Zach turned to Elise and kissed her gently.

"Ladies and gentlemen, may I present to you Mr. and Mrs. Zach Thomas."

Applause erupted from the friends and family members who'd gathered for the ceremony. Zach led Elise down the aisle and they left the church, ready to begin their new life together.

The reception was held in the church hall and everyone had a wonderful time. Zach and Elise stayed for most of it, enjoying being with all the people who loved them. Finally, as midnight neared, they slipped away.

Zach stopped on the deserted walk in front of the church to gaze up at the night sky. "It's a beautiful night, Mrs. Thomas."

"It certainly is," she agreed, leaning against him, enjoying the feel of his arm around her.

"I have one last present for you."

She looked up at him in surprise, wondering how he could possibly give her any more than he already had. She had his love, and that was all that really mattered. "You do?"

"Here." He reached into his pocket and took out the keys to the Mustang. "The car is my wedding present to you."

"Oh, Zach!" She launched herself into his arms as best she could in her wedding gown. "Is it here?"

"I had Rod park it around back. Can you drive it with that skirt on?"

"No, I think tonight you'd better chauffeur me."

He took the keys from her, and they were soon on their way to the honeymoon suite he'd booked at a hotel near the airport. Their bags were already there awaiting them. They would be flying out in the morning to begin their week-long honeymoon in Jamaica.

Zach swung her up into his arms and carried her across the threshold. She looped her arms about his neck and kissed him with wild abandon. He set her from him and hung the "Do Not Disturb" sign on the door. He shut the door and locked it, then turned to his bride. It seemed he'd waited his whole life for this moment, and he could wait no longer.

"I love you, Elise."

Zach needed to say no more, for she was there, in his arms. He helped her shed the dress, glorying in the loveliness of her. Soon they were together on the soft width of their bed, exploring the beauty of their differences.

As his hands traced paths of fire over her sensitive flesh, a fever of need grew within Elise. This was Zach . . . her love. She gave herself over to the excitement his caresses created in the heart of her. When he moved over her to make her his own, she opened to him like a flower in bloom. Sinking deep within the feminine heat of her, Zach knew the meaning of true bliss. She held him tightly within her, loving the sensation so new and precious. They were one in body. He began to move, and she met him in that sensual rhythm as old as time. Ecstasy was theirs as they reached the peak of pleasure together. Enraptured, they clung to one another, knowing true love.

"You know, my horoscope was right that day of the charity fund-raiser," Elise said in a soft, sleepy voice as she lay in her husband's arms.

"What did it say?"

" 'The future holds unlimited potential for happiness for you as long as you are honest with yourself and follow your dreams.' " She sighed and nestled closer to Zach. "I followed my dreams, Zach, and they brought me you."

He drew her up to him for a soft kiss. He had found his heaven in her embrace. "I like the way you dream, lady."

That simple kiss ignited the fire of their desire again, and all thoughts of horoscopes were forgotten. They came together in perfect union again, giving and taking in love's most sacred way.

They would live happily ever after.

BOBBI SMITH

The LADY & the TEXAN

"A fine storyteller!"—*Romantic Times*

A firebrand since the day she was born, Amanda Taylor always stands up for what she believes in. She won't let any man control her—especially a man like gunslinger Jack Logan. Even though Jack knows Amanda is trouble, her defiant spirit only spurs his hunger for her. He discovers that keeping the dark-haired tigress at bay is a lot harder than outsmarting the outlaws after his hide—and surrendering to her sweet fury is a heck of a lot riskier.

___4319-X $5.99 US/$6.99 CAN

Dorchester Publishing Co., Inc.
P.O. Box 6640
Wayne, PA 19087-8640

Please add $1.75 for shipping and handling for the first book and $.50 for each book thereafter. NY, NYC, and PA residents, please add appropriate sales tax. No cash, stamps, or C.O.D.s. All orders shipped within 6 weeks via postal service book rate. Canadian orders require $2.00 extra postage and must be paid in U.S. dollars through a U.S. banking facility.

Name_____
Address_____
City_____ State_____ Zip_____
I have enclosed $_____ in payment for the checked book(s).
Payment <u>must</u> accompany all orders. ❑ Please send a free catalog.

Elaine Fox
Leigh Greenwood
Linda Winstead

Three Heartwarming Tales of Romance and Holiday Cheer

Bah Humbug! by Leigh Greenwood. Nate wants to go somewhere hot, but when his neighbor offers holiday cheer, their passion makes the tropics look like the arctic.

Christmas Present by Elaine Fox. When Susannah returns home, a late-night savior teaches her the secret to happiness. But is this fate, or something more wonderful?

Blue Christmas by Linda Winstead. Jess doesn't date musicians, especially handsome, up-and-coming ones. But she has a ghost of a chance to realize that Jimmy Blue is a heavenly gift.

___4320-3 $5.50 US/$6.50 CAN

Dorchester Publishing Co., Inc.
P.O. Box 6640
Wayne, PA 19087-8640

Please add $1.75 for shipping and handling for the first book and $.50 for each book thereafter. NY, NYC, and PA residents, please add appropriate sales tax. No cash, stamps, or C.O.D.s. All orders shipped within 6 weeks via postal service book rate. Canadian orders require $2.00 extra postage and must be paid in U.S. dollars through a U.S. banking facility.

Name_____
Address_____
City_____State_____Zip_____
I have enclosed $_____ in payment for the checked book(s).
Payment <u>must</u> accompany all orders. ❏ Please send a free catalog.

Surrender to the fantasy...

Indulge yourself in these sensual love stories written by four of today's hottest romance authors!

CONNIE BENNETT, "Masquerade": When shy, unassuming Charlotte Nolan wins a masquerade cruise, she has no idea that looks can be so deceiving—or that her wildest romantic fantasies are about to come true.

THEA DEVINE, "Admit Desire": Nick's brother is getting married—to the woman who left him at the altar two years before. And when Nick sees them together, he realizes he wants Francesca more than ever. But little does he know that she, too, will do anything to have him in her life again.

EVELYN ROGERS, "The Gold Digger": Susan Ballinger is determined to marry for money. She doesn't believe in love at first sight—until she meets Sonny, a golden boy who takes her to soaring heights of pleasure—and gives her so much more in the bargain.

OLIVIA RUPPRECHT, "A Quiver of Sighs": Valerie Smith is a lonely writer with an active imagination. But she's missing one thing: experience. Then she meets Jake Larson, a handsome editor who takes her writing—and her body—to places beyond her wildest dreams.

___4289-4 $5.50 US/$6.50 CAN

Dorchester Publishing Co., Inc.
P.O. Box 6640
Wayne, PA 19087-8640

Please add $1.75 for shipping and handling for the first book and $.50 for each book thereafter. NY, NYC, and PA residents, please add appropriate sales tax. No cash, stamps, or C.O.D.s. All orders shipped within 6 weeks via postal service book rate.
Canadian orders require $2.00 extra postage and must be paid in U.S. dollars through a U.S. banking facility.

Name_____
Address_____
City_____State_____Zip_____
I have enclosed $_____ in payment for the checked book(s).
Payment <u>must</u> accompany all orders. ❑ Please send a free catalog.

HOLIDAY ROMANCE ANTHOLOGIES

Trick or Treat by Lark Eden, Lori Handeland, Stobie Piel, and Lynda Trent. From four of romance's most provocative authors come the stories of four couples as they experience the true magic of Halloween, and the ecstasy of everlasting love.

___52220-9 $5.99 US/$6.99 CAN

Midsummer Night's Magic by Emma Craig, Tess Mallory, Amy Elizabeth Saunders, and Pam McCutcheon. In the balmy heat of the summer season, four couples venture into the realm of the wee folk and spirits, and in doing so, learn the true meaning of passion.

___52209-8 $5.50 US/$6.50 CAN

Dorchester Publishing Co., Inc.
P.O. Box 6640
Wayne, PA 19087-8640

Please add $1.75 for shipping and handling for the first book and $.50 for each book thereafter. NY, NYC, and PA residents, please add appropriate sales tax. No cash, stamps, or C.O.D.s. All orders shipped within 6 weeks via postal service book rate. Canadian orders require $2.00 extra postage and must be paid in U.S. dollars through a U.S. banking facility.

Name_____

Address_____

City_____State_____Zip_____

I have enclosed $_____ in payment for the checked book(s).

Payment <u>must</u> accompany all orders. ☐ Please send a free catalog.